THE MOSTLY TRUE STORY OF
RUDABAUGH & WEBB

MIKE WATT

Encyclopocalypse Publications
www.encyclopocalypse.com

Contents

For Dave and J. J.

ACKNOWLEDGMENTS

This book came about almost accidentally. I was researching Dave Rudabaugh for something else entirely and kept coming across huge gaps in his history. Once Billy the Kid enters Dave's story, it stops being about Dave. The stories told were *never* about J. J.

As Father Francis Stanley wrote in *Dave Rudabaugh: Border Ruffian* (1961) (a book I'd never have known about were it not for my father, Western historian Bill Watt, who found it through a Pakistani P.O.D. press, of all things): "I give you Rudabaugh because no one else has." For this same reason, I give you both Dave *and* J. J.

Big thanks to Edison Soto for copyediting the Spanish profanity.

Thank you, too, to my wife and my eternal sounding board—"Can I read you something?"—my partner, and my love, Amy Lynn Best.

In addition to the invaluable *True West Magazine*, I used the following sources to put together this weird puzzle of two men history had virtually forgotten:

- *Dave Rudabaugh: Border Ruffian* and *Desperadoes of New Mexico*, by Fr. Francis Stanley.
- *Mysterious Gunfighter: The Story of Dave Mather (The Early West)* by Jack DeMattos.
- *Trailing Billy the Kid*, by Philip J. Rasch.

- *Bat Masterson, The Man And The Legend*, by Robert K. DeArment.
- *The West of Billy the Kid*, by Frederick Nolan.
- *My Life on the Frontier, 1864–1882*, and *The Real Billy the Kid; With New Light on the Lincoln County War*, by Miguel Otero, Jr.

And against my better judgment:

- *Pat F. Garrett's The Authentic Life of Billy The Kid —* notes and commentary by Frederick Nolan

Mike Watt
February, 2024

THE MOSTLY TRUE STORY OF
RUDABAUGH & WEBB

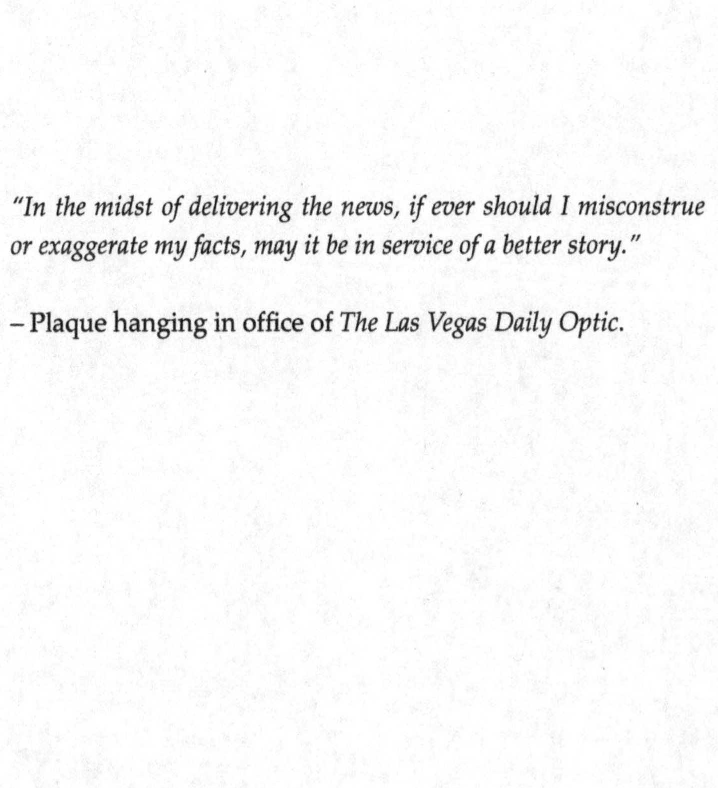

"In the midst of delivering the news, if ever should I misconstrue or exaggerate my facts, may it be in service of a better story."

– Plaque hanging in office of *The Las Vegas Daily Optic.*

Chapter 1

The Kinsley Train Job

Dave Rudabaugh, frequently the most wanted outlaw in the Southwestern territories, raised his glass and saluted his companion. "The first time I met J. J.," he said, "he had a gun to my head."

John Joshua Webb, frequently a lawman, most recently in the employ of the great Bat Masterson, touched the brim of his hat in return. "Made it easier to arrest you."

Sitting in the dim recesses of The Gadfly saloon, a slap-back-and-board structure erected the previous week, Lute Wilcox, as the City Editor of the *Las Vegas Gazette*, served as both spectator and reporter. Lute's eyesight had failed him at birth, and each waking had him peering through another layer of silk. Fortunately, his memory had improved as his vision hazed, and he would later recount the pair's conversation verbatim. Mostly verbatim.

Though close enough in height and weight to share shadows, Rudabaugh and Webb were a display of contrasts: the darker Rudabaugh, with his droop mustache and narrow, suspicious eyes, train robber, rustler, and horse thief, in and out of prison like a preferred customer, attempting to turn his back on his illegal ways; Webb, fair haired and thick-bearded, the smiling, genial lawman, who had been of late toeing the waters of criminality. Longtime and unlikely friends, their time as hired guns fighting the so-called "Railroad Wars" under Masterson ended with settled territory and nary a shot fired. They did this or that a while in Dodge City, and then rode together into the New Town side of Las Vegas, New Mexico, eager to get something going.

"You should tell him about the Kinsley train job," said Webb, egging on his companion, Rudabaugh. Many drinks were already downed as Dave knocked back another. Storytelling was inevitable. As was, Lute noted, confession.

"I should tell you about the Kinsley train job," said the outlaw, in his cups and rare voice. "I'd been riding off and on with a pair of skunks, Mike Roark and Dan Dement. Good enough cutting out cows, but neither had the head for planning. We did a couple of stages, some good takes, some bad. Papers started calling us 'The Trio,' which sit better with me than 'The Roark-Rudabaugh Gang,' particularly as both those fools t'weren't nothing but drummers and card cheats a'fore I came along.

"Anyways, Dement has his pea brain set on robbing the *Pueblo Express*, train coming in and out of Kinsley with a payroll, he says. Three times him and Roark call me in from Wolf Creek and three times they call off the job. First time, they didn't know when or where the train stopped. They thought we could just find it. Next time, the weather was too foul, couldn't see the train if we was riding a'top it. Third time, sons'a bitches never even made it out of the fuckin' saloon. I was ready to quit the lot of them when they called me down a fourth with a bona fide schedule.

"We blacked our faces with coal soot and took over the depot shack. There's a safe there—with maybe two thousand in it, we think—but the rube on watch's got no key for it. Stationmaster didn't trust him and took it home. Train stops as it should. We get on. Engineer sees us, panics, throttles open and jumps. So now we's on a train with no conductor. Half the fools we was with scatter soon as the guards start to fire. Roark and I get into the store car and there ain't nothing! The train was coming *back* from Kinsley. Payroll already been dropped off."

At this, Webb's quiet chuckles increased in volume and burst. Normally, you couldn't get three words out of Rudabaugh, master of taciturn hostility, but rarely had he an audience. Encouraged, Dave continued. "Now, I been on some bad takes with trains. It's always a risk. Hell, me, Milt Yarberry and Dave Mather, when we was still crotch-bald we took a train in Arkansas—not even baggage aboard and the dozen trainsmen had about six bits total between them. So I says to Mather, 'Take the lanterns!' Which we did. And the window curtains, some of the seats.

"But this Kinsley train? Roark's idiots left us behind holding nothing but our cods! I was madder than hell! I booted Roark off and we lit out. Tramped through the snow and wind and misery with piss-all to show for it." The outlaw was on his feet now, using the narrow space between the slat tables for a stage.

"We get to the meet-up at this cow camp south of Dodge, and I can see right away there's men in the trees covering the cabin. Dement and two of his crew was right behind us, we crest the bend and spy them ahead with their hands up, kneeling in the snow, and I now know we're in for a fight. It's Masterson hisself who hollers from the dark that we should put up our hands and Roark does just that. Tosses a brand new Henry rifle into the mud like a …Who them uneducated Bible fellas?"

"Philistines," said Webb.

"One a'them," said Rudabaugh.

Lute gave Webb a thin smile. "Are you his thesaurus?"

"Hey now," said Rudabaugh, angling a finger at the newsman. "None of that talk. J. J.'s my friend." Lute held up his hand in apology. Dave went on. "Anyways, I'm past tired and cold's made me numb and I'm still belching fire from the botched job and wasted trips, I actually start to think a gunfight is the perfect way to end this partnership, even if a grave is all I get out of it. Then I hear the click of J. J.'s Schofield just behind my right ear."

" 'Don't do it, David,' I said."

"That you did. 'Don't die for these fools,' is what you said next. So I didn't. I tossed my gun down."

"Then I made you toss the other two."

"Shut up, this is my story."

"Kinda *our* story," said Webb.

"You make it sound like we's married," grumbled Rudabaugh, whiskey slurring his words now. Turning back to Lute, he pointed a finger. "I wan' make one thing clear," he said, "I never betrayed a friend. If it'd been Mather or even Yarberry, no way I would have given them up."

"You asked me for advice," said Webb.

"I was facing a noose for rustling. I got caught on the stupidest job ever pulled and it weren't even my fault. Not my plan, anyway."

"So I said—"

"So *J. J. said*—" Rudabaugh continued, " 'David, you should turn State's Evidence. That's where you tell your part of the story and blame it all on your cohorts.' Like I said if Roark had—I mean, posse'd killed Dement on the road behind us, so I pinned a lot of it on him in the end. Less on Roark, but they had him already on a murder charge. Anyways, the State let me go, time served. Pardoned, I guess. I had the paper. Then I wandered back down South a while looking for straight work, found myself somehow on Masterson's side of the Railroad War."

Webb snorted, "Wa'n't no 'war.'"

"That's my point. There was barely feelings hurt. Only war was between the bankers and … them others."

"Politicians."

"Them assholes," said Rudabaugh. He rocked on his heels a bit then recovered. "I spent the whole summer twirling my gun and chowing rice with the coolies."

"Chow with the Chows," said J. J. in a kind of sigh, whiskey warming him too.

Dave helped himself to another pour. "So anyways, that ended, and J. J. told me that Masterson might rescind my pardon somehows."

"Pressure from the moneyed parties," said Webb, "embarrassed the railroad had to hire outlaws to ensure their progress." He held up his hands, fingers spread. "Dirtied up their white gloves."

"So here we are now," said Dave, finally taking a seat. "Gonna try my hand at being a lawman. Worked for pimps like Masterson and the Earps."

"Luke Short," added Webb.

"Short's all right," said Rudabaugh. Webb just shrugged.

Lute leaned forward and poured himself a shot, his first, from the dregs of the bottle, and of Webb he asked, "When do you take him to meet the Judge?"

Webb smiled, mischievous and secretive, almost winking at Rudabaugh, all with affection. "Shortly and soon, Mr. Wilcox. Shortly and soon."

Thus began the most violent and deadly period in the history of Las Vegas, New Mexico, the Meadow City within the vast desert, choking on new railroad steam.

TWO TOWNS DIVIDED BY THE GALLINAS

The railroad came to Las Vegas on July 4, 1879, and with it came the outlaws.

– The Daily Optic, August 18, 1879.

Las Vegas, New Mexico—pronounced *Ve-has* by all but the rubes—was established as part of a Mexican land grant in 1835 to the settlers there whose roots could be traced back to the early 1600s. The settlement doubled as a fort, designed to be battened down against attacks by the Apache Indians. Originally called *Nuestra Senora de Los Dolores de Las Vegas Grandes*—"Our Lady of Sorrows of the Great Meadows"— the town was built as one-story adobe houses encircling the large central Llano Plaza where stock could be driven to safety.

In this plaza stood a large windmill meant for pumping from the town well, designed by architect and mechanic, Orlando Smith, and approved by town commissioner, Jose Santos Esquivel. The town paid the sum of $137.00 for the contraption. Though long disused by 1878, the battered windmill stood as a reminder of the town's resilience against not only the threat of savages, but also the frigid winter weather, which belied the Montezuma Hot Springs' reputation for a 'welcoming climate.' Its healing waters attracted thousands of visitors every year, accommodated by the grand Hot Springs Hotel, boasting one bathhouse for hot mineral soaking and another for mud. Outside, swirling snow could be had without charge.

With the railroad progressing across the country, the interesting decision was made to put a commuter station in not Las Vegas proper, but rather a mile East of Llano Plaza. To the dismay of the citizens of the already established town, on the East side of the Gallinas River, a clapboard-and-tent city sprouted up almost overnight, offering drinks, gambling, and strange ladies. By the end of the first week, permanent structures stood where there had been first only canvas and audacity.

The West side of Meadow City, almost instantly rebranded as "Old Town," was inhabited by and thrived under citizens Mexican and otherwise, who'd made the town their home for more than thirty years in a manner most decidedly non-segregated. It had its share of crime, certainly, including the ruffian gang run by Hilario Romero and his brood of cousins (as well as numerous unrelated Romeros, the name being as common among New Mexicans as "Smith"). Most of these worked under the auspices of the most honorable Vincente Silva, among his "Forty Bandits," sometime later to be called "The White Caps." In whispers, Silva was known as "The Man with the Red Beard." In public, Silva was addressed as "*Jefe*" or Don with both fear and respect. Silva was also a benefactor, a prominent citizen in Las Vegas. Such was often the case with great men.

It was a blessing, then, that much of the undesirable element that had arrived in Las Vegas prematurely of the trains rapidly emptied into the burgeoning East side, and took with it the even less desirable that had made their home the alleys and gutters of Old Town. There was a stampede for claims on the suddenly valuable land.

East Las Vegas, this newly established Precinct No. 29, was home to seven newspapers, four of which were owned by the same two publishers who ran them in competition. John H. Koogler was the owner and publisher of, primarily, *The Las Vegas Gazette*, and employed Lucius "Lute" Wilcox as the City Editor.

Chief competitor was Russell A. Kistler, owner and publisher of, primarily, *The Las Vegas Weekly Optic* (formerly *The Otero Optic*, and soon to be rebranded *The Daily Optic*, which owed its existence to a loan from Las Vegas' wealthy banker, Don Miguel Otero, Sr.). *The Optic* also employed Lute in the same position.

These two newsmen, Kistler and Koogler, enjoyed an enmity that rivaled any gun-toting foes whose tales of violence daily graced the stained pages of their papers. Koogler the Republican, Kistler the Democrat, and their four papers offering a variety of conflicting views, in order to best ensure advertising from all parties. Even beyond politics, the pair was ever at war. If Koogler wrote about his support of unifying the two towns, Kistler would screech that *"Greasers would be in charge!"* Venom spit in both directions. Each loathed the other, spied upon the other, worked daily and nightly to undermine the other. Such, as Mr. Samuel Clemens would indicate in his own writing, was the credo of the newspapermen.

Meadow City had multiple saloons, liveries, stables, restaurants, barber shops, tailors, and enjoyed one ice cream parlor. While gambling was forbidden in Old Town, it was tolerated in New, depending on which watchman was on duty and when. Convictions and fines of $50.00 were levied at whim.

The town boasted a number of organized bands along with many social and bachelor clubs, including "The Firing Out Club" organized by Miguel Otero, Jr., son of the banker. This club's reason for being was to convince the young men of their ranks that marriage was a sin against machismo. This convincing took the form of drinking to excess on his bachelor's swan song, then binding the plastered bridegroom into a mattress and leaving him afield.

Music could be heard on the streets on all hours, from the mariachis and tinkling pianos in Old Town, to the buskers with banjos and accordions in the New. At any time of day and well into the night one could hear *Suwanee River* or *Whiskey in the Jar* or *Muldoon's Picnic* or *Dixieland* or a variety of Mexican and Spanish ballads. Harmonics spilled forth from every saloon, up and down every street, mixing with the cacophony of wagons, and horses, and laughter, and screaming, and gunfire.

Multiple freight services competed for trade just beyond the depot. One in particular was Adams Express Company, frequented by "Whiskey Jim" Greathouse. It was said he got his nickname from selling liquor to Indians at a time when it was contrary to wisdom. He was now a White Oaks rancher and stage stop owner and a man of considerable wealth. All along the route to La Questa, Anton Chico, San Miguel, Puertocito, La Manga, and now Las Vegas, Greathouse had business interests, some of it ill gotten, much of it legal. Few could say they had otherwise, and many would be more reliant on the former than they'd ever admit outside a confessional.

There were those that called him "Big Jim," a slur on his

height, being less than five-foot-eight-inches tall. Still, he didn't seem to take offense.

As the railroad made its bucolic way West, opportunists of all stripes set their sights on the burgeoning town. When the first train arrived in Las Vegas on July 4, 1879, amidst much ballyhoo and revelry, it is true that the outlaws came with it. The politicians, and other whores, were already there.

Whether it had taken place in the dead of night or in the purity of day, the fact remained that Justice of the Peace Hyman G. Neill, soon to be nicknamed "Hoodoo Brown," was quickly established as New Town's Coroner and, for all intents and purposes, was second only to Lord Jesus Himself.

CHAPTER 3

YOU DON'T GROW OLD IN THIS BUSINESS

John Joshua Webb was the eleventh child born to Job and Mary Webb. In keeping with his given name, Job found all his offspring a burden, but that was to be his life. He made his feelings known to his children, too, that all Webbs were meant to toil and suffer on this earth before returning to Jesus. By the time he was fourteen, John Joshua was done waiting around for Christ's redemption.

In 1871, he left behind the graves of his parents, taken by sickness in Osage County, Kansas, and headed West, for work and—for a twenty-four year old man who'd seen little of the world beyond wagon roads and scrub towns—a soup spoon of adventure. Panned for gold in the Black Hills a spell, worked as a miner in camps that would have him, a buffalo hunter when they would not. As a buff hunter, he took pride in eliminating more than his share of the silly species, the hides bringing in plenty of money, enough so that he once employed a team of eight men, and they could each clear two hundred buff in a day.

Returning to Kansas, Webb found himself in Dodge City at a time when prestigious men had gathered in the names of law, order, and of course, commerce. Bartholemew William Barclay "Bat" Masterson, having won his election for sheriff of Ford County by just three votes, was unpopular in town for all of a month, after which he was accepted as inevitable. Soon after accepting his position, Masterson replaced his political and personal enemy, city marshal Larry Deger, with his brother, Ed Masterson. By the end of that week, Deger relocated to points otherwise and the Masterson brothers more or less assumed ownership of Dodge.

Playing both sides of the Owl Hoot Trail was nothing revolutionary and the Mastersons took naturally to the contradiction. While they managed their business interests in Dodge, they could not ignore the various outlaw gangs plaguing the rail lines and wagon routes. One in particular, alternatively known as "The Trio," "The Rudabaugh-Roark Gang", "The Roark-West Gang," and "Those Motherless Bastards," it was unknown how many men actually comprised the group. Reports conflicted as to whether they were a band of ingenious villains or a collision of half-wits that lucked into crimes and proved just as lucky with evasion. These were mostly young men, of course, as it was difficult to grow old in such business.

Unwilling to accept such interrupt in commerce, by January the Moneyed Interests decreed that something had to be done, and the Mastersons were to do it. Thus, Bat deputized men known to him as trusted members of society: Kinch Riley, Dave "Prairie Dog" Morrow—the only man to have killed a white buffalo and the third man to make that claim—and a newcomer, John Joshua Webb.

* * *

John Radebaugh had the distinction of being one of the very first casualties of the war between the States. A member of Silbey's Brigade, he succumbed in battle in 1861. He left his five children fatherless, his wife a widow, and the family forced to travel back and forth across the burgeoning Midwest—Missouri to Kansas, Illinois to Ohio, to Indiana then back to Ohio again, forever fleeing hardship. Somewhere along the line, the name changed spellings. They were now the Rodebaugh clan.

Mrs. Rodebaugh found herself forced into situations many widows faced, and into the profession also went her three daughters. Her eldest surviving son, David, having apprenticed at several liveries and stockyards, found a talent in handling horses. An even greater talent for stealing them.

Told in no uncertain terms that whoring was more honorable than thieving, Dave left his family behind and meandered into crime. Though still spelling his name *Rodebaugh* on documents legal and official and damning, another metamorphosis occurred, though this time in pronunciation, and so now drifted Dave *Rudabaugh* south to Arkansas, trailing cattle, riding drag on drives, working ranches, trading with the Arapahoe. As with usage of that tribe's dialect, so too did his Spanish grow from negligible to understandable and he could communicate a little better than many others he encountered.

Within these cow camps, he took up with two of similar skills: Milton J. Yarberry, otherwise born as John Armstrong, under an assumed name to hide from a murder charge; and David Mather, said to be a Harvard graduate and of a family who claimed kin to the great Cotton Mather, without whom none of this Western Expansion would be necessary. Mather, with his breeding, his trademark suit of royal blue, and beneath his treasured mustache a constant slight smile that hid his true feelings, earned a nickname that followed him into adulthood and to the grave: "Mysterious Dave Mather."

Rudabaugh was himself slandered with a less favorable sobriquet by Wyatt Earp: "Dirty Dave Rudabaugh," read the writ drafted by Earp, with the new nickname and spelling, "so named for his aversion to soap and water … " Damned lies. He wasn't a fan of shaving and wore a shadow at all times of the day, but he was as regular a washer as anyone on the trail.

The law came for the three in the form of the upstart Marshall Earp—not for their prominent and frequent stage robberies, but for the murder of some rancher. While Yarberry was often guilty of shooting without thinking, at this point in their careers neither of the Daves were prone to bloodshed of any kind. That the rancher's name remained unknown to them raised question as to the existence of this poor victim in the first place. It gave the citizenry an excuse to turn vigilante against them. Arkansas became inhospitable for the ruffian gang and they fled to Texas where they parted ways.

Within two months, Yarberry would pick up another murder charge and a $200.00 bounty would chase him back into Texas, where he joined up—and reportedly performed honorably—with the Rangers.

Mather drifted as well, and was frequently listed in news reports amongst other names, when stages were robbed, shops held up, on and on. Perhaps some of these stories were circulated by the man himself. The nickname was apt. He would eventually stray into Dodge City and find modest stakes there.

Rudabaugh, the man no one called "Dirty Dave" to his face, spent a terrible winter in the Black Hills of South Dakota, lasting almost one full day as a gold prospector before deciding the icy creek waters yielded less reward than stage coaches. He hooked up with a group called 'The Texas Gang' for a while, using the clapboard mining camp of Deadwood as their headquarters. After a while, they were known as the 'Dunc Blackburn Outfit,' after their vicious ringleader, and spent most of their time making Wells Fargo pay for its sins. Blackburn was killed by Scott Davis in '77 and the gang broke up.

Another peril, the Sioux, even in their dwindling numbers, encouraged Dave's return south. Rudabaugh worked well alone, but preferred the cover and safety of partners. He made frequent attempts at straight jobs, liveries, stockyards, the like, but the needs of business left him frustrated and bored, and his employers usually sore for want of an employee, or a full cash register, or, on occasion, teeth.

Encountering other such layabouts and miscreants in dark saloons, Dave met up with Mike Roark, Dan Dement, and Ed West, and where they lacked in shrewdness they made up for in sand. They found success robbing construction yards, making off with supplies and funds before the camps had fully unpacked. Sometimes, a gang could take the same yard twice in a month, the turnover for security detail high and unreliable. Occasionally, lead was exchanged —not every sentry dozed at his post. Still, they'd made enough of a nuisance of himself that the Santa Fe line paid for Wyatt Earp's temporary commission as a U.S. Marshal.

* * *

Even at the beginning of his career, Earp was a man considered bound for greatness. And if it wasn't an opinion offered voluntarily, Wyatt would happily open the bidding.

Putting other interests aside—among them epic plans for gambling parlors throughout the Southwest—Earp rode out to Fort Griffin, Texas, hot on the trail of Dave Rudabaugh.

Earp had a friend in Fort Griffin, a saloon owner and to no small degree mentor, John Shanssey. Shanssey owned the largest saloon in town, The Bee Hive, and no one came to Fort Griffin without watering themselves in the Hive. Rudabaugh had indeed frequented The Bee Hive within the week, but unfortunately he'd lit out the day before Earp's arrival without leaving a forwarding of address.

"He spent most of the night playing cards with John Holliday," Shanssey told Earp. "The dentist fella and sharp."

"I know of Holliday," Earp would later relate to Stuart Lake, his biographer, while recalling the conversation. "He is a killer of men, John."

"Perhaps," replied Shanssey, "but if anyone knows where Rudabaugh went, it would be Doc."

While Holliday had little to offer beyond insults of Dave's character—"He yattered on about heading North, so I would search in that direction. Kansas is North of here, so I'm told." Earp found himself taken with the gambler's straightforward and antisocial demeanor, thus beginning a life-long friendship between the men.

Rudabaugh and Holliday would find themselves adjacent again and again over the next slim decade of their lives. Dave and Earp would only meet once, many years later: amidst blood and gunfire in Iron Springs, Arizona, that left at least one man dead in the water, but neither Rudabaugh nor Earp would sustain even a scratch.

* * *

In Kinsley, taking the wretched Dave Rudabaugh alive was proof of Bat Masterson's success and ferocity as a lawman, so the newspapers said. Businessmen across the country could rest in the knowledge that their wares would be safe, at least as far as Kansas.

Escaping the noose via loophole, Rudabaugh was still unsettled by informing on his partners. "Friends" or not, they'd been saddle mates, for however brief a period it had been. Saving his own neck left him raw.

This rawness was something that Webb recognized and was surprised to see it present in a man so reportedly unrepentant and dangerous. Upon signing his name to the confession, sealing the deal, Rudabaugh emerged from the dark courthouse a free man, and it was Webb who offered to buy him his first drink of freedom.

"You brought me in," said Dave. "Hell, you could have killed me that night. Then you set me up with a lawyer, get me free. Now you wanna buy me a drink." He looked at Webb hard, through the eyes of a man who has killed, regardless of how he'd planned his day a'forehand. "What's your play?"

Webb smiled, extended his hand. "If your reputation is anywhere near true, you could'a taken all of us, 'stead, you listened to me. Man who can kill me and doesn't? I'll happily buy him a drink."

* * *

On July 31, 1878 Dave was meant to be mucking stalls at Charlie Polk's Dodge City Livery when Webb climbed the fence and bid him hello. Shirtless, the white glare coming off his chest in stark contrast to the dark tan of his face and hands, Dave dunked his head in a rain barrel and scrubbed his neck. "*Hola*, J. J.," he said.

"I bring news." Webb swung his long legs over the fence and dropped down. Dust puffed up and he waved it away. "Masterson's gonna pull your pardon."

"How's he doing that?"

J. J. shook his head. "Ain't proper for a lawman of his silk to muck around with the Owl Hooters. He's getting proper shamed in the press. So examples have to be made. I have other rounds to make, but I'm telling you first."

"Obliged," Dave said, shaking water out of his eyes. His hair was getting too long and it felt greasy against his sunbaked neck. "You give me a few minutes, I'll ride out with you."

"Ain't you got work to do?"

"Here?" Dave spat into the dust. "I'm making six bits an hour. I drink more'n that." He grabbed his work shirt from the post and shrugged into it. Not an impressive man to look at, thin and wiry, like a scarecrow after a middling-sized meal, but there was always a look in his eyes of bored violence wanting for any excuse to cut free. It was this look he wore as Charlie Polk came through the door, red to the scalp with anger.

"Rudabaugh! There's shit in all six stalls! Where the hell —" He stopped short of entering the paddock, lingering in the shelter of the doorway, seeing Rudabaugh with another, and not immediately recognizing Deputy Webb. "What's this? Where you think you're going?"

"Resigning, Polk," said Dave. "You can take care of that dog meat on hooves your own self."

"No you don't, you sombitch," said Polk. "You owe me two dollars' worth of work."

Dave shrugged into his braces and spit into the dirt

again. He reached into his pocket and pulled out the hammered tin star he'd been issued by Masterson the day he joined the Atchison-Topeka "deputies" and never returned. He flipped it into the dirt at Polk's feet. "That might buy two bucks worth of something." He and Webb turned to the gate to leave.

"Wait a minute," said Polk, now with a sly smile that put neither man at ease. "Let's put your talk to test. I say you owe me two dollars. You say you're a gun sharp."

"When'd I say that?" asked Dave, in a low voice.

Polk heard the growl but kept his courage and soldiered onward. He held up the star. "You shoot this out the air like Annie Oakley," he said, "and we're square."

Dave gave Webb a look. Webb shrugged and planted his ass on the fence bar. To J. J., Dave said, "I ain't heeled." Without a thought, Webb took his pistol and handed it butt-down over to Dave. "Fine," he said to Polk. "Flip the tin and keep your eye on it." He cocked the Colt.

Polk did as he was told. His thumb sent the star skyward and Polk watched it with his full attention, waiting for the report of the pistol, certain the bullet would miss. Polk watched the star descend, without noise accompanying. And as it dropped past his nose, Polk's eyes focused on the yawning tunnel of the Colt's barrel not six inches from his face. The noise he emitted was comical and inimitable.

"We square?" asked Dave.

As Polk nodded and watched the pair depart, he realized he'd pissed himself, the stream of urine running down his boot and heading towards the star imbedded in the dirt.

* * *

Dave had his doubts that what Webb said to him was true. His pardon was from the State of Kansas, and he doubted even the great Masterson had the juice to turn that around. He thought, rather arrogantly perhaps, it was more reasonable that J. J. was ready to move on and just wanted the company.

Webb and Rudabaugh were first seen meandering around Las Vegas, NM, in August, 1878, both together and separately. As usual, they were the study in contrasts: Webb dressed neatly in long coat and linen shirt, black buckskin boots, flat-crowned black sombrero, always brushed and handsome; Rudabaugh dressed in whatever he'd passed out in, unshaven, uninterested in fashion of any sort, taking pride only in his tan Stetson, low crown, wide brim.

Once the owner of The Lady Gray public house in Dodge, Webb missed the saloon life and became stakeholder and partner of Holliday's Saloon on Centre Street. Some minutes later, he'd joined up as a deputy for Marshal Joe Carson. Rudabaugh went to work for Whiskey Jim Greathouse who'd bought a stake in the Adams Express Service. Some nights Dave would sling drinks in The Gadfly or Baca's Saloon in Old Town, or other such places. That was their public persona.

Some folk were fooled.

CHAPTER 4

MIKE GORDON HAD NO NOSE

The so-called "Railroad Wars" of 1878 were waged less in the canyons and more in the courthouses and newspapers. The Moneyed Interests represented two parties: The Atchison, Topeka and Santa Fe Railway, and the smaller Denver and Rio Grande Company. The disputed territory: The Raton Pass, a 50-mile corridor through The Royal Gorge Canyon in Colorado, so narrow it could only accommodate one set of tracks. Sharing was not an option.

The Denver and Rio Grande was given the right to lay the track. They hired guards to protect against sabotage. Undeterred, Atchison, Topeka and Santa Fe Railway hired the great Bat Masterson to form a similar army. Among those recruited, with J. J. Webb as proxy, were Mysterious Dave Mather, Doc Holliday, and Dave Rudabaugh. Despite occupying the same end of the bad man spectrum, the latter two men did not get along and gave each other a wide berth as they eyed each other crossing Front Street in Dodge. As a matter of truth, in a contest of who had more friends, neither man would come out winner, though Rudabaugh could always be seen with one in particular. Always Webb. Where there was one, inevitably you would find the other.

Ultimately those working for Masterson and the AT&SF interests would find themselves on the side of Denver and Rio Grande, after the sufficient bribes were paid into Bat's pocket. In the end, D&RG completed the line, and did so relatively bloodlessly.

While the newspapers reported with breathless glee that bloodshed was carving furrows on either side of the Gorge, the truth was that any shots fired were done in boredom and over the heads of the laboring coolies. Battles involving rocks and clubs were frequent, often among men on the same side. Over time, listening to the language of the Chinese workers, even the white men got to insulting each other with *"bok gwei!"*

One of the very few casualties of The Royal Gorge War was J. J. Webb. In an attempt to intervene in fight between two drunken factions, J. J. received a brick to the mouth, resulting in the loss of his left eyetooth. Rumor had it that it was Masterson who paid to replace the missing tooth with one of solid gold. After the initial shock, the gold tooth became a thing of pride with J. J., and he flashed it often with a smile wider than his formerly.

In misfortune, the tooth did not fit as well as J. J. liked and he was a frequent patient of Dodge City dentists. Of those famous jawbreakers was Dr. John H. Holliday, his compatriot in the Railroad Wars. As a dentist, Holliday was an accomplished card player. Yet, it was during a routine re-fitting that Webb told Doc about new opportunities arising in New Mexico, new towns popping up along the rail lines, lawless and inviting.

"I thought you were a man of the law, Webb," said Doc,

wiggling the bridge back into place. J. J. responded in vowels until Doc withdrew his hand.

"How many men you know had their character changed by the badge?" asked J. J.

"Meaning?"

Webb paused a moment, tonguing the tooth and checking the fit. "Meaning," he said, wiping his mouth afore drool dampened his beard, "a tin star don't make a skunk into a lion."

"Makes a skunk feel like one."

"That's the difference," said Webb, his tone bitter.

Masterson had been a hero to him, but more and more he'd revealed his true colors. For Webb, a man who'd drifted West in search of something large, he'd viewed the Masterson brothers—Bat and Ed—as big men, as paragons. There was a phrase that Webb had yet to learn: "never meet your heroes."

"We should both go to Las Vegas," said Webb, pronouncing the 'g' as an 'h', as was proper. "There's already an end-of-the-line camp set up across from the Mex' side of the Gallinas. Train gets there in June."

"And what should we do there, John?" asked Doc, being unusually familiar.

"Hang your shingle," said Webb. "Open a saloon. Rake the rubes in poker."

Holliday considered the man for a moment. Las Vegas was infamous for its healing hot springs, if not the lie about the mild winters. It had been Doc's experience that John Joshua Webb was a generally upstanding man, quiet and righteous minus piety. Doc would have to admit that, as much as he did anyone, he liked Webb as a man, and admired his sense of right and wrong, a quality he himself so often lacked. Seeing the man in moral quandary made Doc take pause.

As if queued: "You might want to talk to Bat as well," said J. J. "He's getting some gaff for hiring outlaws on the Denver dime. He's yanking pardons."

"I am not wanted for anything." Indeed, he'd been cleared of an assault on a man named Charlie White in Dodge, Doc's bullet merely splitting the belligerent barman's hair while answering an insult.

"Make sure Bat knows that," said Webb. "He does not care for you."

"He said that?"

"Your feelings hurt?"

Doc shook his head. He could count on one hand the men for whom he had genuine affection and still have fingers left over. Still, Holliday took the hint. By the end of June, "Holliday's Saloon," with Webb as a backer, opened on Centre Street in Las Vegas, in the form of a canvas tent hung from a single back slat wall. Plans were in place to add on to the joint: walls and a floor were considered *de riguer*.

Dave Rudabaugh was there, sitting in a corner and playing with an errant thread poking from the canvas, when Mike Gordon showed up calling for Polly. Polly Nome was just 16-years-old, hired to serve drinks, wipe the bar, whatever the old Mexican bartender, Miguel Romero, couldn't or didn't want to do. She was a sweet girl, plain, soft spoken and rarely; at sixteen, she seemed made to bear many fat children. Gordon felt that too.

"Polly, y'all get out now, girl! We's leaving!" Gordon wouldn't enter Holliday's. He feared Doc. Like many, Gordon had bought into Doc's reputation, as much earned as self-generated. *"That bandy-legged killer,"* The Gazette branded Doc, and Gordon, *"poor, inoffensive."*

Mike Gordon had no nose and often forgot to affix his leather replacement, causing consternation among townsfolk and tears from children. The facial appendage had been bitten off by an outraged gambling opponent who'd caught Gordon cheating. Seizing Gordon's head between his hands, the gambler took hold and chewed until his teeth met at the bridge. It had taken half a minute and ruined the game for everyone.

The loss did nothing to improve Gordon's character, nor did the inevitable and unimaginative nickname that followed, "No-Nose Gordon." When he was not pursuing odd jobs he wasted his time in gin mills. Doc Holliday had taken an instant dislike to the man but tolerated Gordon's coin. Polly, sadly, became the object of Gordon's misapplied affections.

Polly had already been engaged once, to a handsome young man who'd worked as a shotgun rider for a freight company. An accident with the wagon on the trail—details were sparse—put an end to Polly's romance and Gordon looked to fill the position. Polly however preferred those with facial features intact, particular as she was.

Doc had warned Gordon to stay out of the tent whether the dentist was present or not. Gordon, in return, recommended that Doc join "The Lunger's Club," meaning the consumptives that sat on the long mourner's bench outside The Plaza Hotel in Old Town, basking in the sun and waiting for death. That cemented their relationship.

For his part, Dave didn't regard Gordon one way or the other. He was just another passerby in the busy bustle of the Las Vegas day.

"Polly! Get out here now, girl!" screamed Gordon. An empty whiskey bottle hung loose in his left hand, his right hovering over the butt of the gun stuck in the waistband of his piss-wet pants.

"Polly!"

"Shut the fuck up!" said Dave.

Gordon ignored him. "I'm here to kill or be killed, you don't come out!"

Though willing to oblige, Dave didn't then yank his gun. Seemed rude to rob Doc of the opportunity.

Polly glanced at him once over her shoulder, grimaced, turned away to mop a table. Gordon threw back his head and screamed, his leather nose flipping up and coming to rest on his forehead, giving him the look of an infant rhino. He yanked his gun and fired a shot into the tent. The bullet tore through Miguel's trousers, right at the crotch, but fortunately the bartender wore his trousers loose.

Holliday had been playing solitaire in a corner opposite the bar. He'd been drinking all morning, which explained why he did not immediately get to his feet. He merely glanced up at the shot and said, "You'll not do that again, No-Nose."

"To Hell with you!" Gordon responded with a second shot. The floor exploded in splinters inches from Doc's boot.

It was then that Doc Holliday rose to his feet and, without reel to his step, crossed to the entrance of the tent and fired from within the cool shadow. Though a notoriously middling shot with a pistol, this time Holliday's bullet flew true. Blood blossomed from Mike Gordon's chest. He dropped both gun and bottle into the mud and reeled backwards. "Mother—!" he screamed. A call or a curse, no one could say.

Polly screamed and cowered in the corner by the bar. Gordon staggered away, leaking like an unbunged barrel.

Doc returned his gun to its holster and his ass to the chair, and placed a Red Nine on a Black Ten.

An hour or so later, a tanner named Kennedy, who'd occupied the tent next to Gordon, found the man writhing on the ground, unresponsive and blood-caked. He sent word over to Marshal Joe Carson.

For her part, Polly's compassion won her over and she had Gordon moved to her room in the St. Nicholas Hotel, a room paid for by her employer and the new occupant's killer. The sawbones from Old Town was summoned, and Dr. M. M. Milligan reported that things were hopeless for No-Nose Gordon.

When Gordon took his last bubbling gasp, Sheriff Carson, who also served as the City Marshal, was called upon again. He then summoned New Town's newly arrived coroner, Justice of the Peace Hyman G. Neill. With Neill came his personal bodyguard and deputy, a hulking creature, all blond hair and beard and muscle, whose name may have been "John Schunderberger," but went by the mononym of "Dutchy." Upon arrival, Dutchy took his place outside the door and remained there, silent as a sphinx.

Striding into the room, filling it with his personality if not his moderate frame, Neill paused a long moment, examining the body. He *"hmmed,"* to himself, ran a troubled hand through his thinning hair. His eyebrows were thick and two-toned, white over black, with the outer edges oddly curled, giving the impression of horns. With grim visage, he proclaimed Gordon's death: "Natural Causes."

"He was shot!" Polly protested.

"Naturally," replied Neill.

Polly shook her head. "What kind of man … " she began to cry. "I need to get away from you. You make me feel … get your *hoodoo* out of my room."

Turning her back on the men, sobbing as Dutchy took Gordon's body away—carried under one arm like a sack of grain—Polly resolved to leave Las Vegas as soon as she could. That would likely require yet another gentleman to provide that passage for her. Ideally, he would have his nose and could survive wagon crashes.

* * *

The Judge made his home in Close & Patterson's Variety Hall, a handsome building owned by partners George Close and the little-known and seemingly gossamer M. Harold Patterson. The Variety Hall boasted guest rooms, two saloon areas, a dance hall, a gentleman's cigar lounge, and a restaurant. Up the spiral staircase were the offices and doves' quarters. A large sign hung over the bar as declaration: *"Everyone entertained in the best possible manner."*

If the elusive Mr. Patterson, whose other business interests kept him in towns east, had few acquaintances in Meadow City, Judge Hyman Neill was a nearly unknown commodity. Scant details were little more than rumors. Some said he came from a respectable family in St. Louis, others'd placed him in Missouri. He'd once been a printer's devil, employed to wash ink-soaked rags. His final words to his publisher were allegedly, "Set fire to your damned rags and shove them up your ass!" Sometimes reported with more decorum as, "Wash your own damned rags!", depending on the audience.

Where he'd met up with the monstrous Dutchy, none could say. Abundant rumors about the man-mountain were even wilder. It was whispered that Dutchy had come face-to-face with the Crow Killer, John "Liver-Eating" Johnson, and lived to tell of it, better still that Johnson had emerged for the worse. It was rumored he'd been forced to run the arrow gauntlet by the Apache in Texas, that he'd wrestled alligators with the Seminole in Florida. None could say for sure. If reports came that he'd been born on the moon, few would argue against it.

The fact was Neill and Dutchy arrived from Dodge City with apparently bona fide credentials from various moneyed and respectable interests, bearer bonds, writs of government, proclaiming him both J. o'P. and Coroner, but without benefit of election or approval by anyone whose names sounded even vaguely familiar.

But official was as official did. There was trade to be done, and freight to move, whiskey to drink, cons to run. Anyone with the time to take notice of the comings and goings of their betters would be advised to find more meaningful engagement.

First order of business: personally installing Joe Carson as Marshal. Then other officials of Neill's choosing were put forward in an ad hoc election, himself included, for permanent coronor. Saloonkeeper Bill Goodlet had been put up as an opponent to the Judge to give the illusion of democracy. Goodlet's profits were already booming barely a month in and he had no desire to split his focus.

Neill had become familiar with Joe Carson back in Dodge City. With Carson came loyalty and few questions. People liked his easy-going nature and disarming smile. A tobacco-stained beard was his sole deficit. He was also married to a fine and handsome woman, near half-a-head taller than her husband, and pleasant of disposition. Neill counted Mrs. Carson among Marshal Joe's exploitable assets. Should it ever come to that.

Things fell into place rather quickly. Marshal Joe was deemed trustworthy by the businessfolk both legitimate and otherwise, and therefore attracted upstanding deputies. Among them, John Joshua Webb and Mysterious Dave Mather. Rudabaugh would be found wherever Webb was; deputizing was as good a way as any to keep an eye on him.

The word "Hoodoo" followed Neill around. Close & Patterson's Lady Mabe, who managed the women, both doves and dancers, took hold of the word and gave it a surname: "Hoodoo Brown." The judge reminded her of an ex-lover of hers long past, who went by the name of Brown, and who'd given her the same ill feeling. The Christening was complete and stuck fast.

The man himself enjoyed the appellation, always delivered in hushed tones and with those responsible crossing themselves after. Both *The Gazette* and *The Optic* referred to him as "the man in the shadows."

From his vantage point in his rooms in Close & Patterson's, Neill could watch the entire town as it grew from camp to civilization. He had a keen instinct for recognizing men who'd parked themselves on a fence, legally-speaking. There was no shortage of colorful characters among them, with rainbow names attached. The *Gazette* and *The Optic* were fond of spending column inches on lists of fanciful monikers: *"Rattlesnake Sam, Cock-Eyed Frank, Web-Fingered Billy, Hook Nose Jim, Stuttering Tom, Durango Kid, Handsome Harry, William P. "Slap Jack Bill" Nicholson, "Little Jack" Allen, John "Bull Shit Jack" Pierce* (politely printed as "Bull Shot Jack"), *Selim K. "Frank" Cady,"* and, of course, *"Mysterious" Dave Mather."* There was even a "Jordan L. Webb," lurking about. Lon Chambers, a confederate of Pat Garrett, would refer to these appellations as "consumed names."

"*History*," Lute Wilcox would write in his journals, "*is little more than lists of names, assumed and Christened, given and given back.*"

The particular Webb in which Mr. Neill was most interested was John Joshua. In Dodge City, Neill'd had more than one run-in with both Mastersons. There was bad blood. Money had not exchanged hands when it should have, or so one side contended. In Dodge, when the Mastersons were about, Webb was often close behind. Now Webb was in Las Vegas, absent Mastersons' upstanding influence. When a man is outside of a guiding hand, he can easily go astray. Arranging side paths was one of Neill's special talents.

* * *

" 'Dirty Dave Rudabaugh' ?" Dave slapped the latest issue of *The Gazette* down on Lute Wilcox's desk. The near-blind author flinched at the flap. He took the paper and held it close to his nose. Then he put the paper down, felt around for a specific pigeonhole among the many set in the wall behind him, and withdrew a rolled yellowed poster. He unrolled it for the benefit of his accuser.

"*Wanted,*" he read, "*Dirty Dave Rudabaugh, so-named for his aversion to soap and water —* "

"Bullshit!" said Dave. "That there is—what's the word?"

"Slander," said J. J., lingering in the doorway, arms crossed, showing off his gold tooth within an amused smile.

Wilcox shrugged. "I didn't write the notice."

"Ya'll wrote that article! Slander's what it is, all right!"

"Actually, it's in print, therefore it's 'libel.' " Wilcox shrugged, spread his hands. "I can print a retraction. 'Not-so-Dirty Dave,' I could call you."

"Obvious Dave?" offered Webb.

Rudabaugh pointed back at the door in agreement. "See? 'Mysterious Dave' Mather. *That's* a decent name. A right … " He looked at Webb.

"Sobriquet?"

Dave made a face. "The fuck?"

"Nickname," Webb amended.

Again, the great train robber pointed a finger in Webb's direction, perhaps at the word hanging in the air. "That," said Dave. "Who the hell called me 'Dirty Dave' ?"

Lute tapped the poster. "I believe that was from when Wyatt Earp was pursuing you."

"Wyatt Earp," said Dave. "We ain't never met. But he has made an enemy of me. I see him, I'll kill him."

Dave Rudabaugh would get his chance in September. Earp and Mattie Blaylock rode into Las Vegas for a very brief stay, and when they departed, with them went Holliday and his paramour, Big Nose Kate Elder, whom Dave had never met but had admired at a distance, removed both from Doc's reputed violence as well as her own. She was not the unhandsome woman the cruel nickname implied, but even she used it in reference to herself. Again, he was reminded that these names don't often come self-applied, but can follow you forever.

Unfortunately for 'Dirty Dave,' he'd been out robbing stagecoaches outside Raton for a full week, under newfound Judge-proven protection, when the Earps came and went. The Holliday Saloon went from tent to construction to abandonment in just four months. Webb had sold his interest some weeks prior to the exodus so the joint was not his problem.

For his part, Judge Neill felt some trepidation with the arrival of the unpredictable Earp faction, and he relaxed quite a bit when Holliday departed with them.

It was time to put his plans into motion.

CHAPTER 5

TELL IF MUMFORD KICKS

While he should have been hauling grain sacks for Greathouse, Dave was instead malingering outside of The Gadfly with Whiskey Jim's sheepdog, Burt, when Webb arrived and made the official recruitment. "Dave," he called. "You are officially deputized."

Dave didn't need to be told twice. He jumped to his feet like a startled frog, eager for anything other than work. "To do what?" Burt looked up and yawned, then returned to his midmorning doze.

Webb walked back towards town with Dave on his heel. "Know Jim Allen?" Webb asked.

Dave thought for a second. "Waiter or some such over at St. Nicholas? Little guy?"

J. J. nodded. "Goes by the name of 'Spence.' He just shot a drummer called Mumford."

"Any particular reason?"

Webb shook his head. "Argument over eggs. Mumford cuffed him. Two minutes later, Spence borrows a gun from the cook and puts a bullet in Mumford."

The facts in the case fit about a dozen similar situations that ended in the same way. Dave shrugged. "So what?"

"So now Dutch Henry and Pete Phillips and a whole drunken committee want to string Allen up and nobody can find the Judge."

"What's that to do with me?"

"I need a favor," J. J. said, and that was all he had to say to satisfy Dave, but he continued on anyway. "Stand outside St. Nick's. Doc Milligan is upstairs with Mumford. He'll flash a thumb up or down if he can get the bullet out. If Mumford kicks, you come find me first."

Nodding, Dave leaned up against a post and lit a cigarillo. "Leave it to me," he said.

Leaving it to Dave, Webb resumed his duties as deputy under Marshal Joe Carson. Marshal Joe had gone to Santa Fe on Judge's business and would be gone another day or so. That left Webb and Mather in charge of the peace. Mather took Spence Allen into custody and they wagon-rode into Old Town with the unlikely "Bull Shit Jack" Pierce, quickly deputized to ride shotgun, the only man that Mather felt could trust that early in the day. At the very least the only one sober at the antiquated hour of nine AM. New Town's jail was still under construction and would remain so until 1881, thus they rode to the little San Miguel County six-cell jail the Mexicans called *la perrera*, "The Dog House."

This left Webb to search New Town for the Judge. He'd already made like a dust devil to Close & Patterson's, but Neill's offices upstairs were vacant. None of the doves there, still rousing to the new day, could say to a certainty where the Judge had gotten to, for none wanted to be wrong—or even correct—lest they earn the Judge's wrath delivered by Dutchy. Lady Mabe, the madam there, who managed both the doves and the dancers and them that overlapped, could do only so much against the giant.

Webb found Mabe upstairs in one of the plush red-and-gold-trimmed smoking lounges. She had a cigar clamped between her teeth and was barking orders to two boys in waiter aprons. "I want you to go over every inch of these couches. You see a burn, circle it in chalk. Dutchy'll take it down to Anderson's when he gets back—" Ole Anderson had set up shop at the end of Centre Street, doing upholstery and whatnot.

"Where is Dutchy?" asked Webb.

Lady Mabe turned her eye on him. "What?" she said. She was a short woman, broad-shouldered and dark of hair, with the biggest, brownest eyes Webb had ever seen. He loved those eyes—most men loved those eyes—but when they were filled with anger and belligerence, as they were at present, they flashed a gaze best averted. Still, Webb had a duty.

"Dutchy," said Webb, cocking a questioning thumb over his shoulder, "or the Judge?"

"Hyman ain't here," said Lady Mabe. "Dutchy neither. They went up to Otero."

"Know when they'd be back?"

Lady Mabe picked up a brass ashtray and sent it sailing in J. J.'s direction. Her aim was off. It went past him, wide, and clattered in the hallway. "I ain't his personal secretary!"

Tipping his hat to ward off additional ashtrays, Webb spun on his heel and went down the curving staircase two steps at a time.

With the Judge absent, Spence Allen didn't have many friends with any particular power. Even as it grew up and out, Las Vegas was also growing nastier. The "good, decent" citizens were as eager for violence as the so-called bad men who had drifted in from Dodge and Santa Fe and White Oaks and Fort Sumner and Old Mexico. Sitting in St. Nick's, big rancher and reformed horse thief Dutch Henry Borne was stewing with tanner Pete Phillips and who knew who else, waiting to throw Allen a necktie party.

Feeling helpless, Webb went back to the sheriff's office, with a distant and futile hope that Bat Masterson might have wandered in to be useful in the situation. His luck consistent, he only found Rudabaugh waiting instead. "Got the thumbs down from your sawbones," he said. "Mumford kicked."

"Who else knows?"

Dave shrugged. "Mumford for certain."

Webb's stomach dropped. The biggest problem was that Mumford wasn't just "some drummer." He'd come in from Leavenworth, Kansas, in town on business for several deep-pocketed outfits and was known to Don Miguel Otero, owner of Otero, Seller & Co., and president of the San Miguel National Bank. Craning his head out the door, Webb could already see a small group growing larger as they progressed up Bridge Street towards Old Town, towards the jail holding Allen, with only the Mexican jailers—and Mather—between them.

Quickly, Webb crossed the room and opened the rifle cabinet, chucking to Dave a Winchester and a box of cartridges. "I need you to run as fast as you can up to the jail in Old Town," Webb said, loading a second rifle for himself. "Anyone gets near Spence, you shoot them. Don't you hesitate."

Dave took exception to that last part. How many men had accused him of murder? Yet here was his best friend painting him as slow to action. There was a word for it, but Dave couldn't think of it and damned if he'd ask Webb.

Cutting down National Avenue, Dave ran the mile in

record time. He'd briefly considered swiping a horse—to use in his official capacity—but he'd woken up energetic that morning. Plus, it was more exciting than shouldering grain bags at the Express Service all day.

As he ran, several of the camp's dogs ran with him. Dogs liked Dave Rudabaugh, as he was usually generous with his slops, so the half-dozen or so collies and coonhounds kept with him over the bridge. Lazy Burt was not among them.

Once across, he stuck to the crisscrossing side streets and came to the jail on the Pacific Avenue side. Peering round the corner of the adobe structure, he saw the now-considerable mob, big Dutch Henry at the lead, rifle in one hand looking like a toy. Beside him, Pete Phillips, winding a rope into a noose.

Rudabaugh entered the jail through the rear entrance. He passed Spence Allen in the cells. "It was all a misunderstanding!" Spence shouted. "I never meant to kill him!"

"Shut the fuck up," said Dave.

Mather had the front door open and he stood tall but alone in the doorway, like a Palace Sentry, his own Henry rifle held in a relaxed grip. The morning sun bathed Mather in halo. Rudabaugh felt he was backing a saint in some painting. Neither Pierce nor the jailers were anywhere in sight.

Now, Mather and Dutch Henry had history and not that long ago. In leaner days, they'd stolen horses together, but only Dutch Henry had done the time. Still, Mather didn't think the big man was dumb enough to advance. So to the crowd, Mather called out, "You men go home!" The tenor of his voice relayed his authority and did not quaver.

"Not without Allen," said Dutch Henry. The men in the mob agreed with taunts and insults. "And we'll go through you, Mather. Try us and see."

"Try me and see," said Rudabaugh, sliding the barrel of the rifle over Mather's shoulder.

Dutch Henry was unmoved. "Just the two of you? You can't take all of us."

"Nope," said Rudabaugh. "But I can take Pete." He adjusted his aim. "You hear that, Pete Phillips? Next person takes a step, you lose your head."

Pete Phillips stopped in his tracks. He was a tanner. His trade was animal skin and harsh chemicals. It was his lot that the trade would do him in, not a bullet. Hearing his name said by Rudabaugh froze his bones. He cast a quick and imploring glance around. "Don't look at Dutch Henry," said Dave. "He's about to get you murdered."

Pete put a hand on Dutch Henry's shoulder. Outside of a spit-wet handshake to seal a deal, nobody ever touched Dutch Henry. The mob stopped advancing.

"Go on, you men," Mather repeated. "You shall not hang anyone today."

"Get the fuck out!" said Rudabaugh, adding punctuation.

Once the mob had dispersed, Mather closed the door and locked it. As of by some miracle, Mexican deputies appeared. Both Daves found themselves surrounded. The eldest, Joaquin Romero, smiled widely at Mather. "We can take over now, *señor*. Your friend will not be harmed."

"Mayhap I will stay around to ensure that," said Mather. Romero shook his head, his smile still wide.

"No need, *señor*," he said. "You have my word as a Deputy appointed by Don Vincente Silva himself."

Rudabaugh spat on the floor, but Mather did no such thing. Silva was known to him—and to many in Las Vegas—as the honorable and venerable leader of Old Town. He was also the operator of *La Sociedad de Bandidos*, one of the most ruthless gangs of *vaqueros* on either side of the Gallinas.

The message from Romero was clear: Silva was in charge, not the *gringo* lawmen. Whether Spence Allen would ever emerge from that cell or not, it would be by no say of either Dave.

The other deputies were smiling now, their hands resting idly on the butts of their pistols. Mather stood his ground, but Rudabaugh felt the drop in temperature. He put a grubby hand on Mather's brushed shoulder. "Let's go, Mather."

Rudabaugh opened the door and Mather backed through it, keeping his eyes on the deputies, watching Allen's chances evaporate.

CHAPTER 6

THE DODGE CITY GANG

The Judge— he'd gotten used to being called "Judge Neill" and "Judge Brown" interchangeably —did not reappear in Las Vegas until the end of the week. By the time his coach arrived, a midnight mob had already visited the Old Town jail. Money had been exchanged, the back door left open.

Jim "Spence" Allen, as well as the three other prisoners inside—two white vagrants and a Negro muleskinner who'd killed his employer's mare in petty revenge—made their escape on horses readied for them. And them that paid for their escape followed behind them.

The posse caught up to Allen and the others at Aguilar Hill, just outside of Chaperito, eating dinner at a campfire without a care in the world. 'They'd been freed, therefore they were free,' was the sum of their attitude. Furthermore, the men approaching, recognized as their liberators, were certainly coming to join in on the celebration.

The wagon returned the next morning with the bullet-riddled corpses stacked like sheep carcasses. The bodies were then laid out in a neat row on the platform of the plaza's windmill.

The Judge pondered all of this. There was an unofficial Vigilante Squad making noise in Las Vegas, and not only the bored and bloodthirsty sought membership. Beyond ruffians like Dutch Henry and his ilk were honorable men like Colonel James A. Lockhart, bankers like Jacob Gross, the orator Rush J. Holmes. All had made rumblings at the disintegrating safety of Old Town since the erection of New. Violence met with violence was as inevitable as the sunset. Neill had Dutchy keeping an eye on things, but the big man couldn't be everywhere.

Neill gave word that he and Dutchy were to be in Otero, but in truth, they'd returned to Dodge City, just under Bat Masterson's nose, to tie up some loose threads left behind in a previously hasty escape. Neill returned with several small bags of gold on his person, a gun reportedly belonging to Frank James (and would be sold as such regardless), and a small stack of papers—writs, land holdings, deeds. He had plans upon plans already in motion. Now, before him, was a volunteer army.

Having men in his vague employ *demand* an audience was something new and Neill found it amusing. He wasn't a man fast to temper—mistakes were made in the heat of anger, and he loathed those kinds of miscalculations. Like the men who built this country from nothing, wrestling the land from the savages to make it suitable for society, he employed rougher, dimmer men to do the things beneath his station.

There he was in his own elegant offices at the top floor of Close & Patterson's, the sumptuous space filled by the asses and elbows of the rough characters in his hire, leaving grease stains on his filigreed wall paper, his embroidered pillows catching on their rough clothing, and they were wanting *justice.* "Something has to be done," implored Webb. "Vigilante mob can't just up and kill men in the middle of the night. We need some kind of law here, Judge."

"Especially when Joe is indisposed," said Mather, referring to now-Marshal Joe Carson, not present and presumably seeing to his other duties, though the good-natured man was more suited to chair-making than peacekeeping. Carson was well liked enough in camp that it made him an inefficient lawman. Which was what the Judge liked best about him.

Neill glanced behind him, at the ever-present Dutchy, his hulking shadow since St. Louis, when they were both young pie-bald grifters. As usual, Dutchy's face was a mask of impassivity, frightening in its dullness. In its absence, Neill found meaning. There was validity to what the men wanted. Certainly, Mather, Webb, Carson had all found themselves on the shadier side of the streets on occasion, but still had the reputation as upstanding men. Forgivable sinners.

The skunks in the room—Rudabaugh, Pierce, Nicholson—you could see it in their faces: a fellow had been injured and the outrage had to be addressed, so that they could be free to go about their business of robbery, thievery, and general mayhem outside of Las Vegas.

So interesting was the situation, Neill frequently stifled a laugh. The complaint, the ironic thirst for *order* in a place of thriving chaos, was so very delicious. It fit perfectly with Neill's own plans for grifting his way into the White House. Not as President, no, no. The President was too visible. Secretary of War, that was a position with room to breathe. First Las Vegas, then Santa Fe, then the Territories as they achieved statehood. Opportunities abounded for the man who could control his wits, his desires, and his minions.

In Dodge City, Masterson had accumulated about him a small collective of upstanding killers, his brother, Ed, and

Luke Short among them. Bat euphemistically called these men "The Dodge City Peace Commission." In public, they were *The Law*, past acquaintances be damned, and Neill felt it best he and Dutchy got the hell out of Dodge. With Masterson embattled in a bitter re-election campaign—the good folk in Dodge none too thrilled with the bribery that changed his railroad alliance to suit Denver—Neill was free to move about the rest of the Territory. A joke occurred to him.

"Boys," he said, "Your demands have not fallen on deaf ears, of that I can assure you. Webb, you are known to me from Dodge, as is Mather, I know you both to be decent men. Joe Carson is as fine a man as ever I've met. Unassailable character, yes, it is true. But he is only one man, is he not? And is that not the point of this gathering? Friends, I have seen the light. It is my honor and duty as a Justice of the Peace of this fair city in its infancy, to protect the citizenry, its wellbeing, its property, and its future. Henceforth, you shall all be marshals, under my direct authority."

Behind him, Dutchy grunted only loud enough for Neill to hear. Approval or disapproval or amusement or phlegm, the Judge couldn't say.

"As the official peace commission, go forth and be this town's protectors. Save us all from the outside influences of bunko men, card sharps, carpet baggers, snake oil salesmen."

Tin stars would be purchased, as would notices in all of the local papers. *The Gazette* and *The Optic* both found The Judge to be an excellent source of information. At any rate, he provided as much entertaining fiction as the editors themselves often produced. He dubbed his own commission, unofficially in every print mention, "The Dodge City Gang," specifically to annoy the Mastersons, three hundred miles away.

As "The Dodge City Gang," the individual members were often called upon to meet with The Judge in private. Oaths were sworn, often over the bounty posters of the newly duty-bound. Signatures were signed in blood only metaphorically.

By night, one faction of The Dodge City Gang would commit crimes all across the Territory. By day, the other faction would go to work covering the tracks of the first. It didn't weigh easily on Webb, nor on well-meaning Joe Carson. But money was coming in. No more tents, no more sleeping in hay lofts, or on unswept floors in the backs of store houses.

For Carson, it meant that he and Hattie could build a house on Front Street, remove themselves from the St. Nicholas.

For Dave Rudabaugh, it meant he could pack out of Whiskey Jim's bunkhouse and into one of the new bachelor rooming houses. Webb had purchased a house on the left side of Simmons' Rooms at the end of Centre Street, where Dave finally planted, behind the St. Nicholas Hotel.

It was at St. Nick's that J. J. began courting a handsome young widow named Bonnie Hommacher, and he started to feel like the man his mother had hoped he'd be. He kept his tin in his pocket. It seemed more likely the badge would be a target, as it had been in Dodge and which had ultimately done in Ed Masterson, by way of example.

Webb, Mather, Marshal Joe, and Bill Goodlet sat down with the Judge one afternoon and hammered out the basic laws they would enforce. No guns in the variety halls or saloons. No gambling permitted in joints known for trouble. No public drunkenness. No using the alleys for outhouses.

No sleeping in the thoroughfare—a tent city could be erected for the itinerant until they could successfully move on, integrate, or be murdered.

For The Gang, there was one rule: No committing crimes in Old Town.

"Go about your business in the Territory," Neill suggested, to much squirming by Webb, uncomfortable with *any* talk of crime, an attitude the Judge found childish. "But keep the hell away from Old Town."

" 'Cause we ain't got jurisdiction there," said Webb.

"Because we require the use of their Dog House," said Mather.

"Because Silva runs the fucking Forty Bandits," snarled Dutchy from his corner, startling the hell out of the others.

Mather and Webb cast their wide-eyes at Neill, who shrugged and said, "He's not wrong."

"What's that got to do with the price of beans?" said Webb.

"Silva is likely having this same conversation with the Bandits right now. Old Town is no safe haven for the greasers either, as they have their own Mex Henrys and Pedro Pedrossons calling for blood on their side. Leaving aside the fact they got the only working jail either side of the Gallinas—a fact I'm perfectly fine with until things settle down—we don't have the manpower to go head-to-head with the Bandits *or* a Mexican lynch mob. So keep your heads down West of the Gallinas. Anywhere else, you get pinched, use a common alias. Dutchy and I will get you out."

"Common alias like what?" said Goodlet, the least likely man in the room to wind up behind bars.

"Rumplestiltskin," said the Judge, irritated and eager to

end things. "Fuck do I care? Dutchy's real name is Samuel King. Use that."

Now it was Dutchy's turn to look surprised, in the form of a slightly raised eyebrow and an utterance like a tripped-over dog. With that, the Judge closed his books and waved the two men away.

"I think he lied about Dutchy's name," said Webb, as he and Mather descended the polished blonde staircase.

"Well," said Mather, "if ever I am arrested, I am certainly not using 'Dutchy.' "

CHAPTER 7

"SERÉ COMO EL TOPO."

In 1872, Hilario Romero and several other members of The Forty Thieves rode into Las Vegas amidst gunfire and shouting. There was much to celebrate as they had finally defeated Gregorio Lopez and his band of *Lobos*. The two factions of bandits had clashed innumerable times over the years, each side claiming bodies in attrition for the bodies claimed before. Hilario himself had hung Lopez's head by its hair from his saddle horn.

Don Miguel Antonio Otero, whose son would one day be Governor of all New Mexico, sat outside The Exchange Hotel, overlooking *la plaza*. He was with Don Vincente Silva and they were enjoying the cool summer sunset over cigars and *cervezas*.

Some of the younger children of the town followed behind the horses, reaching up for rides or cactus candies. Otero took notice that one boy stood on the street by himself, drawing in the dust with a stick, taking little notice of the parade, only flinching at the gunfire. Setting his cigar aside, he called the boy over. "Linolito!"

Pequito Lino Valdez waited until the horses stamped by,

then he crossed the street to see what the man wanted. *"Por que?"*

"Why do you not celebrate?" Otero asked him while Don Silva smoked. "Do you not want to be big and strong like Hilario? Or Desiderio, his cousin?"

The boy shook his head and spat into the dust. He'd seen his mother, father, and all his aunts do the same when the banditos were mentioned. "No," he said. *"Seré como El Topo.* The freedom fighter! He fights for the people!"

"What people?" asked Otero.

The boy spread his arms wide. *"All* the people!"

"Gringos?" asked Otero.

"Si!" said the boy.

"The Negro? The Apache?"

"Si! *Si! All* the people!"

"The Comanche?"

Linolito balled his hands into fists and put them on his hips. *"All* the people. *¿Me repito?"*

Otero laughed mightily as he flipped a coin to the boy and dismissed him. Settling back, Otero relit his cigar, and Don Silva finally spoke.

"I do not know of this 'The Mole,' this freedom fighter," said the Mayor of Las Vegas, thoughtfully and with suspicion. "Who is he?"

Otero laughed again, and blew a smoke ring out into the purple evening. "He does not exist," he said. "The boy's father, Miguel Valdez, told his children stories to entertain them and send them to sleep."

"He inspires them to be heroes," said Don Silva, nodding in approval. *"Bueno."*

"Your Forty Thieves killed Valdez last winter," said Otero, managing another ring before his cigar extinguished once again. "He owed you money."

"Oh, well," said Don Silva. "That is not oppression. That is business."

Nine years later, Don Silva would again sit on the balcony of The Exchange Hotel, and look down upon the men who came and went in the Plaza beneath him. He did not have Don Otero for counsel this day, nor did he particularly need him. The problem before Silva was a simple one. Across the Gallinas, the white politicians had brought with them the criminals. The Mexicans had only just rid themselves of the local Apache, and now the *gringos* were here to provide the violence they'd been so lacking. His *banditos*, known now as *las Gorras Blancas*, "The White Caps,"—so named for the hoods they wore during their plunder, a fear tactic mimicking the *gringo* Ku Klux Klan in the South—had been instructed to do no wrong within town. Leave the *crímenes* to the *gringos* who would not be able to hide their crimes, but whose crimes would provide the White Caps cover.

The White Caps were notorious outside of town, but tolerated so long as they remained so. Yet, Silva could not help but notice that with the expansion of the East Side, the people of Old Town noticeably relaxed when Hilario, Desiderio, or Joaquin Romero walked the Llano Plaza. Having their own gang of outlaws was somehow a calming notion to the people of The Meadows. To keep his citizens from mounting vigilante mobs in Old Town, Silva decided that it was time for the western end to have their own peace-keeping force, something more visible than the weathered deputies that kept the little jail clean.

Hilario was easily persuaded. He'd been lately spending less time terrorizing ranchers in the Territories in favor of guarding the Gallinas bridge with intensity. Hilario Romero was a hulk of a man, and his shadow rivaled that of their windmill. The people of Old Town respected him and were eager to forgive his wayward past. The good people who'd made Las Vegas their homes, their places of business, felt the corruption seeping towards their doors.

"I want you for Sheriff," said Silva to Hilario. "The town wants you."

"One year ago, I would have disagreed with you, *jefe*," said Hilario. "One year ago, I would have bartered and pleaded and perhaps even escaped into the night. But now …"

He thought of the mob of white men descending upon the jail, demanding the release of prisoner Allen. The *gringos* used their jail, relied on their deputies, to protect *their* criminals. Had he been there, Hilario would have shot the prisoner, the mob leaders, and perhaps the deputies, for cowards.

Lingering within the shade of the Mayor's office, Silva offered Hilario a cigar while they discussed the most important issues. They came to the point of trustworthy men. "I trust all of the Forty Bandits like brothers," said Hilario. "My brothers have robbed me blind. I've done the same to them."

Silva nodded. "That's the obstacle I have encountered." He smoked and thought. "We need to appear unassailable. The people must know they are safe on this side of the bridge." Silva stood. There was a pain in his leg, a wound from his wild youth that pained him when he sat too long. It labored his thinking. Silva went to the window, exhaled a plume of smoke and stared out.

Across the street, at the South end of the plaza, manning his *tio*'s vegetable cart, was Lino Valdez, who went by Antonio now, and was *pequito* no more. Antonio Lino Valdez, the young man had grown up every bit as forthright as his father's fictional *Topo* ever could have been. He was liked by the young and old alike and respected, as far as respect by peasants took you.

"Do we have five like him?" he asked Hilario.

"No," said the new Sheriff. "I don't know four like him."

Silva nodded. His cigar had gone out. "Round up the three you do."

Chapter 8

Having A Good Year

August 18, 1879: a Barlow & Sanderson stagecoach was nearing the village of Tecolote, New Mexico, when it was robbed by three masked men. John Clancy, Jim Dunagan, and Antonio Lopez were arrested for the robbery. Though no name appeared on the warrants, the arresting marshal was J. J. Webb. None of the three men were convicted. Reportedly, they were shown to the border by two deputies, one of them being "Bull Shit Jack" Pierce. The other was unknown, but wore a "tan Stetson and three pistols."

A few weeks later, on August 30, B & S suffered another hold up. The crime was not clean—a passenger was wounded—and a posse from Santa Fe rounded up Selim "Frank" Cady, Slap Jack Bill Nicholson, "Bull Shit Jack" Pierce himself (his name entered into the record as "Bull Shank"), and Jordan L. Webb (no relation), all with ties to the Dodge City Gang, and each giving their names initially as "Samuel King." They too escaped conviction.

Months later, Dave Rudabaugh would confess to this crime, naming his partners as, "Las Vegas Marshal Joe

Carson (deceased)" and "a man named Joseph Martin, who lit out soon after. Don't know what happened to him."

On October 14, 1879, a train was robbed outside the Las Vegas area by "several" masked men. The robbers wore canvas hoods and were "quite terrifying" in presence. As reported in *The Optic*, *"The marauders made off with $2,085.00, three pistols, and all the lanterns on the train."*

Three men, Charlie Bassett, Chalk Beeson, and Harry E. Gryden, of Dodge City, Kansas, were hired by the Adams Express Company to investigate the robbery. The posse was assembled by John Joshua Webb. The masked men were never found, nor was the money recovered, nor the pistols, nor the lanterns.

* * *

It was not lost on J. J. Webb that he was just as responsible as any for cultivating the notion that Las Vegas was rotten with criminals seemingly immune from the law. He'd learned by then that "reputation" was what others made of you. The Earps and Mastersons were well-respected men of the law, *by reputation*. By riding tall, J. J. kept his reputation in the positive end of the public's assessment, even if he did wear gloves to hide dirty hands. For certain, no one yet booed him from the street as he passed.

For his part, Webb enjoyed spending the money paid by Barlow & Sanderson, also the other bosses and bankers, while giving the Dodge City Gangsters a wide berth. His reports were circular and comical. Those who were wanted had always just left, or had covered their tracks, or had turned to dust devils before their very eyes. The appearance of "something being done" was all that really mattered to the Moneyed Interests. The charade brought comfort to the shareholders back East. Insurance covered the losses, and the Dodge City Gang split it all equally.

Shamefully, it didn't take more than a minute for Webb to accept his share of the spoils. The posse jobs paid $4.00 per day, with one of those dollars to be split amongst any deputized. There was a dollar bonus for every man arrested and brought in. On a good weekend, he'd pocket eleven. The daily deputy position paid no better. Dave and his skunk jobs would always yield more. As far as Webb was concerned, the Gang was just ripping off the moneyed interests traveling throughout the territory. Why shouldn't he benefit? The only virtue in poverty was inedible piety.

Despite his increased fortunes, Webb remained a man of modest means. He opened an account in Old Town's San Miguel National Bank, established by the Oteros and off limits to the Dodge City Gang and the White Caps both. His money was safer there than in his boot. Never one to gamble, drank when others did and scarcely any time else, he was rarely sure what to do with the cash that accrued. On Sundays there were horse and dog races, but he never won big enough to develop the habit. J. J. bought interest in local establishments, particularly a large part of Close & Patterson's, which seemed like a sound financial move and proved out. Even with the Man in the Shadows lurking eternally above, the Variety Hall and Saloon sections were always filled with raucous revelry. He entertained notions of establishing another saloon of his own.

When he was not working, blistering his ass on a horse during a typical reach-around searching for those whose home addresses he knew by heart, J. J. also had trouble filling his time. He slung drinks in the C & P, and doubled his shifts for Marshal Joe Carson, giving relief to Hattie Carson who preferred her gent home nights.

There was, of course, the criminal element outside the Gang to contend with. A day hadn't yet passed without someone's blood pooling in a hoof print. The papers took such delight in reporting in massacres, their pages read of little else, even if come morning no one could recall the specifics of this or that horrid event, or even meeting its participants. Stories made for a good breakfast read.

Bonnie Hommacher assumed kitchen duties at the St. Nicholas. Seeing as the joint's previous cook had provided Jim Allen with the gun used to murder Mumford, a vacancy in the kitchen had been inevitable, and followed a hasty midnight resignation. Bonnie accepted the position gratefully. An unattached woman, she had meant to wed Charles Marsh in the Spring, but pneumonia put an end to Charlie before the last snow fell. Bonnie came from hearty stock, necessary for survival in the borderlands. She hadn't come to Las Vegas in a clay pot. J. J. found her independence attractive and terrifying.

Living behind the St. Nicholas made daily dining there convenient, so J. J. and Rudabaugh frequented the restaurant. They'd found the grub there preferable to the other joints, cheaper too than C & P's, which was also a hike away. Bereft of a single pious trapping that would give its "Saint" appellation weight, instead the modest dining room felt homey and warm, but practical. Butcher paper protected the linen tablecloths as best it could. The plain serving plates did not match the delicate china on display in the breakfronts. It felt like a smart operation.

Once Bonnie assumed stove duties, the quality of the food had improved considerably. But it would be almost a full month before Bonnie realized that the shy lawman had been courting her.

It started with handsome gratuity. Bonnie wasn't sure the

one named Rudabaugh could work out figures, but his igno-
rance always worked out in her favor, paying with crumpled
notes and more coins than should be. Some men, particularly the others on the so-called "Dodge City Gang," were
never generous, but whatever Rudabaugh left, Webb would
leave double. Plus the lawman always smiled at her, with
the smile reaching his bright blue eyes, not to mention that
gold tooth of his. Rarely spoke to her, and couldn't meet her
eyes when he did, but always smiled.

When she came through the doors, Webb instructed
Dave, by way of shin kick, to take off his hat and stand in
her presence. Hard kick, too, from the responding yelp. Two
or three instances later, the ruffian needed no further
encouragement and henceforward nearly bowed in her presence. Like the lawman, Rudabaugh rarely spoke to her
directly, preferring to mumble his orders to Miggs the
waiter. With Webb, it was with boyish shyness and was not
smallishly endearing. With Rudabaugh, she kept her purse
in the back.

For another week, the gratuity came with a wild flower,
usually wilted and fussed-over crushed, plucked from a
neighbor's yard. To Bonnie, they were sonnets.

One early September morning, a pair of drummers were
harassing the new waitress, the colored girl, Jenny Freeman.
When Jenny was five, she got caught out in a rainstorm and
was splashed by lightning. The electricity painted her body
with a grapevine pattern, standing out white against her
dark skin and running the length of her left side, from the
top of her neck to the back of her calf. This gave her the nickname of "Lightning Jenny." In later years, long after leaving
Las Vegas behind, "Lightning Jenny" would lead her own
gang of outlaws, plaguing mail routes throughout New
Mexico and Arizona. But on this morning, she was 17-years

old and being abused by two rough characters still drunk from the night before.

Bad language was hurled Jenny's way, and then so was a lead cup. The cup missed Jenny's head, bounced against a wall, and then rolled to a stop beneath J. J.'s boot as he came in with his shadow. Rudabaugh looked rough and sleep-eyed, but Webb was instantly alert. As Bonnie hurried through the kitchen door to Jenny, she watched as John Joshua took charge.

J. J. crossed from door to wall in three strides. With his pistol, he clubbed the first ruffian behind the ear, dropping him like a grain sack. The second, with the gutter mouth, Webb cracked in the face with butt of his Colt, and blood sprayed across the table. Rudabaugh caught the falling man and said, "Now you clean that up!" Slamming the man hard onto the table, Rudabaugh wiped him around, sopping the blood into his striped suit coat.

J. J. ordered the man released. Rudabaugh dropped him to the floor. Webb took hold of their collars and hoisted them to their feet. To Lightning Jenny, he said, "Do you wish to press charges, miss?"

Jenny, unaccustomed to white men addressing her with respect, kept her eyes down and shook her head. Then Rudabaugh spoke. "You wish me—hey, miss? Hey? Do wish *me* to press charges?"

Something passed between the pair then—the gunman and the free girl—that began as shock and quickly became a shared giggle. Lightning Jenny guffawed. "Naw, sir," she said, and touched her fingers to an imaginary hat brim, "Appreciate it, though!" Rudabaugh laughed then too. Bonnie found the joy on his rat face to be almost as unpleasant as his normal blank scowl, but Jenney seemed delighted.

"Well, you keep his fuckin' teeth as a souvenir." Dave toed a pair of white triangles her way, and she snickered again at the absurdity.

"David," said Webb. "Comport yourself."

Dave gave him a sour look but the smile didn't dissipate. "Pardon the French."

"I speak a little French," said Lightning Jenny.

Keeping hold of the collars, Webb shoved the pair through the swinging doors, hurling them into the muck of the thoroughfare. He returned to the parlor wiping his hands on his vest. Rudabaugh had already claimed a seat at their normal table, still snickering with Lightning Jenny over their shared joke, whatever it happened to be.

To Bonnie, Webb quickly doffed his hat and lowered his eyes. "Ma'am," he said. "Apologies for the roughness." J. J. quickly took his seat by Dave, who shook his head at it all.

"How the sand just leave your hourglass like that?" asked Dave.

"Hat," said J. J. Dave grumbled and removed his Stetson.

Bonnie didn't forget the quiet action, nor Webb's demurring as she entered. Violence was a daily event in Las Vegas, and sometimes that spilled into the St. Nick's, but this event had been something different. And after that day, she saw Webb differently.

Rudabaugh too, but mostly John Joshua.

* * *

In late September, the Dodge City Gang got its one and only peek behind the Judge's veil. "Screwnose Martin" Murphy, who worked at the Mercantile, proposed to baker Hettie Docherty. It would be the first formal wedding in New Town. It would also be the Judge's first to preside over. The method, he realized with cold terror, completely foreign to him. He'd been to only one wedding, an uncle's. He was six years-old and fell asleep almost immediately, and unfortunately standing, falling backwards onto the chapel floor. So as officiate, he had concerns.

With New Town lacking anything resembling a church, the ceremony would be held in the Variety Hall of C&P's, on the very stage where every night the dancer girls kicked up their legs, often *sans culottes*. But necessity trumped decorum.

Pacing back and forth in his offices, trying to both learn the methodology and imagine the blocking, the Judge worked himself into a lather of profanity. Eventually, he kicked open his door and called first for Lady Mabe, then for Dutchy. He rallied his troops on the stage. J. J. had been loitering outside with Dave Rudabaugh when the Judge's call issued forth. Dave tagged along for the entertainment, choosing to linger in the back to avoid participation.

"Mabe, you stand in for Hattie," Neill demanded, mopping a sheen of sweat from his high forehead before it dripped into his mutton chops. "Dutchy, you're Screwnose."

"No," said Mabe.

"What's that?" said Neill, whirling on her and dropping his notes. "What's that?"

"You're like to wed me to this great walking outhouse by accident," said Mabe, jerking her thumb at Dutchy. "I been to lots of weddings. I'll tell you when you get something wrong."

"Fine," said Neill, huffing and dropping his papers again. "Fine," he repeated, gathering them from the floor, standing on one, ripping it in two instead of lifting his foot, then swearing again. "Webb! You're Hattie!"

A deep red hue crept up from beneath Webb's collar and

overtook his face in two steps. "It's *Hettie*," he said, stamping up the steps. "And this is beneath me."

"Quiet!" the Judge ordered. He pointed at the stage where Webb should stand. Dave smothered a laugh, but the noise carried through the empty hall. Webb shot a hateful glance over his shoulder. Rudabaugh bit loudly into an apple he'd snaked from a table on the bar. That noise carried too and the Judge winced. "Quiet! Now … " and then he returned to muttering over his papers. *"We're gathered here together to celebrate the union of …* What'd you say? Hattie or Hettie?"

"*Hettie*," answered Webb and Mabe in unison. Dutchy remained stoic.

"Hettie," said the Judge, making a note. "And … what the fuck is Screwnose's Christian name?"

"Screw*cock*," answered Mabe. The laughter resulting sent the Judge back into a rage.

His bible hit the far wall.

Soon he had Webb and Dutchy facing each other—rather, Webb faced Dutchy's collarbone and lower half of beard—with Webb miming holding a bouquet, his face redder than the two apples Dave chawed down. As the Judge paced, Mabe followed, making fussy adjustments for her own amusement. For his part, Dutchy stood and did as instructed, like an obedient oak tree. Webb stewed with Dave's laughter pinching at the back of his neck.

"Okay, do you Hettie, take Screwnose Murphy—"

"For the love of God, will you call him 'Martin' ?" said Mabe.

"Do you take *Martin?*" The Judge stared hard at Webb.

"Christ," said Webb, and glanced at Dutchy. "If it'll get this over with, I fucking *do*."

The Judge cocked an eyebrow at Dutchy. "Screwnose—goddamn, uh, Martin? Do you?"

Dutchy nodded.

"Speak up!" shouted Dave, spitting apple.

"By the power vested in me—"

"Yeah, that's the part worried me too," said Mabe, stepping back.

"Skip that," said Webb.

"I'll skip what I want to skip!" said the Judge. Then, "Don't tell me what to skip and what to add." His hands were sweaty and had stained the pages.

To everyone, seeing the Judge foam like this was astonishment. Here was a man who ordered murder like a meal, fussing over a wedding.

When the day came for the blessed event, the Judge managed to mumble his way through it all without too much consternation. The important bits got said, the rings were exchanged and the bride got kissed. The festivities spilled out into the thoroughfare, as C&P's didn't allow gunfire celebration within.

Rudabaugh and Screwnose had never met, nor had he any past exchanges with the new bride. That did not stop him from slicing a large piece of cake for himself nor spinning Hettie a turn during the bridal dance. He did, however, restrain himself from running off with the nuptial purse, even though it was sitting unattended just inside C&P's. He felt that showed growth of character and later bragged to Webb about his restraint.

"You want a prize for not being a skunk?" asked Webb.

"I denied my nature," said Dave. "Don't I deserve it?"

"That and more," said J. J. "That and more."

* * *

The drummers who'd caused such a fuss in the St. Nick's at the beginning of the week reappeared near the end. They were cousins, Yoke Milner and E.Z., the latter's initials lazily repurposed into the nickname, "Easy." They'd ridden throughout the Territories for some months, making little more of themselves than nuisance, though it was suspected that Yoke was responsible for the death of a stable boy in Otero. The pair came to the Meadow City seeking the same as so many others: violence, adventure, notoriety.

Following their humiliation in the St. Nick's, the cousins Milner had laid low enough, sticking with the tent slums closer to the rail station, The Gadfly and the like. But they'd kept their eye out for the sheriff's deputies, watchful for a revenge opportunity.

It was Yoke who'd approached Dave Rudabaugh Saturday morning. On this rarest of occasions, Dave was working, a sack of horse feed over each shoulder, special delivery from Greathouse to the L.V. Livery on Centre Street. With the ruffian so encumbered, Yoke Miller thought he'd found the occasion. As he stomped down the wooden walkway, dodging grocers, meat carts, the like, Yoke found his sand draining away the closer Rudabaugh got.

Yoke retained enough grit to impede the man's progress on the walk. Swallowing hard, he jabbed a forefinger into Rudabaugh's sternum. "You tell your lawdog friend me and my cousin are coming for him," he managed, his throat suddenly a cracked desert. "You too, you sumbitch."

Rudabaugh didn't drop the sacks, nor did he do anything but fix his dark eyes with a bored stare. "Ya'll ain't still staying at the St. Nick's?" he asked, his tone even.

"What the fuck is it to you?"

"Well," said Dave slowly, "you go gather up your cousin,

go back to the St. Nick's, pack your *mierda*, and get the fuck out."

"Why don't you come help us pack?" said Yoke, the question hissing through his teeth while the rest of him wondered why he'd even ask.

Rudabaugh sighed. "You caught me in the midst of a duty," he said. "It'll take me eleven minutes to drop this off and walk back." He looked up at the sun, made a quick calculation. "See you at half-past."

Pushing past the drummer, Rudabaugh continued on his way towards the livery. Yoke watched him go and felt his life go with him.

Neither Milner could be considered much of a hard case. They were troublemakers, true, but a man half-filled with salt could glare them into submission. Masterson served them notice in Dodge, as had Luke Short. Another reason they'd preferred the border towns and end-of-the-lines. After taking another few seconds to recover, Yoke ran down the walk towards the St. Nicholas Hotel and Cousin Easy.

Rudabaugh proved punctual. Bonnie Hommacher was standing outside, cleaning her hands on her apron and scowling at Dave as he approached. "Those two men are upstairs with guns," she said, her tone accusatory. "I hadn't trouble with them all week."

Nodding, Dave stared past her into the hotel. "Go see if you can find J. J.," he said to her. "Tell him to lay low."

"Jenny's upstairs," said Bonnie, "in the Number Three."

Dave nodded again. "Maybe find Marshal Joe, too."

Bonnie didn't wait for an escort. She hurried off towards Carson's office and hoped John Joshua would be there.

"You here to see us out, Rudabaugh?" called the other one from somewhere upstairs.

It was cooler inside than out, and it took a second for

Dave's eyes to adjust. Yoke was upstairs on the balcony, a Navy Colt in his hand. Dave drew his Schofield with his right hand and mounted the steps. "Where you at, Jenny?"

"I'm here," came the small voice through the closed door to Number Three.

"You okay?"

"I'm buying a gun tomorrow," said Jenny.

Dave laughed but his face didn't show it. "Don't blame you." He stopped at the top step, his gun leveled on Yoke. "You can come out, Jenny. These bad men ain't gonna hurt you."

Slowly, the Number Three door cracked, then Jenny came out, her eyes wide and watchful. Dave kept his eye on Yoke as she came towards him. "You go on now and find Marshal Joe," he told her.

As she passed him close, she whispered, "The other one's behind you in the Number Five."

"I know where he is," said Dave, eyes still on Yoke. "You go on."

As she passed him descending, he took another step up, now fully on the landing.

"We gonna deal with you," said Yoke.

Later, when asked, Dave will say he heard the Number Five door creak, alerting him to the presence of Easy Milner, but in truth, he'd heard no sound. Something pricked at the back of his neck and that was all it took for him to yank his Colt from the holster with his left hand and fire straight-armed behind him, plowing a hole through Easy Milner's gut.

Blood bloomed from Easy as he spilled back into room Number Five, splintering the door crashing against the wall. Yoke threw himself sideways against the railing and fired. Dave launched against the doorjamb of the Number Four—

screaming, *"Chinga tu madre! Bok gweilo!"*—and kept both pistols going. Grey smoke filled the space between the two men as bullets zipped by, wood exploding around them. Dave fired twice more and through the smoke, he heard a gurgling scream as Yoke's body hit the floor hard.

Both his guns empty, Dave kept them trained on the body anyway. He still had his third, another Colt's .45, in the cross-draw ready to roar. Dave risked quick glance behind him to ensure Easy was not on the advance. He was not. He was on the floor and partially on the wall, body stiff.

Limbs splayed through the struts of the railing, Yoke Miller was dying badly. He had three holes in him, including the one that had removed a good portion of his face, leaving a crater that bubbled blood like a mountain spring over the side of the balcony, pattering down onto the serving tables below. Yoke's body convulsed with each gurgling gasp, crimson spitting through the wounds in his chest.

Dave stood a moment, waiting. Only when Yoke finally emitted his death rattle did Rudabaugh return his guns to their holsters. A minute or so later, Marshal Joe was there, with both Mather and Webb backing him, guns drawn, but unnecessary. Dave removed his belts and held up his hands, as was customary.

"Guess I'm spending some time in Old Town," he said descending the staircase, walking wide of the blood creek trickling from the Number Five. Marshal Joe took his guns, then his arm.

* * *

"Was he wearing his badge?" the Judge asked J. J., who shook his head.

"It don't even have a pin," said Webb. "I think he wears it on a string around his neck."

"Well? Had he produced it prior to shooting? Had he warned them they were dealing with a peace officer?"

"Dave is barely a deputy," said Webb, realizing he was being unhelpful.

"Did he do *anything* to indicate he was law?"

Webb shrugged. "I wasn't there," he said. "I was here with you."

There was a problem. The Millers had come to Las Vegas at the Judge's request. Granted, it was a request he had made over a year ago previous in Dodge City and forgotten about. There was nothing official to connect the dead men to him. Still, it was a relationship he'd best see buried with the deceased.

"Let him stew in the Dog House for a while," said the Judge, scribbling a writ in his authoritative hand, "then produce this."

Webb glanced down at the paper. "'*It is my estimate that David Rudabaugh conducted himself with the duty of his office in the slaying of—*'" Webb looked up. "You left the names blank."

"I usually do," said the Judge.

* * *

The events at the St. Nicholas Hotel did not warrant more than a few lines in any of the newspapers. *The Optic* ran the longest piece, naming the cousins and saying that they were killed "by a deputy during the course of his duties." Rudabaugh was not named in any of the notices.

The Gazette ran nothing about it at all.

* * *

Marshal Joe Carson left Dave at *la perrera* in the charge of Joachim Romero, and both with a full bottle of whiskey. As far as an afternoon in jail went, Dave found this was more pleasant than many in his past. He and Joachim drained their bottles, singing *Amorcito Corazón* and *Via Condios* and *Molly Malone* and *I'll Tell Me Ma*, until both men passed out from the drink.

When he awoke again, Dave found a clean-shaven young Mexican man smiling down at him, his foot up on the bars. Dave's Spanish failed him as he mumbled, "*¿Estoy aquí?*"

"*Si*," said the young man. "You are here."

It took him a moment to gather himself. His head had an angry mule in it. "I don't know you," he said.

The young man shook his head. "*Me llamo* Lino," he said. "Valdez."

"Good to know you," said Dave, groaning as he sat. Deputy Valdez stuck a tin cup of water through the bars and Dave was grateful for the kindness and said so. Valdez nodded. "My friends show up yet?" Dave asked.

Valdez misunderstood his question. "Don't worry, *señor*. If men come, I will not give you to them." It took a second for Dave to parse the meaning. He looked up at the man and saw him in a different light. "No matter how much money I'm offered," said Valdez. There was no joke in the Deputy's tone. None of the wink-and-grin you got from the other Mexican deputies in Hilario Romero's employ that said you would not be protected, you were not their problem, you were their profit. Deputy Lino Valdez was implicitly saying the opposite. And meant it.

It wasn't that Dave held Mexicans in particularly low regard, no lower than he held a man of any color, he reckoned. It was more the matter of seeing a lawman as honorable made the matter a puzzler. Dave nodded, touched his brow. "Much obliged," he said. And Valdez grinned back at him.

Sometime before sundown, J. J. finally showed up with the Judge's writ and Lino released Dave without fuss. The pair had killed time playing cards and telling filthy jokes. By the end of this particular bout of incarceration, Dave Rudabaugh left his cell with the feeling he'd gained something, though damn him if he could figure out what.

* * *

In light of the events of the past week, Bonnie Hommacher felt obliged to reward her unofficial-official protectors with a home-cooked meal.

"You cook for us every day," Webb complained as he shrugged into a clean-brushed suit coat, newly purchased for the coming evening.

"Well, now I wanna do it for friends, not customers," she said, picking a hair from his shoulder with affection. "To say *thank you*." They were a the modest sitting room in the St. Nicholas. Other guests were present too, pretending over tea and newspapers not to notice the pair.

He eyed her with suspicion. "To me *and* David?"

Bonnie sighed. She found it as hard to hide her dislike for Rudabaugh as it was her affection for John Joshua. "He looked out for Jenny," she said. "*Even though he's the one put her in danger*," she didn't say.

"He's like to make you uncomfortable," Webb said. "That is his nature."

"Don't matter," said Bonnie, finding another hair on his lapel. "It's the thing to do."

"He might want to bring Jenny with him."

"John Joshua Webb, why would that make any difference to me?"

"Some folks might—"

"Some folks might shoot themselves in the foot 'cause their boot's too tight," she said. "I got nothing to say to 'some folk.' Jenny's a good girl," she said. *"That deserves better than David Rudabaugh,"* she didn't. Aloud: "I presume he owns cleaner clothes than the duds he goes around in?"

"If'n he don't, he will."

"Good," she kissed him lightly on the cheek, then again out of sheer fondness. "Now you hustle him over here by five o'clock. I just got in some beautiful steaks."

Webb didn't have to be told twice. As far as he was concerned, the sun rose and set at her command. He hurried off towards his digs and found Dave dozing in his room.

"Bonnie's cooking us dinner," he said, kicking the foot of Dave's bed to rouse him.

"I et," Dave mumbled.

"That was breakfast! Get up."

Dave turned over, tossed his pillow over his head. *"Bok gweilo,"* came the muffled insult. He was still regretting emptying the bottles of whiskey with Lino Valdez in the Dog House and wished to regret in peace.

Webb kicked the bed again then went to the near-empty closet where Dave kept his few belongings. He found a brand new tan frock coat and trousers flung over the rod without hangers. A decent pair of low boots, more or less polished, occupied a corner next to a bag containing random stacks of currency, purloined weaponry, other effluvia typical of Dave's occupation. "I can't believe you just leaving evidence of your crimes lying about."

"Go 'way!" said Dave into his pillow.

Webb tossed the clean clothes onto the pile of Rudabaugh on the bed. "I'll strip you nekkid and stuff you into them duds, you don't get a move on."

That got a frustrated growl and the pillow hurled in Webb's direction. "Goddamn it," Dave groused, then gave J. J. a hard look. "This is important to you, ain't it?"

"It is."

"Goddamn it, then," Dave said again. "Go on, get out. Go perfume your feet. I'll be down shortly."

"You swear?"

Dave tossed a boot at him. "Fuck outta here!"

True to his word, ten minutes later, Dave was downstairs and walking with Webb towards Bonnie Hommacher's home on Front Street.

* * *

Bonnie agreed that having Jenny present might make John Joshua's less civilized companion better behaved. Though Rudabaugh had never comported himself in any sort of rough manner in the St. Nicholas—prior to the shooting, of course—neither had he ever presented himself as the perfect dining guest. Indoors, he was a dog on its hind legs. Yet her free girl helper had taken to him, and Jenny was good company. Bonnie also knew that the two men would outright forget to invite her if it were left up to them, so she sent a little Mexican boy—

Felix, ever ready for errands—over to Jenny's with the invitation.

Jenny arrived in a lovely yellow dress she'd purchased at Robb's Mercantile that afternoon. The shade muted the white tattoo left by the lightning and though she felt even more eyes on her when she walked about town wearing it, the dress had a lovely flow and it made her want to twirl. Since receiving Bonnie's invitation, her feet scarcely touched the ground, floating like a daffodil on the wind.

The men arrived at Bonnie's door sheepish and hat-in-hand. Jenny fussed about them, hustling them to their seats. While Bonnie's attention was strictly on John Joshua, she found amusement in Rudabaugh's sullen awkwardness. Seeing him stumbling and mumbling helped gauze somewhat his violence that stained her memory.

For his part, Webb's heart was like to leap from his chest and scurry out the window. Seeing his rough compatriot in the home of a woman he held so high made his hands sweat. What was he doing, bringing Rudabaugh into such an environment? Like bringing a badger to a salon. Whatever a *salon* was. He'd heard the Judge mention them once or twice. Still: moron move.

The four of them gathered in Bonnie's modest little dining room, the men sat awkwardly as the women served. Eating off the China plates ringed with blue roses come all the way from San Francisco. Steak, potatoes, beans, cornbread, all the hearty things men loved.

While Bonnie and J. J. made mawkish small talk, Dave focused his entire concentration on various commandments handed down to him by Webb the entirety of their walk: No chewing with his mouth open, repress any appreciative belch or wind, keep his elbows off the table, put his silverware down when he wasn't using it. Too many rules just to chaw a meal. But it mattered to J. J., so he'd do his best.

He looked up and found Jenny smiling at him with amusement. "What?" he asked, with no little embarrassment. By God, that girl had a smile on her.

Jenny shook her head. "Nothin'."

"You seen me eat before."

"Usually, you hunker over it like the drummers gonna take it from you." She parodied him hunched over the plate with suspicious eyes.

"I do not," said Dave, smiling in spite of himself.

"Do too." She looked down at her meal, suddenly embarrassed and too aware of her surroundings. shifting potatoes around with her fork.

Without looking up, Bonnie came to her rescue, "And don't he always leave a hell of a mess behind!"

The remark caught Dave the right way and he snorted out a mouthful of beans into his hand. Horrified, Webb kicked him, but he continued coughing. "Sorry," he mumbled, and gave Jenny a bug-eyed look in recrimination. She giggled.

With sly eyes, Bonnie gave J. J. a look and a smile that he'd feel in his heart forever. Finally, he let the gate swing open and a smile bloomed beneath his mustache.

"So, uh … " said Dave to Jenny, with mischief. "What'd you do with them teeth I give you?"

Jenny guffawed, even Bonnie snickered, shamefully, into her napkin. Webb kicked Dave under the table. "Will you quit kicking me?" said Dave.

"Kick him again!" said Jenny.

And thus the pretext of high-toned civility left the modest dining room, leaving only four people to enjoy a pleasant evening.

For once, the sun set on Las Vegas without witnessing further injury.

CHAPTER 9

FOUR BASTARDS IN VEGAS

In January 20, 1880, four white idiots rode into Las Vegas with the intent to raise Hell. They were John Dorsey, William Randall, a man named James Lowe who traveled under the name of West, and Thomas Jefferson House, better known to his friends as Tom Henry. As soon as their horses were stabled at Llewellyn & Olds, they began their drinking. Beginning at The Tin Five, a whiskey tent at the mouth of Centre Street, they swilled their way down the thoroughfare. Once they reached the rental tents at Blanchard Street, bottles on planks laid across stumps, the four took an hour off to rest. Soon they were at it again before the initial drunk had even run its course.

"We are four bastards here to drink up every drop of rot gun in the place!" Dorsey announced in Close & Patterson's. "We will kill any sumbitch tries to prevent us!" Piss, vinegar, sand, but no sense.

Had Rudabaugh or any the Skunk Faction been in town, the Four Bastards might have had their revelry cancelled earlier, but the disreputables were out in Raton, pestering the stagecoaches. This left the law enforcement to Webb, Mather, and good old Marshal Joe Carson.

At first glance, it would be a difficulty to state the difference between the Dodge City Gang and the Four Bastards. Perhaps the level of obnoxiousness. The Dodge City Gang could be loudmouthed boot-scrapings, but they were accepted as a more or less necessary evil. This new foursome didn't know who could be trifled with, who couldn't be, who *shouldn't* be. Each minute was a study in rude behavior. They believed the law was as ephemeral as silk in flame. The Bastards mean to keep the fire burning.

While the quartet had made nuisance of themselves throughout the town, they'd found a favorite in Close & Patterson's, pawing at the women, scrapping with the men, interrupting the entertainment, all in the name of simple belligerence. Until blood was shed, or until the Skunks arrived, the Marshal Joe would keep out a wary eye, not intervene. Even with Webb and Mather at his back, Carson was hesitant to confront the armed men. Confrontations delay a return to a happy wife and a hot meal. Hattie was always waiting for Joe Carson to return.

Every joint on the East Side had the prerogative to disarm their customers. Patrons were meant to be congenial about it. The Dodge City Gang had let gambling slide so's all could have a good time, the drinkers should keep up their end. Marshal Joe's primary job each day was to maintain his watch. At each liquor stop, he'd remind all present to check their guns; usually they had, sometimes they had not. Of the Four Bastards, Marshal Joe opted for vigilance, but from distance. Reticence should not be mistaken for cowardice. Joe Carson hadn't come to this rough country as a fool, nor had he reached the age of 41 by accident.

On the morning of January 22, Thursday, the Judge woke

early to gunfire. A bullet exploded through his floor, showering him with splinters and threads from his favorite Navajo rug. He could already hear Dutchy's mighty hooves clomping towards his door through the adjoining and hidden hallway connecting the bodyguard's rooms to his. "I'm all right!" he called, his voice bringing the giant skidding to a stop on the other side. "Send for Carson."

When Marshal Joe arrived, Neill was wrapped up in a fine silk robe of his preferred colors, red and gold, giving him the feeling of some Chinese Emperor whose whims *would* be obeyed. "Those four," said the Judge, pointing vaguely at the floor. "I want them gone."

"I can put them all on nuisance charges—"

"Go downstairs and take their guns away," said Neill. "Cocksuckers shouldn't be heeled inside."

Carson couldn't argue with that.

Descending the staircase, Carson kept his eye on the Four. They were in the large ale room, Lowe and Henry at the bar, and Randall and Dorsey at a table, all four keeping Lady Mabe's girls squirming hostages. As he reached the floor, Joe Carson couldn't help but notice that Dutchy had not descended with him.

At the door of Close & Patterson's, dutiful as he'd ever been, was Dave Mather. Ol Mysterious had his hands at the ready, one at hip and one at cross. He'd once criticized Rudabaugh for wearing his three.

"If you fail to hit with one of two," said Mather, "what will three do for you?"

"I make people madder'n you do," was Rudabaugh's shrugged reply.

Mouth suddenly full with brick dust, Joe tried to swallow and wondered where Webb might have gotten up to, but there was no time to inquire. With Mather at his back,

Marshal Joe Carson addressed the party. "You four," he called out. "Let go of those girls, turn over your pistols to the Lady Mabe there, and quit making idiots of yourselves."

The Four Bastards turned open-mouthed to gape at the newcomer. They'd driven off most of the other customers, so it was the girls—Sadie, Nervous Jesse, Carless Ida on the floor and in hand; Cockeyed Liz and Lady Mabe behind the bar, with Mike Redd fretting and tending—the bastard quartet, and just the two lawmen in the elegant and now seemingly cavernous room. The painted odalisque that hung above the bar seemed to be lounging in naked judgment of all.

"Who the fuck do you think you are, law dog?" demanded Tom Henry. "We will kill you and go back to our drinks!"

The four men laughed. It was an ugly sound. Still, they stood and let the girls loose to give themselves more room.

"I'll arrest the lot of you," Joe said, his voice and hand steady, gun still holstered.

"You hear that?" said Lowe. "Arrest us for what, Marshal? Having a good time?"

"Get out, old man," said Randall in a low growl. "Before we bend you over and fuck you too."

Joe Carson was famously a kind, generous man. In their nine years of marriage he'd never been unfaithful to Hattie, He didn't use rough language, he'd never intentionally hurt a man, never failed to apologize for a slight. So appalling was threat from Randall, Carson drew his pistol. "Now!" he said. It was the last thing he said.

Opening fire, the four men dove for cover. Lady Mabe and Cock-Eyed Liz dropped down with Mike Redd. The air filled with choking gray smoke. In all, they counted forty shots.

Carson managed only a single shot, sending a bullet through Dorsey's left foot. For ten solid seconds, Marshal Joe's body was held aloft and dancing by the bullets tearing through him. He took nine slugs total before his legs dropped him to the boards.

From his place at the staircase, Mather emptied both pistols. With his Navy Colt, he blasted a chunk from Tom Henry's thigh. With his Schofield, he blew candlelight through William Randall, splashing him across the table. James West also took a couple of slugs, including one across his temple that left him twitching on the floor.

Before the smoke cleared, Tom Henry and James Dorsey had dragged themselves panicked and bleeding through the back door, escaping to the stable on National Avenue.

Five bullets had pierced Mather's long blue-black coat, but never touched his person.

* * *

Mrs. Carson, Hattie to all who knew her, watched her husband cross into Close & Patterson's with Dutchy as escort and her entire body went cold. She worked in the Porter Bakery and she was then caked with flour, standing vigil on the sidewalk boards. Something terrible was going to happen to her Joe.

Since the installation of the Dodge City Gang and its separate faction of untrustworthies, Hattie had grown more and more anxious. Joe was comfortable in Las Vegas. They'd been able to afford a house off National Avenue, and though it was a modest affair, she'd worked hard to transform the structure of oaken planks into a loving home. These past few weeks, so many ill omens had appeared to her. Just that morning, a cardinal had dashed out its brains flying into their sitting room window. A terrible portent.

When she heard the first gunshots ring out from the C&P, she ran down to *The Optic*, calling for Lute Wilcox. "Lute! They're killing my Joe!"

What assistance she thought the near-blind City Editor could bring, of that even Hattie was uncertain. But he'd been an ally in the past, and her panicked brain summoned his name before any others.

With Lute on her arm—she providing him as much stability as the other way around—Hattie crossed the thoroughfare with great trepidation, terror growing with each step. There was gunsmoke *billowing* through the swinging doors of the Variety Hall. As her foot reached the platform, her wonderful Joe Carson came spilling out of the building.

She screamed because she couldn't recognize him. He was a hunk of bloody meat walking unsteadily on rickety man-legs. The left side of his face was gone and she couldn't bear to look upon it. Catching his body, she crumpled with him into the mud. Lute kept his hand on her shoulder as she sobbed and cursed in unladylike language and held her poor Joe and wailed.

Later, while his friends arranged a coffin and the ladies around town brought her food and much sympathy, Hattie sought out Lady Mabe. The two women were known to each other in Dodge City, many years back, before life had brought them both to their current stations in Meadow City. "Someone is going to pay for my Joe," Hattie said, while Lady Mabe kept her whiskey glass full.

"That damned judge," said Mabe, angling her chin in the direction of Neill's rooms upstairs. "And that skunkape a'his."

"Sent my Joe to his death," said Hattie.

"Sent your Joe to his death," said Mabe.

They toasted to Joe Carson, the man everybody liked.

"I told Webb," said Hattie, her breath momentarily caught on the hook of another sob, "I tol' Webb, 'you bring those motherless cunts back alive.' I don't care—that's the word. The *right word*. 'Cause I want to kill them myself."

"Then they string *you* up for murder," said Mabe. "Kill, then hang, then kill—that's this goddamned town."

"I got rights," said Hattie. "And after I kill them four … " She glanced up at the ceiling, nowhere near where the Judge kept his offices, but Mabe got her meaning all the same.

It was no secret among the ladies of Close & Patterson's that the Judge had his eye on Hattie Carson. There was always a change in his demeanor when she was around. Less of his gruffness or his penchant for huffily repeating himself. When Miss Hattie was about, the Judge made Dutchy hang back so as to not frighten the woman—as if the stout frontier widow could be cowed by any man. But to the Judge, she was a delicate flower.

After another slug or several, Lady Mabe suggested the unspeakable. Hattie nodded. "I had the exact same thought," she said, throwing back another for herself. "He wanted my Joe out of his goddamned way."

Lady Mabe nodded. Then nodded again. "Well … " she said, and emptied the bottle into their glasses. "Dead soldier," she muttered.

If Hattie caught it, she didn't let on. "My Joe always said he loved my patience. 'Hattie,' he'd say, 'you could win a staring contest with a shadow.' Well, we'll all see just how patient I can be."

"Real patient," said Lady Mabe.

"Real patient," said the newly widowed Hattie Carson.

CHAPTER 10

ONE MAN TO A SAIL

Leave Las Vegas and take the Mora Wagon Road thirty miles north, you'll wind up in the picturesque town of Buena Vista, and find its name no lie. Located in Mora County, Buena Vista was home to a verdant field that spread throughout Sapello, La Cueva, Guadalupita, Cacon, Rociada, and the town of Mora. Buena Vista was also home to farmer Juan Antonio Dominguez. A patient and generous man, Dominguez had a number of empty cabins on his land that he frequently offered to weary travelers. He'd never regretted this. Someday, he knew, a stranger will reveal himself to be *Cristo*.

Sometime in the past few months, Señor Dominguez chanced to meet Tom Henry and James Dorsey on the trail. To these travelers, he offered his usual accommodations. In return, they did not murder him in his sleep. He felt this a good deal. They came and they went, sometimes together, sometimes with other men. They did not bother him. To him, they said as they left this final time, "We're going to Las Vegas to become gods among men!" That was Tom Henry. A joking man.

On the night of January 25, 1880, Juan Antonio Dominguez left his adobe dwelling and rode his burro up to the main fence of his property. There were a dozen men there; many were deputies he knew from Mora County accompanying the men he did not know. To the lead, a *gringo* with a blonde beard on his chin, and pale sad eyes, Dominguez said, "They are inside, in my own home. Please do not damage it too much." Webb nodded in response.

"Go and be absolved of your sins," said "Slap Jack Bill" Nicholson and laughed up his sleeve as the little Mexican farmer turned his burro away from them, leaving the gate open to allow the men passage.

The night was moonless but the stars were doing their jobs. "I'm in the lead here," Webb said, reminding the group a third time. There'd been mumblings of sedition throughout the posse. He thought that entreating Sheriff John Dougherty and his men from Mora County would put rest to any suggestions of hanging Henry or Dorsey from the nearest tree in Buena Vista, but everyone's blood was up. Dougherty had provided six men, adding to Webb's posse consisting of himself, Rudabaugh, Mather, Nicholson, plus a section of the honorable men, deputy and businessman William L. Goodlet, Bill Combs, Lee Smith, and Ben Muldoon. "Bull Shit Jack" Pierce hadn't been seen in town much since abandoning Mather at the Old Town jail. Shame was a hell of a thing.

Outside the shack, Webb announced their presence. The two killers inside, who'd put Joe Carson in the ground and made his Hattie a widow, gave the posse no trouble as they came limping out into the snow, hands up. Tom Henry's wound had taken all fight out of him—the thirty-mile trip had almost killed him as it was.

"Come on, skin that thing," said Rudabaugh, his

Schofield in hand, waiting to let it loose on John Dorsey. Dorsey told himself that he was no fool, but the fact was he'd been born a coward who whooped and hollered with sand borrowed from others. During the trip back, Rudabaugh and the others goaded Dorsey, described what the rope would do to his body, bringing tears from the phony Owl Hooter.

"You should put a stop to that kind of talk," said Sheriff Dougherty to Deputy Sheriff Webb.

Webb grunted, then repeated without passion, "I will personally ensure the safety of these men," he said. "They will not die by frontier justice today."

"What about tomorrow?" asked Dorsey in tremble.

Rudabaugh and Nicholson kept up their bullying while the rest of the company rode in silence. Once they were clear of Buena Vista, Dougherty and his men peeled off, bidding the company well and offering prayers to the unlucky pair tied to their saddles.

Seeing the split as a bad omen, Tom Henry made an offer. "I very much doubt if we will be given any show," he said to Webb, pain in his voice. "Now, here's what I propose: If you boys will give me my horse, which you are trailing behind the wagon, and allow me a start of a hundred yards, you may shoot at me with all your rifles, and I'll take a chance of getting away."

Were Webb to offer the matter up to a vote, Henry wouldn't make it the hundred yards. "Can't do it, Tom," he said. "Got my duty to uphold."

* * *

The posse tossed Tom Henry and Jim Dorsey into the Dog House cell with their former saddle mate, James West, who had already copped to his alias, officially booked as James Lowe, and was suffering his own wounds on the bare mattress. Tom Henry confessed to the given-moniker of T.J. House, and that was the name entered into the record. More names. "*…assumed and Christened, given and given back.*"

As Webb stood guard, the three prisoners spent part of the afternoon interviewing with Lute Wilcox. All three insisted that their true stories were told. They had come up from Texas together, eager to leave behind the hard work of ranching for the excitement and adventure of rustling. The newly-minted legend of Las Vegas' lawlessness had tantalized them like the aroma of fresh baked goods.

At thirty-three, Dorsey was the oldest of the group and insisted he was innocent. "I weren't even wearing guns in the joint," he complained to Lute. None of the witnesses would corroborate this. He insisted he'd just come along due to his friendship with the killed Randall.

Lowe barely spoke but to complain about his wounds and his lack of doctor care. "You saw the doc," House barked at him. "Quit crying over some grazing. I'm the one lost most his leg!"

"You are all goddamned fools to been taken alive," muttered Lowe.

Near the end of his telling, House leaned in close to Wilcox. "It's all a bad mix-up. Truth of the matter, we was invited here," he said. "I met up with your Judge, that Hyman Neill, back in Dodge about a year back. He said he always had work. We was just waiting for his word."

This admission would eat at Lute until well past what he thought rational. Webb, too. Neither man was under any illusion of what kind of judge the Judge was. J. J. had taken his share of the gains won by the many, many crimes committed by the Dodge City Gang. This confession made a strong case, however, that Marshal Joe had been commissioned by the Judge to do murder.

Lute mounted his old horse, Dodger, who knew the route between the towns well enough Lute didn't have to bother with steering. The world was a haze through his ever-weakening left eye. Webb caught up quick. "You can't print that," he said.

"Which?" said Lute, attempting a cool detachment, but wrestling with a creeping nausea.

"You know the bit," said Webb. "Dutch Henry and the mob will be at the C&P with a noose for Neill."

Lute nodded and prodded Dodger into a trot. In the end, he opted to omit this passage from his article for *The Optic*. For his piece in *The Gazette*, he referred to an *"implied connection between the four and Las Vegas' own Man in the Shadows who held offices at Close & Patterson's."* He did not speak of it further to any of the Dodge City Gang, not even to Webb. Much later, he would regret this.

With the murder of Marshal Joe Carson the leading topic in all the papers, and with the *Gazette* doing its best to top *The Optic* with gory details, Lute argued with Kistler that perhaps in deference to widow Hattie Carson, they eschew from repetition, particularly the bits about the state of Joe's corpse, still cooling in the Gallinas, awaiting shipment. Kistler scoffed at the notion and corrected his own spelling of the word "arterial."

* * *

There is good reason to believe that the three remaining of the Four Bastards would have survived to trial had it not been for the funeral procession for Marshal Joe Carson.

His body was prepared for transfer by train to family in

Houston, Texas, where a plot was awaited him in Glenwood Cemetery. Hattie was eager to get him out of Las Vegas, but she would not be accompanying her husband on his final journey.

The Rogers Mortuary had wrapped Joe in linen and placed him in a coffin bought by the Dodge City Gang. He was loaded into a hearse drawn by two black Morgan horses and the Mariah led the procession through New Town, across the Gallinas Bridge, through Old Town and around the Plaza, before turning back towards the rail station. Hattie rode in a simple wagon driven by Sam Denver, a friend and neighbor. She wore her mourning dress and a black veil. The Gang marched behind her, but she paid no notice to any of them.

The majority of businesses in New Town closed for the hour, their proprietors and many of their customers joining the procession. Those who watched from the walkways threw flowers into the path. There was tremendous weeping on both sides of the bridge. In Old Town, a mariachi played *El Adios A La Vida* as the Mariah passed through the Plaza.

When the train departed with Joe aboard, the crowd broke up, unsettled and not eager to return to their daily rituals. Sam Denver returned Hattie to her empty home and she closed the door behind her, refusing all visitors.

Rudabaugh and Nicholson drifted back to the Gallinas Bridge. They passed a bottle between them and stared hard in the direction of the little jail in Old Town, the Dog House, and imagined the men inside. And what they'd see done to them. Imagination, fueled by the booze, turned to planning.

* * *

Saturday Evening, John Joshua Webb paid a candid visit to Hilario Romero at his home. Webb removed his hat as the big Mexican sheriff opened his door, his body filling the doorway. "*Que?*"

"There's gonna be a mob coming for those three in *la parrera*," Webb said. "Won't be nothing I can do about it. Are your men up to it?"

Romero didn't answer immediately. He stared down at this white man on his stoop. He and Webb were not familiar. Of the New Town *gringo* lawmen, he preferred Mather. Hilario and Mather were of a spirit, he felt: solitary with opinions, watchful, deductive. The New Town *gringo* lawmen were all criminals at heart, Romero believed, but so too were most of the men he had ridden with, and now employed. Hilario Romero was hardly a pure soul. Survival had demanded that he, too, become a *vaquero* and a bandit. But now he was in civilization, and those without blood on their hands were suffering under those that had. He decided, let the *gringo* kill the *gringo*. Leave the Mexicans out of it.

"One man," Hilario said, finally.

J. J. grimaced. "Get rid of him," he said. "Make sure he ain't on duty tonight."

Hilario nodded. "I have business in Raton," he said. "I can leave tonight and I will take Valdez with me." Lino wouldn't like it, Hilario thought, when the truth came out later. But an angry young man is an alive young man.

"I can't trust my men any more," said Webb, a sadness in his voice. Hilario recognized it.

"They want their revenge for your marshal."

Webb spat into the dirt. "They want blood by the bucketful."

Again, Hilario fell silent for a few moments. Finally, he

said, "My cousin will be watchman tonight. Desiderio. Go to his home. He'll have the keys."

"Should we truss him up? Make it look like he struggled?"

Hilario shrugged. "If he insists." Then he leveled a finger at Webb's face. "They do not die here. Take them to your *gringo* town and kill them there. Do not spill blood in my Las Vegas."

Webb nodded, thanked the man, replaced his hat and turned on his heel back towards the Gallinas bridge. He had a long walk ahead of him.

And then another long walk back.

* * *

Heat lightning lit up the sky, followed close by dry thunder. Whatever gods were awake were angry.

John Dorsey screeched as the cell door flew open. "You're hanging an innocent man!" The mob fell upon them, Rudabaugh in the lead, dragging the prisoners half-dressed from their bunks, the wounded crying but protesting less than Dorsey.

"For Christ's sake, John," said Thomas Jefferson House. "Die like a man."

In New Town, a small crowd simmered, passing bottles and muttering vengeance. The crowd became of one mind as Hattie Carson emerged from her home, still in her mourning dress, in the company of the Judge and Dutchy. As the widow and her escorts passed outside the C&P, Cock-Eyed Liz and Lady Mabe joined behind, both women heeled with rifles. A silent order seemed given and the mob began their procession across the bridge and into Old Town, numbers growing with each step.

As he'd been directed, Desiderio Romero gave up the keys to the jail without a fuss. He'd demanded his hands tied to save his reputation, but not many of his neighbors were fooled. Many Mexican faces appeared in windows all along Old Town's main road, but few joined the hunting party. No one crossed themselves either.

Webb and Mather took the lead, but quickly Rudabaugh took over. "You gents fall back," he said quietly. Ostensibly, Mather was the new sheriff of New Town, and Rudabaugh understood that this was a terrible start to a career. Like Desiderio, Rudabaugh hoped to save his friends' faces. Again, no one was fooled.

For his part, J. J. was sickened by the entire thing, no matter how much he'd personally loved Joe Carson. But if he were to interfere with the mob, there would be four men hanged that night.

The crowd brought along a wagon into which to load the prisoners and convey them from town, but at the last moment, Slap Jack Bill Nicholson shouted, "To the fucking windmill!" The crowd cheered.

"Fuck," J. J. whispered to himself, his promise to Sheriff Hilario Romero utterly broken as the crowd became a single-minded force.

The three men protested as they were hustled and shoved towards Llano Plaza. Webb and Mather tried to divert them, but their authority was drowned out by blood-lust. House complained he could not walk, so the crowd hoisted him above their heads and carried him, struggling like a landed carp. Webb watched, useless as a stump.

Dorsey moaned every step. "Please! Please! I don't want to die! I don't wanna die!"

"Shut the fuck up, John," groaned Lowe.

The three bastards were hurled onto the platform. Ropes

were looped around their necks before they could even get to their feet. Looking out at the sea of hateful faces, House tried one final plea. "Don't we get last words?"

"That'll do," said Rudabaugh. He tossed the other end of the ropes around the sail.

Nicholson butted in. "Each to a sail."

Rudabaugh took up the noose around Dorsey and looped it over. "No! No! No!" Dorsey protested. The sail turned and he was yanked to his toes. In the ultimate indignity, his trousers began to slip and he wore no drawers beneath. Hands still shackled, he could do nothing to preserve his dignity. "Pull my pants up—" he managed before the rope crushed his windpipe. He was about a foot off the platform before he commenced kicking.

"May God forgive you," said T.J. House. As he was slowly pulled upwards, strangling and dancing, it was clear the old windmill wouldn't bear any more weight. Dorsey was a foot in the air; House was barely half that. Both men clawed at the ropes at their necks, faces going swollen and purple. House gurgled, "Shoot me."

Taking Lady Mabe's rifle, Hattie Carson blew a hole through Thomas Jefferson House. Chest spilling blood, his body went slack for a moment, then began kicking again.

Rudabaugh cut the two men down, casting a quick look at the remaining Lowe. "Fucking shoot me in the head!" said Lowe. "Don't do me like that!"

The crowd had been hushed by Hattie Carson. They waited for her to move again. House tried getting to his feet, blood pouring from the hole in his chest, but failed and remained on all fours. Blood pattered like rainfall onto the platform. House looked up at Hattie weakly, and begged her, with his eyes and a bloody finger to his temple, to end him. Hattie Carson levered the rifle and blew off the top of

House's skull. He collapsed to the platform. A dozen men and women then opened fire.

At the rear of the crowd, Lute Wilcox silently counted thirty shots. The men on the platform spun around like *piñatas*, their blood painting the windmill, cascading over the platform's edge to the dirt at the crowd's feet. Later, the undertaker would dispatch three men with shovels to collect the bodies.

Lightning flashed, turning the grey clouds of gun smoke white, the blood black, setting enraged faces in sharp relief against the darkness. As the smoke cleared, the anger dissipated with it, the howling ceased. As was often the case following violence, the crowd was left aimless, purposeless, once the bodies stopped moving. Bloodlust sated, justice satisfied. What to do for an encore but return home? Departing, everyone was careful to avoid the eye of their neighbor.

Webb watched the crowd disperse. Mather vanished into the throng as the entire town escorted the Widow Hattie Carson to her home in New Town, still flanked on either side by the Judge and his hulking companion. J. J. stood rooted in place. Though Lightning Jenny had taken up a place near the back, Bonnie Hommacher had not joined the party, and for that, Webb was grateful. He hadn't wanted her to see him part of such a thing. Nor had he wanted to take part himself. But he was the law in Las Vegas. Wasn't he?

Nicholson slipped in some blood as he attempted to jump down from the platform, and he landed quite awkwardly then departed. Rudabaugh lingered. He spit on each corpse in turn, having personally emptied two pistols without mourning the lost cartridges. Dave turned and winked at Webb, as if it had all been in good fun.

Webb took a good hard look at his longtime companion. Rudabaugh was splattered with gore, the blood on his face black in the moonlight. J. J. had seen Dave Rudabaugh in many scrapes. He knew the man was capable of violence, was usually slow to it, opting for menace over murder more often than not. In fact, Webb had never actually witnessed his friend kill *anyone* before tonight. Tonight wasn't Owl Hootery. Tonight had been an atrocity.

He couldn't look any longer. Webb couldn't face his friend who was gleeful through the gore. He turned on his heel and walked down National Avenue, in the opposite direction of the Gallinas Bridge. He couldn't go home. He didn't want to cross back into New Town. Webb wanted something he couldn't name.

It was a long walk back, the longest he'd ever walked. He passed faces brown and white, staring at him in horror from the shadows. With horrible shame, he realized he still wore the star on his chest, the symbol of his office as Peace Keeper of Las Vegas. When he tore it from his chest, the pocket of his fine vest came with it. Blue cloth, tattered, pinned to the star worthless in his hand. With hard emotion stopping up his chest, Webb shoved the star deep into his coat pocket and turned back towards home.

CHAPTER 11

THE BOYS ARE SKIPPING OUT

"One cannot help but notice," wrote J. H. Koogler, under the byline of "Anonymous," in an editorial in The Gazette, *"that when strangers come into Las Vegas, whether on business or for other matters, more often than not, they leave town feet-first, or in the accompany of a mob in the middle of the night. The streets are unsafe, not because of inaction by the local constabulary, but by its very nature. The peacekeepers, known colloquially as 'The Dodge City Gang,' are utterly complicit in these crimes. The line between the law and the lawless has never been thinner."*

Indeed, the events following the death of Joe Carson hung heavily over both sides of the Gallinas. A dreadful pall had descended. The music in the streets had changed from boisterous to dirge. The oh-so tenuous trust was gone between the two sides and the suspicious glares didn't end at the bridge. The decent folk were having trouble looking one another in the eye.

With Joe Carson in his plot in Texas, the mantle of sheriff fell to Dave Mather, already a U.S. Marshal by order of Governor Lew Wallace, and he made his presence known on the streets. He'd been whiling away the evenings slinging drinks in the East Side saloon owned by his now-deputy, Bill Goodlett, but had to give it up to tend to his duties full time. Due to the nature of Las Vegas, he wasn't long for the position.

Joseph Castello had been a telegraph operator at the Raton Pass before hiring out to lead a cadre of men West to continue working on the rail line. A decent man, Castello was nonetheless wrong for the job. The men under his command were a rowdy bunch, many ex-criminals seeking redemption through honest labor, as far as that went. Most succumbed to the permissiveness of Meadow City. Within days of their arrival, both sides of town were as weary of the workers as they were the familiar cutthroats.

When Castello and company first rode in, many of Las Vegas had feared them to be associated with House and Dorsey, seeking revenge for the hanging. Strangers in groups rarely arrived with tidings of comfort or joy. Most in Meadow City saw a strange face and immediately steeled themselves for blood.

One afternoon, Castello utterly lost control. Two of his men began a drunken fight beside the New Town bandstand and none could break it up. A crowd had gathered, first to watch, then threatening to join in and expel the ruffians bodily. Others in Castello's employ were readying to fight the crowd. Not sure what to do, Castello yanked his gun and fired a round into the air.

The gunshot only made the angry crowd angrier and they surged forward. There was a thin fence between the quarrel and the bandstand, providing a precarious illusion of safety. Sheriff Dave Mather quickly appeared, badge on his chest shining in the sun. "Enough of this!" he shouted, parting the crowd with his approach. He walked tall and straight, clad in blue like a saint.

The drunken men were still up for fighting. Wanting to regain control and authority, Castello jumped down and placed himself between lawman Mather and those under his charge. He leveled the pistol at Mather. "Stay back! I can handle this!"

"Clearly, you cannot."

Whether this statement enraged Castello or humiliated him, the result was the same. He fired wild. Once again, the miraculous occurred and again the bullet only tore through Mather's coat. Within a blink, Mather drew his pistol and shot Castello once, sending the bullet through lung and liver, splashing the men behind him as it left through his back. Blood sent them yelping. Castello staggered a few steps to his right then collapsed half-over the little fence. Mather holstered and ordered everyone to disperse, the battered drunks included. He then sent a runner for Doctor Bryerly and awaited his arrival.

A few days later, Sheriff Mysterious Dave Mather resigned his position. He left his

badge on Goodlett's desk, who stuck out a finger and gave the star a little spin. "Hours too long?" asked Bill.

"You pay better at the bar," said Mather, and left it at that. If there were other reasons for leaving, they went with him. He didn't immediately exit Las Vegas, but was eyeing that direction. During his stay in New Town, though he'd never been disparaged for it, and remained respected on both sides, Mysterious Dave Mather had killed more men than anyone else there.

A fact that dug deep and burrowed in.

*   *   *

Web-Fingered Billy Jones was a decent shot with his custom .44, trigger-guard removed to accommodate his skin-bound trigger- and middle-fingers. He could move them independently but not separately, and he delighted in making children and women sick by wiggling the finger bones, poking them against the flesh sack cocoon. Once upon a time, he'd been a reliable stable man and a decent rider on drag. In Dodge City, he'd made the acquaintance of both opium and gin and never again left their sides.

The Skunks would use him sometimes, as a runner mainly, untrustworthy he would be with any real responsibility. Meager was his pay for cleaning outhouses throughout New Town; it all went to drowning his nervous system in various poisons. Web-Fingered Billy was down to a single set of clothes. Once a month, he would pay the forty-five cents for a shower and laundry at Sjorgen's bathhouse. More and more often, charitable citizens would pitch in to lessen that interval.

If there was any description for Billy beyond the noting of his physical aberration, most would choose the word "harmless." But on the afternoon of February 28, 1880, the usual concoction had darkened Billy Jones' spirits, and he expressed his woe by firing bullets into the paint-wet side of The Gadfly Saloon. As the first lead pierced the wood wall, the dozen or so lurkers within rushed the back door, so no casualties were had. Nonetheless the sheriff was summoned and J. J. Webb appeared on the scene.

"I'm Web-Fingered Billy Jones!" he screamed at invisible critics. "I shit lightn'n'! I c'n call down th' thunder! I…" And so on, firing here and there to punctuate his raving.

With Mather's resignation came J. J.'s promotion. Just his turn to wear the star, it seemed. J. J. took in the scene while curious folk gawked from the alleys and doorways. Billy

Jones was reeling on his heels, the upper half of his body scribing an imperfect circle independent of his legs. Having emptied his pistol, he dropped bullets while attempting reload, the pistol more or less balanced along his strange fleshy hand. A more pathetic tableau J. J. couldn't imagine.

"For God's sake, Billy, drop the gun," Webb said, irritation giving his words their full weight. He was still haunted by the recent past. He saw constantly the lightning flash revealing the bulging eyes and tongue of Thomas Jefferson House. Then he saw the fury-crazed faces of the crowd, his neighbors and friends. This town was consuming the half-decent people. First Joe Carson, then Dave Mather, so many others. The poison was leeching into the Decent Folk on both sides of the river, them civilized and hearty, trying to make something of their lives.

The last thing J. J. wanted to do was harass a poor wet-brain in the middle of the street, but the pitiful creature was still armed. "Billy—" he said, and was then interrupted by the .44 in his face. Billy reeled again, but the gun was steady. "—*you*, sher'ff!"

With a sigh, Webb swatted the gun away and brought his own Colt upside Billy's head, knocking the drunk to the ground. He commandeered a horse and motioned for two drummers to load the man over the saddle. Webb arresting the webbed—the japes wrote themselves.

Leading the horse towards the bridge, Webb saw angry faces of the citizens emerging from the dim recesses of buildings. He walked this gauntlet of disapproval the full length of the road and turned towards the C&P. The sun was high and hot, but an icy chill followed J. J. Few had any love for Web-Fingered Billy, so why the contempt? For him in specific? Or for the Dodge City Gang entirely? There were more than a dozen faces he remembered from that night at the windmill. Those same faces howling for murder in the night were now casting their judgment upon him. Hypocrisy! They held him responsible for not preventing their decent into Hell.

He looked for but did not see his Bonnie Hommacher, and for that, he was grateful. To see such a look of disappointment on her face would murder him.

The upper windows of Close & Patterson's were open. Neill leaned on an elbow, his own face matching the disapproval of the townsfolk. Webb knew, of course, that Billy Jones was one of the Judge's confidants. Neill paid the man in dope, even for useless information. He treated his dogs well. Officially, as far as that went, Web-Finger Billy was one of the Gang. And you didn't go against the Gang. "Where you taking poor Billy Jones, John?" asked Neill, the only man to call him by his first name.

"The Doghouse," Webb answered, keeping his eyes forward.

"Cut him loose, John," said the Judge. But Webb didn't stop. So he called out again, with more urgency and his full authority, "John."

"At the moment, I'm 'Sheriff Webb,'" he said, not looking up, not yielding the satisfaction. "And I'm arresting this man for his own good and for the good of the community." Finally: "Your Honor."

"'The community,'" Neill repeated. The contempt smelt of shit as it rode the word.

Webb didn't turn. Reaching the bridge, Sheriff Webb and his quarry continued on their way, accompanied by the silent judgment of the onlookers. In whose service, Webb wondered, had been his defiance of the Judge?

It was time to move on. Before he caked himself in too

much more of Meadow City's dirt, the town famous for its baths of healing mud.

* * *

Watching Webb's back, Neill thought to himself about how narrow the window has become between appointments of sheriffs in Las Vegas. That very morning, he'd remarked to Dutchy how it should have been J. J. as sheriff all along, but the man constantly rejected the office. Now that the position had been thrust upon Webb by default, Neill was positive it was the right choice.

"The right choice," he said to Dutchy, "for the town." He chewed his cigar. "Not so sure for us."

"No?" asked Dutchy. He wasn't particularly interested in the answer, just the action he'd be soon asked to take.

"That man suffers from a surfeit of conscience. Sooner or later, a man like that forgets his position. Abandons responsibility for a higher calling."

"Like priesthood?"

"Like sainthood," said Neill. "Once men attain sainthood, they become utterly useless."

* * *

At four o'clock in the morning, March 2, 1880, Michael Kelliher, in company with William Brickley and another man named Gidlow, entered Goodlett & Roberts' Saloon and called for drinks. Kelliher called himself a salesman, but wasn't clear on the type of wares he peddled. He and Brickley rode into town together, met with Gidlow, and the three paraded themselves through town, making sure it was known they were going around armed.

99

At The Gadfly, they refused to turn over their guns to barman Ryan. Being accustomed to drawing breath, Ryan didn't push the issue.

As they passed by the Close & Patterson's, Hyman Neill took notice of the three, and Kelliher in particular. He thought he knew the man. He called Dutchy over and the two discussed the past, as far as Kelliher went, to ensure the right man was being fingered by memory. Concession was reached. Kelliher was there to do them harm. The Judge sent for Webb.

"Got men in town with guns," the Judge told him, remembering a backroom deal, long before Dodge City, that had salted a successful run. Followed by a subsequent midnight escape. "Can't have that," said Neill. "Can't have that."

Webb sighed. He had a sour feeling in his gut. It didn't get better when the Judge said, "Take Dutchy with you."

The Judge's sidekick mountain stood silently in the corner of the room, where he slept as far as Webb knew, and likely how. Officially, Dutchy was a Town Marshal. Webb had never seen him act in any capacity other than bully. "Don't need him."

"He's going anyway."

Without another word, Webb replaced his hat and left the room with one of God's lesser apes in tow.

Goodlett & Roberts' was a fair joint on the east end. It lacked the pomp and circumstance of the C & P, but it boasted an atmosphere fancier than the piss-stained wood slats of The Gadfly. When Webb and Dutchy entered through the back, they found Kelliher and William Brickley at the bar. Gidlow they didn't see. Both the men at the bar were well-heeled, guns in deliberate display.

J. J. had his pistol drawn when he entered. "Evening, gentlemen," he said.

Kelliher looked up at Webb, then past him at Dutchy, and laughed. It was a mean sound one usually heard after a dog yelped in pain. "I won't be disarmed," said Kelliher. "Take another step, lawman, and anything goes."

Before Webb could even respond, the report from Dutchy's Navy Colt, inches from his head, blew his eardrum out. Kelliher flew backwards away from the bar, crashing into the chairs behind him, scrambling to keep on his feet and failing. His legs went out from under him and he sat down hard.

Brickley quickly disarmed himself, tossing down his guns and throwing up his hands. Gidlow, entering through the front on return from the outhouse, saw his friend lying gurgling on the floor and took off down the thoroughfare. He would be picked up later.

Leaning against the bar, Webb pressed a hand to his left ear and the palm came away bloody. His vision swam in synch with the throbbing in his head. At the edge of his sight, he watched as Dutchy went through Kelliher's pockets and pressed Brickley into custody, hustling the living partner out the door. Webb watched him go.

One of the bar girls—Webb didn't know her name—went for the doc. Webb righted one of the chairs and sat down hard, waiting for his head to clear. Men came and took the body away. Bill Goodlet himself came down to supervise the cleanup of the blood. Lute Wilcox ambled by for a statement. Webb remained where he was. He answered the questions he could, demurred when he could not. He watched the sun come up and lengthen the shadows outside the bar.

While the lawman was responsive and more or less friendly,

he showed no intention of leaving. The doc checked out his ruptured ear, stuffed in some cotton and bandaged it up, and still Webb remained seated. Rudabaugh was suggested and the suggestion was ignored. Finally, someone sent for Bonnie Hommacher. The handsome widow came in from the bakery with flour on her blouse, and when she entered, Webb fell into her arms. Only then did he allow himself to return home.

A few days later, Sheriff Hilario Romero and his cousin, Desiderio, knocked upon the front door of John Joshua Webb and placed him under arrest for the robbery and murder of Michael Kelliher.

* * *

On his person at the time of his death, Michael Kelliher held more than a thousand dollars. $1,090.00 to be exact, for the purposes of "purchasing cattle on the low," as reported by Brickley. He would later testify that he watched John Joshua Webb relieve the corpse of that money. *After* he shot Michael Kelliher without warning.

This testimony was contrary to the "official" report returned by the Judge's coroner's jury, which *The Optic* published on March 2, 1880:

> *We the jury duly sworn to enquire into the circumstances of the death of Michael Kelliher, here lying dead before us, find that the deceased came to his death by pistol shots, fired with a Colt's revolver, loaded with powder and ball, on the morning of March 2nd, 1880, by J. J. Webb, in the town of East Las Vegas, and Territory of New Mexico. The said J. J. Webb, then and there being a peace officer, and that the killing was justifiable and absolutely necessary under the circumstances.*

Signed by the Jury.

Michael Kelliher's coffin and transport back to Texas was paid for and arranged by Judge Hyman Neill, aka "Hoodoo Brown." Neill was certain everything would have gone back to normal had it not been for a conversation he'd had the morning following Kelliher's death.

Hilario Romero walked into the Close & Patterson's just before noon, with Kelliher barely cold in the doc's office. He smiled warmly to Lady Mabe and asked to see the Judge. "And *just* the Judge, if I may." Lady Mabe took his meaning and hurried upstairs.

The Judge kept a private table at the rear of the dance hall. That early in the day, there were no performances. The hall was empty but for Romero and the Judge. Neill offered the sheriff a drink, but Hilario declined.

"I told your man," he said to Neill, "no violence in our side of the Gallinas. But what do you do? You hang white men from *our* windmill. Your people shoot them to bits. Your *whole town*, Señor Judge. Now, maybe we are not as civilized as you, we Mexicans, but we were here first. But I thought we had mutual respect in Las Vegas."

Neill wasn't used to being spoken to this way, especially not by some greaser with a badge. So he poured himself a slug and knocked it back before fixing Romero with a cold look.

"Those men had it coming. Wouldn't wait."

Romero nodded, then shook his head at the man's arrogance. "Do you know my employer, *señor*? Jefe Silva? Do you know of his White Caps? Do you know how many we are? Or can you tell us apart from Mexicans who mean you no harm?"

Fear took hold of the Judge's chest. "What's that?" he demanded. "What's that?" He poured himself another slug and held it without drinking.

"Maybe it is not us you should fear after all," said Romero. "Maybe your own town will tire of men like you. Maybe the crowd will come for you soon." He smiled wide. "Maybe we will have torn down our windmill by then."

With that, Romero took the shot glass from the Judge's hand and downed the drink. He touched his hat only to Lady Mabe as he left. Then he turned and looked up at Dutchy on the landing above. To Dutchy, Romero said something low and in Spanish.

Dutchy's face turned white.

The Judge remained where he sat at his private table, bottle in one hand, the other empty.

He muttered to himself, "Time to go, Hyman. Definitely time to go."

* * *

On March 3, 1880, *Las Vegas Daily Optic*, having interviewed all the eye-witnesses present in the bar at the time of the shooting, printed the following version of the events:

About four o'clock this morning, Michael Kelliher, in company with William Brickley and another man, entered Goodlet (a member of the Dodge City Gang) & Roberts' Saloon and called for drinks. Michael Kelliher appeared to be the leader of the party and he, in violation of the law, had a pistol on his person. This was noticed by the officers, who came through a rear door, and they requested that Kelliher lay aside his revolver. But he refused to do so, remarking, "I won't be disarmed—everything goes," immediately placing his hand on his pistol, no doubt intending to shoot. But officer Webb was too quick for him. The man was shot before he *had time to use his weapon. He was shot three times—once in each breast and once in the head … Kelliher had $1,090 on his person when killed.*

* * *

Dave Rudabaugh had been in Buena Vista for several nights and had missed the entire show. Riding back into Las Vegas, he saw that Bill Nicholson was mounting up, ready to light out. "They arrested Webb," said Slap Jack Bill. "He's facing a murder charge."

"The hell—why?"

Nicholson filled him in best he could, but the news had filtered to him through talk first, then the fighting reports in the papers. J. J., they all said, killed a drummer named Kelliher and robbed him.

"J. J.," said Rudabaugh, trying to work it out, "*robbed* somebody." He thought of the times he'd tried to include Webb on a stage job, just to show him the fun of it. Webb never took the bait. He'd pocket the odd pilfering, sure, what man was beneath that? But the thought of John Joshua Webb robbing a corpse?

When he'd first been made deputy, Dave made a list of everything he'd ever been pestered for by a lawman: vagrancy, profanity, public urination—all resulting in fines and kicks to the dirt. Strutting around town with his badge on a string, Dave had made an occasional bully out of himself. Once, walking back from the St. Nick, Dave tripped over some bummer passed out on the walkway. Dave cursed him, then searched his pockets.

"I fine you … three dollars and twelve cents … for … " He looked up at Webb.

Webb winked at him. "Loitering."

They split the take.

That was about as dirty as Webb had ever gotten. The man could stomp through a swine pen and emerge with clean boots.

Dave jumped back onto his poor sleepy horse and tore over to the Close & Patterson's.

There, he found the Judge and Dutchy loading bags into a hack. Dave could barely grasp what he was seeing. "You lighting out." It wasn't a question.

The Judge didn't answer and Dutchy pushed past him. Dave followed the Judge back into the C&P. "Judge!" he called. "Judge, what are you going to do about J. J.?"

Dutchy vanished into the variety hall and the Judge mounted the stairs. Dave followed, calling for him. "He was doing his duty, Judge." No response. "How many times you done it for us? When we didn't deserve it? This is J. J. we's talking about."

The Judge went into his office, keeping his back to Dave. He attempted to close the door behind him. Dave caught it with his foot and sent it flying back to splinter the wood wall. "Motherfuck! You turn and face me!" The Judge stiffened but didn't move. He placed his hands on his empty desk, his shoulders slumped.

Dave yanked his gun and cocked it. "You answer me, you filthy fraud." The Judge mumbled something Dave didn't catch. "The fuck was that?"

"Nothing can be done!" the Judge roared. "You want to murder me here? Do it! Murder Dutchy, then Mabe, and whoever else the fuck you want to!"

Dave nodded, then pointed to the desk with his gun. "Open that desk and write out a writ. Say he was doing his duty, or so help me God I'll spray you all over this room."

The Judge turned to him, red-faced and tears in his eyes, *"I can't!"*

"Then you tell them Mexicans that Dutchy killed that drummer. Send your shitstain to the rope."

"You think Dutchy would go for that?"

Dave pressed the pistol to the Judge's head. *"You make him go for it!"*

There was a horrible silence. The Judge winced beneath the barrel and let it press him down, almost to the desk top, but he did not acquiesce. Realizing the truth, Dave lowered the hammer and stepped back. "God damn you. You son of a bitch, god *damn* you."

"I'm sure he has," said the Judge.

And Dave hit him across the mouth with his Colt. The older man dropped to one knee, spitting blood and half a tooth.

"I hear Holliday is in Tombstone, you want that tooth looked at. *Bok gweilo.*" Dave spit on the floor. White froth speckled the Judge's hands. Dutchy came around the corner, carrying a crate of something or other. Dave shot him a look. The big man did not impede him as the outlaw stomped down the stairs.

Once he hit the street, Dave didn't know what to do. Find Mather? He'd never once in his life located Mather on his own. You wanted to find Dave Mather, you checked the corner of your eye until he materialized. Truth was, Rudabaugh wasn't smart enough about the law to know what, if anything, could be done for J. J.'s situation. Not if them who knew the truth weren't willing to tell it.

With murder in his eyes he watched as the Judge left the Variety Hall, fine silk handkerchief held to his bloody mouth. He and Dutchy loaded themselves into the hack. Dave's jaw dropped at the kicker: still in her mourning garb, widow Hattie Carson emerged from the C&P as well, Lady Mabe on her arm. The two women embraced fondly and Mabe watched Hattie mount the hack, take her seat beside the Judge. Driver Nelson Starbird snapped the reins and the hack took off towards the train station. Dave watched them go.

"Ain't no Gang," Dave said aloud and to nobody, not changing a goddamned thing.

* * *

"The boys are skipping out," wrote *The Optic* on March 2, 1880. *"The Grand Jury is in session, you know. H.G. Neill, vulgarly known as 'Hoodoo Brown,' went East Wednesday Night in company with Dutchy, against whom an indictment was returned by the Grand Jury. After the killing of Kelliher, the money in his possession, said to be $1950, instead of only $1900, fell into the hands of Neill, who was Justice of the Peace and acting coroner. Neill paid the funeral expenses and pocketed the balance departing for parts unknown."*

* * *

On Friday, March 5, the Grand Jury submitted its "True Bill," charging John Joshua Webb with the murder of Michael Kelliher. Hyman G. Neill was charged the following day with five counts of larceny. Neill was further charged with absconding with the now-settled amount of $1,900 from the estate of Michael Kelliher.

It was looking as if things were going to go Webb's way. He was well-liked and well-known throughout Las Vegas and San Miguel County. Were it not for his known association with Neill and the Dodge City Gang, his duty as a lawman would have been lauded as commendable. But the fact remained: after almost two thousand dollars of Kelliher's money left with Hoodoo Brown, the bag, so to speak, was left for J. J. to hold.

* * *

Koogler had another paper, *The Las Vegas Standard*, and it relayed a very different story regarding the killing of Kelliher. According to a lengthy peace, there had been a fight that had started in Locke & Brooks that spilled into the street and continued into Bill Goodlet's.

Allegedly, a member of the Dodge City Gang, identified as "S. Boyle," better-known to all as Sport Boyle, goaded Kelliher into a fight by scamming a free drink then demanding satisfaction for the implied insult that he was a moocher. Bored of the man's talk, Kelliher belted this Boyle and fled Locke & Brooks, with Boyle on his heel.

The Standard alleged that this was a conspiracy between Dutchy, Webb, and Sport, to separate Kelliher from his money. When the smoke cleared, Sport was nowhere to be found.

Boyle was familiar to J.J., and Webb couldn't say for certain the last time he'd even seen Sport in town. Why the man was being included in the story, not even Webb could say. Perhaps it was another of Koogler's personal vendettas. Boyle had, somehow, perhaps, done the newsman harm.

Sometime later, after Webb's trial, Killher's brother came down from Wyoming offering a substantial reward for Dutchy, the Judge, and Boyle. No investigation was made. The reward went unclaimed. Sport Boyle, just another face among the Skunk brigade, was never located.

*** * ***

"First man steps towards this jail," said Dave Rudabaugh, "I kill."

Once again, he stood upon the porch of *la perrara*, rifle loaded and ready to spit fire, holding off a mob of angry, righteous, God-fearing folk with murder on their mind. They wanted the Judge. They'd settle for J. J.

Appalling—so many of J. J.'s friends were present in the scowling throng. Dutch Henry aside, there were shop owners who'd owed Webb for stopping robberies, saloon keeps whose joints avoided bloodshed on premises thanks to J. J. Fueled by whiskey, boredom, no little misplaced fury, they meant to punish Webb for the sins of his fellows.

But between them and the prisoner were two: Rudabaugh and the Mex deputy, Valdez.

Both were armed for bear but only one was taking things personal. Lino had been instructed to stay within. Sheriff Romero did not want to send the message that the Mexicans were taking sides. Valdez shrugged and did his duty regardless of the politics. Webb was under his protection and would remain so. If his crazy *gringo* friend wanted to shoot his crazy *gringo* neighbors, it made no difference in Old Town.

Outside, there was arguing amidst grumbling but there was more whiskey than sand shared amongst the angry, and none wanted to be the first to take Rudabaugh's lead. Not a man among them believed he'd hesitate.

Through the crowd came Bonnie Hommacher, dressed in a dark blue dress, carrying a covered basket. She'd walked the mile from New Town, quietly and without escort. "How about me, David?" she asked.

"Naw," he said. "You're okay." He raised the rifle barrel

to the sky to allow her entry. Quicker, he leveled back on the crowd.

Every day since J. J.'s arrest, Bonnie brought him breakfast, lunch, and dinner, with enough for any of the deputies as well. At first, he tried to deny her, he didn't want her to see him like that, incarcerated and shamed. But she'd hear none of it. "Quiet now, Josh, and eat."

While he ate, and gratefully, she would sit with him, try to thrill him with gossip and news from the world outside Las Vegas. She brought him newspapers, including *The Gazette* and *The Optic*, "In case the privy runs out of paper," she said.

All the rags had painted Webb as the foulest sort, replacing the Judge as the purveyor of all evil in Meadow City. Bonnie had confronted Lute on the streets on several occasions, but the editor avoided her gaze. "You know you're killing him," she said to him outside *The Optic*, in a low growl and with sharper additional words. Lute didn't reply. Mr. Kistler would respond to her with barbs of his own, through his open window from the safety of his office.

As a grateful J. J. ate in his cell, he looked out at the handsome woman outside, doting on him even in his sorrowful state. She'd made facing a death sentence more pleasant than anyone could reasonably hope for. "That Mather told me your appeal is building fine," she said to him, a brave nervous smile on her face. Webb nodded, but didn't speak while chewing. "That's good," she said. "That's real good."

The fact was she couldn't fathom why the town had soured on him. She'd tried to appeal to Dutch Henry and the others, but Webb's name turned foul in their mouths. The only people still on his side, it seemed, were present in the jailhouse. Plus Mather, who came and went like a hot breeze. Allegedly, there was an army of supporters back in Dodge

City, all rallying behind Josh's cause. But where the hell was this support in Las Vegas?

Sensing her worry, J. J. reached out and patted her hand, giving the fingers a squeeze. "It's all politics," he said. "I have a letter out to Governor Wallace. I am known to him. I could walk out of here any day now," he said, instead of, *I could be strung up any day now.*

Bonnie fussed with her basket, smoothing a blue cloth over the cover, then smoothing again. "I got biscuits in here for Lino," she said. "And that other." She jerked her chin towards the door and Rudabaugh.

"They'll appreciate that," said Josh. "Dave 'specially. He thinks you don't like him."

"Smarter than he looks then," she thought, then said, "Your partner terrifies me."

An image of Dave flashed through J. J.'s mind, face black with blood, standing on the windmill platform while the insides of three men pooled around his boots. "Scares me too," he said. "Sometimes."

They turned together, and watched the back of the man in the doorway, who had always watched their backs in turn. "Can I tell you something about Dave?" J. J. asked her, his voice softer but thicker than usual. She nodded. "I don't know what everyone else sees when they look at him—or, rather, I think I *do* know, and it isn't a paragon of virtue or a prince among men. He doesn't see that in the mirror either. But I have walked among men I'd been told were giants, and when they caught up to their long shadows, I found them smaller than I could ever fear. Does that make any sense? Big men, real paragons, and they were often the first to say so."

He took a bite of biscuit and chewed thoughtfully. She waited for him to swallow and continue. "Dave has never presented himself as anything but hisself. Never puts on airs, never brags. Good storyteller if you can get him going, but not one to talk your ear off then ask how you lost it." His voice caught in his throat but fought its way out. "That man, at times, can be the biggest man you'll ever meet."

Bonnie nodded, thinking she understood, not sure she agreed. But still, as Rudabaugh came back towards them, she flipped back the cloth and offered him a biscuit. He took one and managed a smile that didn't resemble that of a cornered badger.

To Webb, Dave said, "They gone for now. And if they come back, they'll get more'n they want. I guarantee you that."

Hearing that, J. J. looked up at his loyal friend, then to the marvelous lady who'd been so kind, then down at the half-eaten biscuit in his hand, shame chasing him around the room. How many times had he violated his oath to uphold the law? If things had gone differently with Kelliher, would he have not pocketed his slice? Swallowing hard he started to speak, but Bonnie interrupted.

"Well, I'm due back at the restaurant," she said, gathering her things. She cast a warm smile to her John Joshua, a polite one to Dave. Tears were burning the corners of her eyes and she'd go to Hell and ask for ice water before she'd cry before either of those men. For very different reasons.

Rudabaugh leaned his rifle against the bars, easily in J. J.'s grasp. He even took a step back. "Sky's ugly this morning," he began, but J. J. hushed him. They sat in tense silence until Bonnie Hommacher was away from the jail. Then, to Dave: "Get that thing away from me."

Dave shot him a sour look and took the Winchester back. "*Bok gweilo*," he said, and grinned in spite of himself.

"Dave," said J. J., "you need to go the fuck away."

Rudabaugh stared down at him without response.

Hurling his biscuit down, J. J. shot to his feet, tin plate clattering to the floor. "You're harshing my chances at a pardon."

"I already got this run down from Mather. I ain't going anywhere near the courthouse during your trial. I ain't gonna show up. I ain't gonna say boo to the judge or jury. You ain't gotta worry about none of that."

Webb shook his head. "Get out of Vegas, Dave. For Christ's sake, what's here for you? Lightning Jenny skinned some days back. Mather's heading back to Dodge. Why are you still here?"

No response. The two men stared at each other. Dave whiled the time watching the red creep up from under J. J.'s shirtless collar and head towards his ears. "Answer me, you dumb son of a bitch!"

Slowly, Dave nodded, then adopted the strangest smile. Like a coyote that solved a puzzle. "I ain't no stray dog you can tell to *git*," he said. "I'm here as long as you are. And there ain't nothing you can say otherwise."

With a great sigh, J. J. sat back down on the hard bunk, deflating, defeated. "Dumb loyalty, Dave. It'll get you killed."

"Naw," said Dave. "It's the meanness in me that'll get me killed." They stared at each other for a long moment. "Anyways," He touched the brim of his wide hat and shouldered the rifle. "I gotta get to Whiskey Jim's, but I'll be back."

"Of that," said J. J., "I have no doubt."

* * *

In the St. Nicholas restaurant, Mrs. Etta Pringle breakfasted with her sister, Mary Darby, and their cousins, Eunice Darby and Mrs. Mercy Blatz. Like the rest of the patrons in the crowded room, they were in their absolute Sunday Best, having emerged renewed and sinfree from the Presbyterian church house, around the corner from the dog track. Though they were relative newcomers to Meadow City, Mrs. Etta and her family had a lot to say about John Joshua Webb's current predicament.

"My Charles always said Webb was no different from the rest of those gangsters," said Etta, and the others clucked in agreement, a carefully trained response. Charles Etta was among the moneyed interests, in business across the bridge with Otero, Sr.

"Disgraceful," said Mary. "A thief and a coward."

Bonnie entered with a tray carrying the women's tea. The tea had come all the way from New York City. Etta and her gang were dedicated trend-chasers.

"Ugly man, too," said Mercy.

"Ugly," echoed Eunice.

As she laid out the cups, the saucers, the teapot, Bonnie had not been listening to the hens clucking. Until Etta said, " 'Webb'? More like '*Drab*'!" Which sent the others into peals of chalk-squeal laughter.

Bonnie grit her teeth. The tea was scalding, so pouring it upon the party could be reasonably considered assault. Instead, she retrieved the saucers and cups, the teapot, and replaced them on the tray.

"Excuse me?" said Eunice, with ice dripping from her voice. "Just what do you think you're doing?"

"I don't serve today," said Bonnie.

Etta looked around the room. They were drawing attention from the others at feast. "Clearly you are serving," she argued.

"I don't serve you," said Bonnie. "Today or ever." She looked at them over her tray, and Etta swore that the look was meant to murder them all. Then with a rage she'd never felt, Bonnie used language equally foreign to her tongue. "You cunts get the *fuck* out of my store!"

Humiliated and abused, the women gathered up their accouterment, parasols and clutches, then skirts and dignity, leaving with noses in the air and tears in their eyes. Their flushes deepened when their exit was met with a smattering of applause.

Very quietly, tray in hand, Bonnie announced to the room, but to no one in particular, "If anyone else has a problem with John Joshua Webb, take it with you to some other slop house."

She held her tears until she reached the safety of her kitchen. There the despair finally took her.

* * *

Though the newspapers all announced the departure of Mysterious Dave Mather immediately following his resignation of office, but this news was premature. He had no intention of leaving Las Vegas until after Webb's trial. Mather was placed in charge of the money raised for the defense back in Dodge and he made sure it reached the correct hands.

As Rudabaugh told Webb, Mather had read the outlaw the entirety of the riot act in English first, then Latin and again in Spanish to avoid miscommunication. Dave Rudabaugh was not to go anywhere near the courthouse. Should he encounter any of the remaining stragglers of the Dodge City Gang, he was to send them in the opposite direction.

"The Mexicans are looking for any excuse to hang Webb from that damned windmill," said Mather. "And there are those in this town with the same attitudes."

Rudabaugh made his promise and Mather knew he'd keep to it.

*** * ***

THE TERRITORY OF NEW MEXICO, PLAINTIFF \ AGAINST JOHN J. WEBB, DEFENDANT
 MURDER

David Mathers (sic) and Wm. H. Bennett & E. Roberts and Richard Pendleton upon their oath say being first duly sworn that they were present during the closing argument of the Counsel for the Territory in said above entitled cause & when said argument closed & said above entitled cause was submitted to the jury that they were in the court room and about the door of the court observing carefully what was going on.

They say that when the argument closed & the jury in this case was about to retire and the defendant about to be remanded to jail to await the consideration of the Jury & there being a large crowd of spectators in the court room, all of a sudden the sheriff announced aloud in the hearing and presence of the Court & Jury & crowd that a body of armed men & friends of Defendant were in the court house door ready & intending to rescue Defendant.

The crowd in the house was required to be seated & not a man permitted to leave his seat or get up. This announcement and action of the sheriff created a considerable sensation & excitement.

In this state of affairs the Jury in the night time at a late hour were conducted from the court room to consider of their verdict & remained out all night. No explanation was given to the Court or Jury of this alarm or commotion as they are advised & verily believe, that they are fully satis-fied and evenly believe and therefore state the circumstances aforesaid and announcement of the sheriff was well calcu-lated to produce & did as they believe produce an unfounded and most unfavorable impression in the minds of said against Defendant.

They further state that said announcement of the sheriff as herein stated of the purpose of the friends of Defendant to rescue him & then & there was Wholly unfounded. It was as they know & believe a delusion on the part of the sheriff.

They say that the friends of Defendant were in the house & about the door of the Court room looking on and listening to other people only, and not demonstrating or intending to rescue the Defendant or violate law or do any wrong.

This 19th March 1880 (signed)

David A. Mather

W. H. Bennett

E. Roberts

Richard Pendleton

Subscribed & sworn to by David Mathers (sic), Wm. H Bennett E Roberts and Richard Pendleton before me, this 19th March 1880.

(signed)

F. W. Clancy, Clerk

* * *

"Everyone in the court room is to remain seated," declared Judge Sidney M. Barnes, honorable and venerable and bone tired at the end of a long day. The San Miguel County Sheriff was Desidario Romero, cousin to Hilario, and he wanted nothing more than to execute every member of the so-called Dodge City Gang. He'd daydreamed that Webb's friends would come to liberate him from the little courthouse. He'd hoped for it so much that he'd sent his men out to circulate rumors that Webb was done for, that the jury was paid off. Anything that would coax the scavengers into the trap.

Every time Desidario glanced out the window, his deputy on watch, Juan Martinez, would shake his head sadly. No one was coming. Rudabaugh had been ordered to stay away. The one they called Mather, the *gringo* sheriff until a few weeks ago, was present in the gallery and did not seem to spoil for action. Desidario found that intensely frustrating.

As the defense rested, before Judge Barnes could dismiss the jury to their deliberations, Desidario leapt to his feet, his hand hovering over his gun, the only gun permitted inside the courthouse. "Your honor!" he shouted with much alarm, "Webb's friends are in the street, demanding his release."

The Judge made his pronouncement that no one was to move. Mather remained seated while the bailiff, a man named Hutchins, was sent out to investigate. Desidario seated himself on the windowsill, obstructing the gallery's view of the street. He did so grinning, laughing at his private joke.

A few minutes later, Hutchins returned, belying the report. Sheriff Romero shrugged. "I guess *señor bailiff* scared them off." He then winked at Mather and returned to his seat. The jury then retired.

The joke was for the benefit of those on the Mexican side of town. It was sport, and an odd joke, meant to send a message. Any of Webb's friends not present in the gallery, they said, were still at large and ready to commit more mayhem. It was a reminder that the Judge's departure was not the end of the violence. Stay vigilant.

The jury was not swayed by Webb's character witnesses. Despite assurances of impartiality, for so many sitting there, the Dodge City Gang had been a menace for too long. Webb was a lawman but also Neill's representative. For those coming in late: If they couldn't hang Neill, they'd hang Webb.

At three o'clock in the morning of Wednesday, March 10, the Jury returned a guilty verdict of murder in the first degree. The sentence was death.

Chapter 12

Via Con Dios, El Topo

John Llewellyn preferred the alias of "Jack Allen" and had wandered into Las Vegas with the hopes of becoming infamous. Even in high-heeled boots, the man barely stood at half-past five inches, add to this his inability to grow a proper mustache and most dismissed him as a juvenile. Worse: an amateur. His dream to be known as "Johnny the Kid" was dashed, as most who knew him called him "Little Jack."

He had one living relative, a sister named Annie Chapman, who wrote to him frequently, begging him to return to the simple and honorable life at home. Think of how his life could be as a husband, a father. He kept the letters but rarely responded. When he did, he spoke of his high adventures, his daring escapes and bloody shootouts, always insisting that he had to prove himself. It was a cruel game, reminiscent of their childhood relationship. He could never be contained. Or, she wrote complaining, reasoned with.

Back in September, 1879, before the Kelliher incident, he'd drifted into New Town on a wagon train and immediately set to proving himself by annoying others. Thinking he had the backing of some of the rougher cowhands on the job, he stomped into The Gadfly one early afternoon and immediately set to crawling up Dave Rudabaugh's nose.

Bellying up too close to the man, Little Jack said to him, "You the one they call 'Dirty Dave'?"

Barman Jimmy Ryan quickly found something else to do at the other end of the building.

Dave didn't glance up from his whiskey. "Nobody calls me that," he said.

"I hear you're quite the sharp," Allen persisted. "That you're a killer of men."

"How you hear so much when you never shut up?"

Little Jack slapped the bar in mock anger. In truth, his fearlessness was due in no small part to the half-bottle of rye he'd consumed earlier. "Why don't we go outside and settle things then?"

Slowly, Dave looked Allen up and down and the trip didn't take long at all. He knocked back his drink. "You know what you're getting into?"

"You ain't nothing," said Jack Allen, and backed out of The Gadfly, keeping his hands low and his eyes on Dave.

For the last few nights, Dave had been out hassling a rancher's herd out near Raton and hadn't yet been to sleep. All morning, he'd been drinking, not eating, and felt the urge to murder. Yet, here was the thing, and he'd been jawing over it for some time: while in town, he felt an obligation to Webb to not make trouble. Outside of town, anything went, and the Judge was always good for an alibi. But in town, Dave *was* a deputy after all, for whatever the hell that was worth, and it wouldn't look good for Webb to have a murderer on the payroll.

Then again, what was he to do about such an arrogant challenge?

He glanced around the bar. The only backup were a couple of the Skunks he didn't ride with—Jordan Webb (no relation) was in a corner with "Bull Shit Jack" Pierce, who'd slunk back into town a few days back. But neither could be relied upon that late in the morning. The little man was still outside, shouting insults. Finally, Dave sighed. "Ryan, you got that Henry still?"

The barman pretended he didn't hear the question. Without asking twice, Dave leaned over the bar and snaked the rifle from under the wood.

Little Jack walked backwards down Centre, still taunting, like he was posing for the cover of one of Ned Buntline's colorful dime books. "Okay, you sumbitch. On the count of three, we draw! Ready?"

"No," said Dave, and levered the Henry.

"Wait!" shouted Little Jack Allen, but Dave did not. Advancing, he fired repeatedly at Jack's feet, driving him backwards down the thoroughfare. Allen scrambled to draw his gun but the pistol slipped from his hand. He lost the piece in the mud and Dave kept firing.

Three bullets penetrated the toes of Jack Allen's boots. Newspaper filling the space exploded in tufts and came down confetti. In final insult, a shot between his legs sent Allen splashing into a horse trough, to the delight of all onlookers who pointed and laughed and—for the very first time—cheered Dave Rudabaugh. Allen came up sputtering horse backwash and slime.

A couple of drummers helped an ungrateful and sputtering Little Jack Allen out of the trough while Rudabaugh returned to The Gadfly without a single glance behind him. "You don't know how lucky you are, you dumb quincy," "Bull Shit Jack" would tell him later. And while Little Jack would never admit it, humiliated as he was, a hateful kernel of gratitude burned deep within for his spared life.

* * *

While Dave Rudabaugh had not completed much schooling, he didn't consider himself a stupid man. Ignorant of some things, definitely, but not a fool and with some small amount of good sense. Yet, the dumbest thing he ever did was get blind drunk on April 2 and join in with Little Jack Allen.

By April 2, 1880, Little Jack Allen was the only ally Dave Rudabaugh had left. Mather had vanished into the night after Webb's sentence came down. He'd allegedly gone back to Dodge for a bit, to raise further money for J. J.'s appeal, but hadn't yet come back and there was no report from Dodge that he'd arrived. "Bull Shit Jack" Pierce again slunk away. Nicholson and Cady were rounded up and arrested for a stage job almost a year old. There was no one left to keep poor old J. J. company. *The Optic* had published a photo of J. J. sitting in jail, with the cruel caption of "Wretched Webb."

Rudabaugh sank into a feeling of helplessness the like of which he'd never experienced. Normally when there was trouble, he'd just light out for a new horizon. To do that now would mean abandoning J. J. Though Webb might be bound for the rope in the very near future, Dave was still certain he could do something about it. But J. J. had made things perfectly clear: "Leave it alone, Dave," he said. "Leave me here."

They argued. Dave couldn't understand his friend's thinking. Without a clear path, Rudabaugh malingered in Las Vegas, the last of the Gang, enduring the evil eye from everyone he passed. The more he drank, the less of a damn he gave. On April 2, he started knocking them back early at the Close & Patterson's and made his way backwards towards the rail station.

He ran out of money at The Gadfly. There was a ranch hand he knew lived nearby, Tom Pickett, who still owed him some money from poker a few night's back. Dave stumbled over and kicked at the door until Tom roused from bed, having only just retired from a security night shift at Goodlett's. Irritated but no welcher, Pickett forked over what was owed and accompanied Dave to a new joint, The Summer House, bringing a bottle along for the walk.

Thanks to Tom's whiskey, by the time they landed at Summer House Dave could barely see. He didn't remember leaving Tom behind there when he moved on. He barely remembered leaving at all. Time slipped away from him. He would find himself in different parts of town with the intervals of travel missing from memory. His vision swam as the ground rose and dipped at whim. The bottle in his hand was rotgut rye and went down as smooth as cinders, but it was mostly full, offering generous glugs. So a'glugging he continued.

* * *

Little Jack Allen knew Tom Picket too. Pickett was a former Texas Ranger, looking for a better slice of pie in New Mexico. He now worked for Whiskey Jim Greathouse with another hand, Billy Wilson. For the better part of two days, Little Jack had played cards with the trio at a little table outside the livery.

As they jawed, Greathouse revealed that his fortunes had greatly improved over the past year thanks to a war between two cattle outfits out in Lincoln County. A young

English rancher by the name of John Tunstall got himself murdered by the Jesse Evans gang, in the employ of Tunstall's rivals, Lawrence Murphy and James Dolan, the proprietors of the LG Murphy Co. Still and all, that was frontier business, and would have been left so were it not for neighboring ranchers and the angry young men in Tunstall's employ that vowed to bring the murderers to justice. This loose association called themselves "The Regulators."

The leaders of the Regulators included a young stalwart named Dick Brewer; a mean bastard of an intellectual by the name of Scurlock; an older hand known as Bowdre; and among the other rabble, a crotch-bald child who alternated between identities, McCarty and Bonney among them, though most called him "Kid." Some forty-men strong, The Regulators set out to rid the world of the Murphy-Dolan operation.

While the two factions fought and killed each other, Greathouse and other businessmen in the area took advantage of the struggle. Once the shooting was done, Dolan and Murphy were inconvenienced but continued strong. Some of the Regulators malingered. Brewer got himself killed by a bounty hunter by the name of Buckshot Roberts. News was that Bonney made short work of Roberts and caught a murder charge for it. Though the group had broken up, folks throughout the Territory were on the lookout for this Billy the Kid.

"The Kid's at war with all of New Mexico," said Big Jim Greathouse, chewing on a cigar slightly thinner than a chair leg. "I buy horses from him on occasion. At a fair price, of course."

"Vegas is getting too hot," said Wilson, tossing a bill into the pot, raising his bet.

"The fuck is that?" demanded Pickett, holding the bill up. "This another of your counterfeits?"

Red faced, Wilson snatched it back. "Thought I got rid of these. That goddamned Harvey West bought my spread and paid me with this worthless paper." To add insult to injury, West teamed up with the counterfeiter himself, Sam Dedrick, and the pair turned Wilson's land into the West & Dedrick Corral in White Oaks, and they were doing very well for themselves. It made Wilson spit.

"Barely looks like money," said Pickett. "How was you fooled?"

Wilson shrugged. "It was dark," he muttered. "The hell you want me to say? There's a warrant out for me 'cause of it."

Greathouse laughed. "You're kind of an idiot, aren't you, boy?"

Little Jack Allen found all of this fascinating, but was eager to bring the subject back around to the rustlers out in White Oaks. "So that what you fellas is doing?" he said, perhaps too quickly. "Lighting out to join that gang?"

Greathouse laughed again. "There's no gang," he said. "Billy and Bowdre, mostly. And since Bowdre got married, it's mostly the Kid on his own. Hell, Charlie would'a restarted his cheese factory and went straight again, but Scurlock was his partner and took off to go teach back East." He added to the pot. "Worst cheese I ever et."

"That's all very interesting," said Little Jack. "But what is the action like over there?"

"Action?" said Greathouse. "You make your own action. Unlike the crap you got in your hand."

That lead to an argument, with Little Jack storming off, embarrassed and unsatisfied. These were three more men who would learn soon enough. Goddamn it, no one in Vegas took him seriously. Not since Rudabaugh sank him in a horse trough.

It was Rudabaugh's respect most of all that Allen needed, though damned if he could explain why. Hardly a day'd gone by that the cut-throat's name hadn't been in one paper or the other. Somehow in Allen's mind, that made the man bona fide.

Though considering the events of the past few weeks, with the Gang broken up and Judge Brown out in the ether, Little Jack couldn't fathom why Rudabaugh still lurked about. Near as he could figure—and it was the prevailing theory in town—Rudabaugh was biding his time to spring Webb from the jail. But how much time could one man bide?

The opportunity was before them. Little Jack planned to make his own opportunities, maybe even impress Rudabaugh enough to finally partner up. He'd made a previous attempt at crime some months back, teaming with the Stokes Brothers and Bill Mullen, but those three idiots got themselves locked up for a train robbery that didn't happen as planned. Fortunately for him, Allen hadn't been part of that plan.

Jack Allen was determined to be an outlaw. That was his fate. But first, they had to get to John Joshua Webb.

* * *

To keep business flowing between New Town and Old, the livery owners offered hack wagons to shoppers and keepers. Usually three-seat affairs, covered during lousy weather, topless in the summer, the straights and the bummers, the ladies and the doves, white, brown, black, red, yellow, everyone enjoyed the ride and everyone paid the two-bits for the privilege.

In the early afternoon of April 2, Miguel Otero, Jr., had business in Old Town and found himself in the company of Mrs. Mattie Mennet, formerly Mattie Bell. Her husband, Adolph Mennet, had been a soldier of fortune fighting for Mexico's Emperor Maximillian and who foresaw the doom approaching. He defected first to Kansas then to Las Vegas, as the head of the wholesale and retail department of Otero, Seller & Co. Mattie was to meet her husband at his offices in Old Town. She was quite fond of his employer, as most people liked and respected Señor Otero, Sr., and was pleased to share company with his son that afternoon.

Driving them was a pleasant man, J. Carl Caldewell, who kept mainly to himself, inevitably ensuring a higher gratuity. The hack belonged to J.M. Talbot, entrepreneur and proud band coronetist, whose livery was one of the larger stables in town, and he kept his wagons in perfect working order, particularly the handsome four-seaters that were his pride. There was a certain irony in that Jack Allen was on occasion employed by Talbot as a mechanic. That irony would land later, after Allen, with a very drunk Rudabaugh, flagged down Caldewell just before the Gallinas Bridge.

The pair climbed in. It was a three-seat wagon and Señor Otero moved to sit next to Mrs. Mennet in the rear seat, sparing her the close company of the rough newcomers stuffing themselves into the center seat. Riding backwards, the new passengers were face-to-face with the young woman and her escort. Though boiled, Rudabaugh was present enough to touch his hat to Mrs. Mennet. Allen shifted continuously in his seat, from both the ride and the withering stare Mrs. Mennet had fixed upon him. He was not unknown to her. Rudabaugh neither. The contempt on her face proved that she should never play cards.

The four rode in silence until they reached the corner

outside the First National Bank. There, Otero and Mrs. Mennet departed. Neither party being a shrinking violet type, both would have remained in the hack had they had an inkling of what the pair had planned. Mrs. Mennet, a student of her husband, kept a Derringer in the clutch purse always in her possession. "I would have put one in Rudabaugh's eye, had I known," she would say later to her Adolph. And he would hug her proudly in response.

Caldewell continued a block further and turned left. The jail loomed into sight and Rudabaugh finally stirred. "Hold up here," he said, slurring the command. Caldewell noticed that both men wore their guns, in defiance of all ordinances. Rudbaugh was a deputy no more.

"You men have a good day," Caldewell said, soon as his passengers' boots hit the ground.

"You wait here," said the smaller one, but Caldewell pretended not to hear him. He snapped the reins and the horses put on the distance. Caldewell would be back in New Town before he realized that Rudabaugh had left the bottle of rye rolling back and forth between the seats.

Outside the jail, Rudabaugh was unsteady on his feet, but found slices of clarity with each subsequent step. "This is where J. J. is," he said, perhaps to Allen and perhaps to no one. Little Jack grabbed Dave's sleeve. "Let's go in."

Inside the jail usually seemed cooler, no matter the temperature without. It was an illusion. Within the cells, the air was stifling. *La pererra* had six cells, often filled to capacity, with drunks and thieves and drifters, particularly on weekends. This afternoon, only two of the cells were occupied. In one, the Stokes brothers were awaiting trial for horse thievery. In the center, poor old wretched J. J. Webb.

At the desk sat Lino Valdez, smoking a thin cigar and reading a Spanish novelette. He grinned as Rudabaugh entered. *"Buenas tardes,"* he said, though it was early still. Rudabaugh mumbled a greeting in return and pointed towards the cells. Lino nodded, gestured that they should enter. He paid no notice to the smaller man in Dave's company.

Over the past few weeks, Lino had grown to appreciate Rudabaugh's loyalty to his friend. Webb, too, was a decent sort. Lino hated to think that the former lawman would hang. Of course, he also hated to think the man was a thief and murderer, but life can be a bastard like that. Spending so much time with both men, Valdez felt no suspicion. It was yet another visit from Rudabaugh, and a rare one unaccompanied by a hate-spitting crowd.

As Rudabaugh approached the cell, Webb sat up on his bunk but remained seated. "David, you are as pickled as an owl."

"J. J., we, uh . . ." Dave stopped and looked around. What the Hell was he doing in the jail with Jack Allen? He tried to remember how he'd even gotten there. Had there been a wagon? And a lady in a wagon? It was still unclear.

Allen came up to him close. "We ain't got the time."

"For what?" said Dave.

Little Jack muttered, "Fuck." He jerked his gun and held it on Valdez. "Give up the keys."

Lino Valdez stood up slowly. He did not raise his hands, but he kept them palms out and away from his hips. The young deputy turned a cool eye towards Rudabaugh, who was swaying on his feet while his senses realigned. "I will not," he said. "I have no right to give them to you. And you have no right to ask for them."

Jack Allen cocked his pistol, held it in Lino's face. "This here's my right!" He quick-glanced over his shoulder at Dave. "You gonna back me, you goddamned drunk?"

It was automatic: Dave jerked his gun, but he didn't point it in any particular direction. He reeled once on his heels then stopped, suddenly upright and not swaying. "Jack?"

Allen's attention was fully on the deputy. "We will kill you, greaser! Give me the keys!"

Coolly, Lino realized that Rudabaugh would be no friend here. "You may kill me, but I won't give them up."

By now, Webb was on his feet, as were the Stokes brothers. "Hell, take us too!" shouted one. Webb never could tell the pair apart, had no idea which spoke. His attention was on Dave. "Stop this, David." He spoke calmly. "Don't let this happen."

Dave wasn't quite there. His gut felt heavy and sick. Adrenaline was clearing his head, heart pumping the alcohol away from his brain. "The fuck is going on?" he mumbled.

Allen took a step towards Valdez. "Keys!"

Lino shook his head. He ignored Allen and looked to Dave.

As the world came into sudden and sharp focus, Dave Rudabaugh froze solid. Before him was a dramatic tableau of impending violence. Even with the gun in his hand, he was merely a spectator.

He heard Webb's voice echo in the distance, calling his name.

Lino Valdez stared at him with dark and disappointed eyes.

Again, Jack Allen glanced over his shoulder and saw Rudabaugh, useless as Lot's wife, and anger spit through him. "Fuck this," said Little Jack Allen. He shot Lino Valdez through the heart. The deputy slammed backwards against the wall and fell forward across the desk.

"Goddamned Hell!" shouted Rudabaugh.

Webb threw up his hands and backed up to the wall, shaking his head the entire time.

Little Jack ripped the keys from the corpse's belt and stomped over to the cells. He thrust the ring through the bars at Webb. "Take 'em!" Webb shook his head. "Take the fucking keys!" Allen demanded.

Webb looked to Rudabaugh. "Get the hell out of here, Dave!"

Dave looked at him. "You're not coming?"

Webb held his hands out, gesturing at the mess. "Come with you to where?"

Jack Allen stood in disbelief. "Fuck this and fuck you, then!" He grabbed the front of Rudabaugh's shirt and pulled him towards the back door. "We gotta go."

With sudden clarity, Dave slapped the man's hand away. "What the hell did you just do?"

"Get out of here, David!" shouted Webb. "Go!"

"You dumb *gweilo*!" said Dave to Jack Allen, shoving him towards the door. "J. J.! I'll be back!"

"Jesus H. Christ," said J.J. "Get the hell out!"

Rudabaugh practically tossed Allen overhand through the rear exit. They holstered their guns and pulled their coats tight over their chests. The streets were only beginning to get busy as the business day drew to a close. There was a small crowd gathering across the street from the jail, drawn to street by the gunshot.

A hack was coming around the corner, empty of passengers. Nelson W. Starbird was at the reins. Jack Allen leapt into the street and flagged him down. Starbird drew the horses to a stop and was surprised to find a pistol in his face. Rudabaugh climbed in, keeping the driver covered. "Get us into New Town. Fast as you can and keep your mouth shut."

Quick to understand, Starbird nodded and snapped the reins.

By now, the small crowd of unfriendly faces of all colors had grown to something much larger, and all eyes were on the hack as it moved through Old Town. Fully aware of the attention, both Rudabaugh and Allen let the crowd know they were heeled. Only angry glances were exchanged. "Go to Houghton's," Rudabaugh told Starbird, who knew the hardware store on Center.

Little Jack kept his gun on Starbird while Rudabaugh jumped down and walked inside. His stride indicated no hurry, merely an errand, something for Greathouse. Once through the door, Dave pulled his Schofield on the clerk and ordered two Winchester rifles from the rack on the wall. The shopkeep handed them over readily, with cartridges, and ducked behind the counter. Still unhurried, Rudabaugh tossed a rifle to Allen and remounted the wagon. "Out," he said to Starbird, who did as he was told.

Dave turned to Allen and gave him a look of murder. "You stupid son of a . . . " He wanted a stronger word than *bitch*. None came and there was no one to ask. Dave snapped the reins and turned the wagon onto the La Cinta Road towards Nine Mile Hill. If they could make the mesa without a posse biting them, they'd be okay.

They had no such luck. As their wagon left the town limits, at least six armed men on horseback rounded the corner of Front Street. A single shot rang out behind them and Dave whipped the horses faster. The posse behind them grew five fold as the wagon bucked and bounced over the hard trail.

Dave would never learn the name of the man in the lead, a Mexican deputy called Ignacio Sena, a man of more bravery than sense. Sena was the first to give pursuit, upon a muscled Saddlebred that was among the fastest in Old Town or New. Sena easily pulled away from the other pursuers and managed to close the distance between him and the fleeing hack. Up ahead, there was a sharp turn to the right and Sena saw his chance. He was a good shot with a pistol, even on horseback. He fired a round that pierced the hack's side. To his delight, the hack slowed, the horses rearing. It stopped and Sena too slowed his mount.

The taller of the two men leapt from the hack and knelt in the road without cover, firing rapidly with a Winchester, forcing the horse backwards. Other members of the posse were closing in behind Sena, which was good, as his blood chilled in the realization that he had no additional ammunition. The man with the rifle kept firing, kept the posse at bay, then turned them back.

The other fugitive got the horses under control and the hack rolled forward once again. The rifleman kept firing as he walked backwards, only stopping to climb into the wagon. Sena and the others would have to regroup. Angrily, they watched the wagon grow smaller in the distance.

Back at the New Town limits, spectators had gathered to watch the pursuit through spyglass and binoculars. Betting opened immediately. Those uninterested in gambling were eager to join a posse or bring one about. Within the hour, more than fifty men were in pursuit.

Jack Allen kept the horses running hard, foaming and snorting, while the rough road bit pieces out of the wagon threatening to overturn beneath them. Dave rode backwards, feet braced against the back seat, rifle ready to respond. The pursuers would be on them by and by. They needed to make some distance.

Throughout his life, Rudabaugh was aware that, while luck was fleeting and fickle, when it was on your side it was a friend indeed. Luck had it that, just as their horses were about to give out, they came upon a group of herders. The herders were in the employ of Antonio Montoya, of San Geronimo, the village lying in the hills between Tecalote and La Manga.

The leader of the herders was named Antonio Gonzolez, and he was not fool enough to die for his employer, fair and decent though he was. Thus, when the two armed men demanded horses, who was he to deny them? The horses were not his, but the life threatened was. Who else could say they would do otherwise?

By dusk, the fugitives were long gone. The posse regrouped under the leadership of Hilario Romero and the great Col. James A. Lockhart, then continued onwards. Reaching the abandoned hack outside of San Geronimo, they found the two long rifles empty and discarded. After interrogating the herders and Gonzolez, Lockhart and Romero determined that pursuit was futile. The men and horses were worn out and the night, having swallowed the killers, had turned bitterly cold.

* * *

"It was a bold and desperate attempt to liberate Webb, which failed on account of the lack of nerve and courage on the part of the projectors." Thus wrote *The Optic*. *"How did they imagine that he should get out and escape on foot without arms? It was an ill-advised plan for their object and nervelessly executed. They made a good escape, however, and luckily for them met the mounted herders, otherwise the chances are that the Romero and Lockhart party would have overhauled them, in which case it would be a dead sure thing that they would have been captured."*

* * *

It would take more than five hours for Lino to die. The coroner would declare that he'd been fired upon "with malice and forethought."

Hilario had missed Allen and Rudabaugh by seconds. Upon seeing his young deputy ventilated across the desk, Hilario grabbed up his rifle and chased the hack on foot until he watched it cross the bridge. Winded, he went back for his horse, calling for his cousins to mount up as well.

J. Maria Tafoya was both deputy and cook for the jail. Running in, he first lowered the unconscious Lino to the floor, then reconsidered to move him to the kitchen. Tafoya was a stout man, but short, and could not lift Lino from the ground.

"Open us up," said a voice from behind him. William Mullen and the Stokes Brothers, Bill and Carl, were serving a year for train robbery. They'd gotten away with all of $23. Jack Allen was a known associate. All three were leaning through the bars, beckoning Tafoya.

The cook hesitated. He needed help and train robbers could rarely be trusted. Having no other choice, he warned Webb to stay back—"The hell did I do?" complained J. J.— and levered open the door for Cell #3. True to their words, Mullen and both Stokes boys helped to bear Lino's bleeding body to the butcher block in the kitchen. Having done so, they returned to their cell. Bob Stokes wept. He'd liked Lino very much. He'd never much liked Allen.

While he bled, Lino drifted in and out of consciousness. The bullet had traveled six inches through his left breast, into his stomach, piercing the lining. Belly acid leaked into his body. Family came and wept and wailed while the doctors did what they could. None dared move him from the kitchen.

Finally, just after 10pm, Antonio Lino Valdez drew his last breath.

Hilario had only just returned, hot, and angry, and frustrated, and without his quarry. Desiderio gave him the news. Lino was no more.

Indescribable and surprising anguish seized Sheriff Hilario Romero. He stumbled backwards as if pushed, and teetered on his heels. Desiderio carried a whiskey flask and Hilario demanded it, draining it in just a few swallows. He left *la perrera* and took his pistol from his holster. Firing three shots into the air, he called out, *"El Topo est muerto! Viva El Topo! Via con Dios, El Topo!"*

The sentiment began to echo throughout Old Town. By 10:35, the mourners ceased wasting lead, and gathered to determine a better use for their ammo.

* * *

Antonio Lino Valdez was buried on April 4, 1880, in the Catholic churchyard just beyond the Hot Springs Hotel. His funeral procession was a long one, winding through most of Old Town and much of New, then out along Hot Springs Road.. The women lamented loudly, dressed all in black, sometimes collapsing in the street as they wept.

That night, in the Baca Saloon, Hilario Romero and his deputies were joined by Vincente Silva, Don Miguel Otero, many honest businessmen, and many White Caps as well. A photo of Lino was placed on the bar, surrounded with flowers and lit candles. To the photo, the men raised their glasses. Vincente Silva led the toast, *"Viva El Topo!"*

"Viva El Topo!"

All drank to Lino's memory. They sang songs to him and prayed to his ancestors that he will be well-met in Heaven. As the night drew on, the cheer and sorrow turned to anger. They threw their knives at the Spanish warrants for Rudabaugh and the Judge. Blood oaths were sworn. The windmill would not be torn down until the *gringo* killers were strung from it.

* * *

Rudabaugh didn't say a word for many miles. Jack Allen filled the silence with a steady stream of chatter aimed at the other's back. "White Oaks, that's the plan," he said. "Big Jim —you know Jim Greathouse—he can give us cover. Then after we lay low a couple of days, we find Tom Pickett. He's rustling horses out this way. Remember Pickett? He was usually with that mule-dumb Billy Wilson. Anyways, Pickett was talking about picking off horses with that kid from the papers? Bill Bonney? My god, that kid's crazier than a frog on a hot skillet. Anyways, I'm thinking, we get something going a while, then we go back and try and spring J. J. again. Make that town fear us, right?"

He watched Rudabaugh's shoulders rise and fall in a deep sigh. Then the head came up straight but did not turn. "Why'd you go and kill Lino?"

"Who?"

"That jailor you shot. Antonio Lino Valdez."

"What's it matter to you, one greaser more or less?"

"*Bok gweilo*," Dave muttered. "He was a freedom fighter." He turned slightly in the saddle as Jack came up behind. "He cared about his people. They called him *El Topo*."

Jack felt uneasy. His lower lip twitched as he said, "What's that to me?"

The fire drained out of Rudabaugh's eyes, leaving cold steel marbles in the sockets, now fixed on Little Jack. "You know your problem, Jack Allen?"

"What problem I got, Rudabaugh?"

Rudabaugh eyes flashed in the darkness, pure silver fury. "You're a small man."

"The hell—?"

But Jack Allen never finished the sentence. Dave drew his pistol and blew a neat hole through Jack's chest. Jack's horse startled and snorted and began walking in a tight circle. The little man stared at the spiraling world ahead of him. Blood leaking from his gaping mouth, eyes wide and uncomprehending, he repeated, " . . . the hell?" Then he slipped sideways out of the saddle and onto the ground.

Dave's mouth was too desert dry to spit on the corpse. Reaching out, he snatched the reins of Jack's mount and nudged his own horse forward, leaving the body to cake in the dust.

Later, during the campaign to blame Billy the Kid for all murders ever committed as far back as Abel, *The Daily Optic* would eulogize Little Jack Allen thusly:

Allen was not of a vicious disposition but whisky and evil associates changed him from a peaceful mechanic to a desperado who only commanded the respect that a pair of forty-fives gives a man on the frontier. He came from a Christian family in Atlanta, Georgia, where his sister, Mrs. Chapman, now resides—and his right name was Llewelling instead of Allen. His old companions ought to have happy dreams in their lonely cells when they think of their old comrade they so foully murdered ...

Allen had written repeatedly to his sister, boasting of his

notoriety, often mentioning his compatriots in an awkward code—"D.R." and "D.M.", confounding no one. His dream was to die in a blaze of glory and cement his fame in history.

The land that embraced and devoured John Llewling, also known as "Little Jack Allen," was a mile above Aleman on the Jordana del Muerto, known at the time as "Martin's Well." Those traveling from Socorro to Fort Seldes would not fail to notice the solitary grave there. Some may wonder who would have dug it, or why it was placed beneath a dead juniper tree. Indeed, this is an enduring mystery. Few would associate it with the deeds of outlaws.

Nothing remains now to indicate the spot. Even its name has passed along. Its area on modern maps show it as part of the Elephant Butte Dam. Not even history gives it a passing glance.

So ended the career of the notorious Jack Allen.

CHAPTER 13

HEREBY NOTIFIED

On April 6, 1880, driver Nelson Starbird was shot by an unknown assailant. Seeing the driver shot, passenger George Poindexter leapt forward and seized the reins, steering the wagon off the main street towards Starbird's home, calling for a doctor the entire way. Sadly, Starbird succumbed to his wound shortly thereafter.

It was commonly believed that the intended victim was Poindexter, the manager of (yet another) Romero's Mercantile Company in Old Town. On his person were the evening's proceeds, to be deposited the next morning.

The following day, a group including Col. James A. Lockhart, Jacob Gross, Rush Holmes, Señor Otero, and Bonnie Hommacher—who would not be turned away—gathered in the restaurant at the St. Nicholas Hotel and held the first meeting of a law-abiding and official "Vigilante Society."

On April 8, 1880, *The Las Vegas Optic* ran the following notice:

> *To Murderers, Confidence Men, Thieves:*
> *The citizens of Las Vegas have tired of robbery, murder,*

and other crimes that have made this town a byword in every civilized community. They have resolved to put a stop to crime, if in attaining that end they have to forget the law and resort to a speedier justice than it will afford. All such characters are therefore, hereby notified, that they must either leave this town or conform themselves to the requirements of law, or they will be summarily dealt with. The flow of blood must and shall be stopped in this community, and the good citizens of both the old and new towns have determined to stop it, if they have to HANG by the strong arm of FORCE every violator of the law in this country.
 — Vigilantes

Similar notices were printed on handbills, and they appeared over night tacked to every post and freestanding wall in both towns. The vigilantes were violently opposed to violence.

A couple ruffians scoffed at this, but cast wary eyes to and fro when they left the confines of saloons and slop houses. They were overly courteous now when visiting the St. Nicholas, taking particular care in complimenting Miss Hommacher's fine cooking. There were still men wearing badges, but it was of those without you had to beware.

The so-called vigilantes were also weary of the false reports coming daily from the many Las Vegas newspapers, occasionally *The Optic* but particularly Koogler's *Gazette* and *Standard*. The desire for Hoodoo Brown's blood still burned throughout the two towns and Koogler took advantage of this desire in the name of Capitalism. In both papers, he reported the death of Hyman Neill. On three different occasions.

HOODOO DEAD IN KANSAS! read one headline. Another cried out, HOODOO BROWN KILLED IN CRIPPLE CREEK. LEAVES

NEW WIFE WIDOW. After each case, a day or so later, a retraction would be printed. Somewhere on the page. After the third such fabrication, Dutch Henry and his familiar cadre showed up to bang on Koogler's door, noose in hand. *The Gazette* editor managed to escape through his office window.

Koogler's papers would not mention Brown again until the winter of 1881, when news came out of Caddo, verified, that Hoodoo Brown, also known as Hyman Neill, sometimes known as Samuel King, was found face-down in a wagon rut, shot through the head and chest. *"His wife was not with him,"* the papers reported. Nor was she identified by name.

It was a matter of much speculation at the Close & Patterson's Variety Hall as to the identity of Neill's so-called wife. Lady Mabe and Sadie and Cock-Eyed Liz took a table after hours and toasted a woman long-gone from Las Vegas.

"You think it was Hattie Carson done it?" asked Liz.

Lady Mabe smiled and nodded, with vigor and glee. "She was no wooden Indian," said Mabe. "That woman had brains. And my god, she loved her Joe Carson."

"Hell of a long game she played," said Liz.

"I hope the son of a bitch suffered."

To that they drank again.

* * *

Six months later, an animal-chewed corpse was found outside Meade, Kansas, not too far from Cripple Creek. It had sprawled at the bottom of a gulley for at least a year, or so the Meade coroner could guess. In life, the man had been well over six-and-a-half feet tall, with a full blonde beard, weighing over 250 pounds. Alive, he must have been terrifying. Whoever had put the bullet in his face must have been a brave soul indeed.

The $50 bounty offered on the head of John "Dutchy" Schlunderberger was never claimed.

At that time, no woman named Hattie Carson, nor Hattie Neill, nor Hattie Brown, had appeared on any town registry anywhere in Kansas, much less Caddo. No warrant for "Mrs. Neill" was ever issued.

* * *

After refusing to leave when liberated, J. J. Webb's character was reconsidered by those with enough power. Señor Otero, Jr., would later write,

> *This act on his part counted much in his favor, in the eyes of the community, and his friends made use of it in an effort to persuade the Governor of the Territory to extend clemency. They also showed that the evidence seemed to indicate that Dutchy had done the actual killing and that Webb had been somewhat unwittingly the tool of Hoodoo Brown. After going into the case thoroughly, the governor commuted Webb's sentence...*

No longer facing the rope, J. J. would merely spend the rest of his life in prison. So said Governor Lew Wallace, statesman, scholar, and author of *Ben-Hur: A Tale of the Christ*. For having killed no one, Webb's life was generously spared.

While Dave Rudabaugh was out somewhere in the Territory, John Joshua Webb made his home in *la pererra*.

CHAPTER 14

PICKING FIGHTS WITH THE KID

He was known in Old Fort Sumner as Billy Bonney, and in White Oaks he was called Henry McCarty. Further East, you'd encounter those who knew him as William Antrim, sometimes "Kid Antrim." But most often you'd hear epithets that couldn't be printed.

Tall and lean, with heavy-lidded eyes, his was a face that narrowed as it descended towards his chin. His bare face smiled all the time, especially when angry, and he enjoyed telling jokes at the expense of others. It was impossible to retaliate against his insults. He was unashamed of his beaver teeth and would demonstrate how deep he could penetrate a pie with just those front lathe blades before his other choppers even touched crust. Or criticism could be just as likely answered by pistol shot.

He'd been called 'Kid' for as long as he could remember, but it was Koogler and *The Gazette* that gave Bonney's nickname the definitive article.

"*Eastern New Mexico,*" he wrote in January, 1880, "*has become a fiefdom of a powerful gang of outlaws harassing the stockmen of the Pecos and Panhandle country, and terrorizing the people of Fort Sumner and vicinity. The gang includes forty or fifty men, all hard characters, the off-scourings of society, fugitives from justice, and desperadoes by profession ... The gang is under the leadership of 'Billy the Kid,' a desperate cuss, who is eligible for the post of captain of any crowd, no matter how mean or lawless. Are the people of San Miguel county to stand this any longer?"*

Normally, seeing any mention of himself in the paper made his heart take flight, but this article made Bonney spit nails. *"I have been known as 'Kid' my whole life,"* he wrote in one of his endless letters to Governor Wallace pleading for clemency. *"But never 'The Kid,' nor the captain of a Band of Outlaws who hold Forth at the Portales."*

Wallace was unmoved. Bonney had been writing him incessantly it seemed, begging for clemency, insisting his crimes were done in service of the law. To be perfectly honest, Wallace never read the letters. His secretaries gave him summaries that he rarely listened to. Certainly not all the way.

The Governor had welcomed Koogler's editorial. Not only did it provide the cover he needed to separate himself from any sense of impropriety with the young outlaw, it also added weight to the boy's dangerous reputation. By naming him, Koogler had centered all attention on Bonney, laying all the Territory's rustling and killing and mayhem at his feet, and thereby cementing all public opinion firmly in the negative. This, Wallace reasoned, would help squash any naïve sympathy still lingering for the young killer. Any midnight thoughts of amnesty Governor Wallace might have had vanished in the wake of Koogler's article.

Of course, Koogler had also taken it upon himself to write directly to Wallace, insisting that the outlaw scourge be dealt with, thus spurring Wallace to action. Scribbling a note to W. G. Ritch—his secretary, who knew so much more about Bonney, having read the letters—Wallace wrote, "*Be good enough to prepare a draft of proclamation of reward $500 for the capture and delivery of William Bonney, alias The Kid, to the Sheriff of Lincoln County.*"

Koogler was the first to publish the notice.

Kistler was beside himself. The next few issues of *The Optic* included screeds against the "Billy the Kid Gang." Readers took note of the new celebrity in their midst.

* * *

For all the press that "Billy the Kid" would gather in 1880, when Dave first met the ex-Regulator he was just another face in the bunkhouse. When he rode into White Oaks to meet up with Greathouse and Pickett, Rudabaugh barely paid the young man any notice. In fact, two attempts were made to introduce them before the first handshakes were exchanged. Dave just wasn't interested. His train of thought was on a single line, owned by "Spring J. J. from the Dog House, Incorporated."

Dave was not a voracious reader, but newspapers were as good a way as any to wile away time between thefts. All the papers in Santa Fe had covered the Lincoln County War with much conflicting and confusing detail. The Kid's name was frequently mentioned in block items, usually reading, "*And with them was William Bonney, sometimes known as Kid Antrim.*" After Koogler, he acquired the full sobriquet. When the Murphy and Dolan factions were more or less depleted, The Kid had to struggle to stay famous. But to Dave, all of that was dust.

Talk among Rudabaugh and the Las Vegas cowboys was

casual. They all agreed that there were plenty of ranchers to hassle, cows and horses to cut out and rebrand. Pickett was a good roper. Wilson was useless and admittedly so. Every now and then, after Dave finally accepted the introduction given by Greathouse, Bonney would attempt a word edgewise. Dave would give him a courtesy nod and repeat his last point. "Whatever we get going," Dave said, "I still intend to break J. J. out of *la pererra*. Don't mistake my intentions here."

"Why don't we just ride in and shoot whoever gets in our way?" Bonney suggested.

Rudabaugh gave him a hard stare. "There's half a thousand people between us and J. J."

"I have my Winchester, I'll lick 'em all."

"Yeah," said Big Jim. "You say that a lot, don't you?"

The others laughed, and Bonney laughed with them, but his ears were scarlet and his collar was hot.

Whiskey Jim Greathouse was as much a gatherer of wool as those supposedly shiftless men in his employ. He was a notorious insomniac and didn't care when work got done so long as done it got. That attitude he maintained with himself as well as others. He had no trouble taking this casual talk of crime and plunder indoors.

By the time the sun set over the Greathouse Ranch bunk house, Dave was well at home and once again enjoying the company of fellow Owl Hooters. As much as he could enjoy anyone's company.

Lanterns were lit and a new bottle of Bourbon was opened to share. Billy Wilson told a story about an Admiral he'd met in Santa Fe. "Married a tattooed lady from the circus. Had the Merrimac on one hip, the Monitor on the other—and a port in between for him to dock!"

The men roared with laughter, but Bonney spit into the

dust. He was mad someone else's joke got a laugh. "That's a made up story," he said.

Wilson didn't respond. Rudabaugh was irritated. "Most stories is made up. That's what makes 'em stories. They're . . . what's the word? F-word?"

"Fucked up?" offered Billy. The men laughed. "Or 'phony' ?" And the men laughed harder.

"'Phony' don't start with an 'f' !" said Dave. The word was right there but he couldn't reach it. Without Webb, the point was lost. He was stuck with a bunch of dumb cowboys.

* * *

"Old Fort Sumner" sat inside a crumbling wall, half adobe and half wood. Named after the famed military man Edwin Vose Sumner, the structure's original purpose was the containing and internment of the Navajo and Mescalero Apache, thanks in a large part to the efforts of none other than the great Kit Carson. For five long years, from 1863 to 1868, the Indians made do within those walls, fed on beef sold to the fort by Charles Goodnight and his partner, Oliver Loving. Then just as abruptly, the government shut down the whole operation in '68, selling the buildings and land to landowner Lucien Maxwell. Goodnight and Loving formed their own namesake trail somewhat further west.

Maxwell's son, Pedro Menard Maxwell, best-known as Pete, more-or-less liked and amiable enough, had a sturdy house within the walls, adjacent to Beaver Smith's little saloon with its own modest kitchen. It was in this saloon that ex-buffalo hunter and future lawman Pat Garrett slung drinks on occasion, and jawed away the hours with the remaining members of The Regulators, Bonney included.

Without their mission of revenge for the death of their rancher-boss, the young magnate English John Tunstall, the gang was aimless, restless. They whiled their time away stealing horses and cattle from local ranchers, John Chisum among them, then change brands and sell them below the border to Mex drovers, who would then sell them back to Chisum. It was a game the rancher was tired of playing.

The "gang" that Rudabaugh encountered operating out of, or very near, the Greathouse and Kuch Wagon Stop, was little more than a loose cadre of men whose comings and goings occasionally coincided with animal theft. Beside Pickett and Wilson, both Charlie Bowdre and "Bigfoot Tom" O'Folliard had planted stakes in Old Fort Sumner, with Mrs. Manuela Bowdre, Charlie's half-Mex wife, doing the cooking for "the boys."

"We's called 'The Rustlers'," said Henry the Kid. Dave wasn't impressed.

"You went from 'Regulators' to 'Rustlers'? Cuz 'The Hole in the Wall Gang' was already taken?"

They were leaning against a fence, sharing a smoke and shirking duties, watching the horses exercise. "You shouldn't talk to me that way," said Henry.

Dave turned his head to look at the younger man. "What way?"

"Teasing me like that. Interpreting I'm stupid. I'm not stupid."

Dave wasn't in the mood to fight anyone at the moment. 'The Kid' reminded him too much of eager Little Jack Allen, a blowfly that wouldn't go away, bringing all manner of shit with it. "Fine," Dave said. "I'll lay off." Henry nodded. "Who are you anyway? I mean, what do I call you? 'Billy' or 'Henry' or 'Kid'? Pick one."

"Henry's fine," said The Kid. "Mostly only the Mexicans call me Billy."

Dave nodded. Stubbed the butt of his cigarette out on his boot heel and flicked the remnants away.

Henry was instantly energetic. "You wanna ride out later? Maybe we can—"

"What?" asked Dave. "Eat corn through a fence?" He walked back to the bunkhouse, leaving Henry McCarty shaking with anger. But at least he hadn't called the boy stupid.

* * *

For his part, Dave spent most of his time away from the Greathouse ranch and away from The Rustlers, preferring to cut out horses and cattle on his own, to feed the "Spring J. J. Fund." Dave had long come to the conclusion that he had no head for planning. If you had a job in motion, he was the man you wanted backing your play, but he would never be a mastermind. Of the smartest men he knew, one had tucked tail and fled into the night, the second came and went like a dry wind, and the third was sitting in jail waiting for Dave to come rescue him. It was beyond his ken.

Since their days riding with Milt Yarberry in Arkansas, Rudabaugh and Mysterious Dave Mather had worked out a long-distance messaging system involving a long stretch of desert and a peculiar-looking rock. They set up a similar system just outside of Las Vegas, just as the Dodge City Gang was getting going.

Halfway between Vegas and Otero, there was a short distance of nothing in particular, and in the middle of that nothing was a rock jutting out of the ground like an obscene troll's phallus. It was a description they'd agreed upon amidst some giggling. At the base of the rock was a crevice into which notes could be tucked. They referred to it as "Just-In-Case Rock," and only the pair of them knew about it. Not even J. J. was privy to its existence.

Since leaving Vegas in his violent rush, Rudabaugh hadn't ventured as far as Otero, but he'd suspected there was a message waiting for him at Just-In-Case. He'd left a pile of money and weapons behind in his room, and while he'd held a sliver of hope that Mather had recovered the stash before the Romeros, practicality and familiarity with luck told him otherwise. Without a kitty, he'd have to start a new fund. Guards could then be bribed, doors left unlocked.

So long as it was someone else doing the bribing, he realized. If he showed his face anywhere near Las Vegas, the Romeros would blow it off.

* * *

Jorge Hernandez was just thirteen-years-old when *Señor Bil-ee* began using him as a messenger between Old Fort Sumner and White Oaks. Sometimes he'd have to ride all the way to Coyote Springs and back, but Señor Bil-ee always let him take his pick of horses from the Greathouse stable, and Señor Big Jim would usually flip him a coin when he returned the animal healthy. Another coin would greet him if he fed and stabled the mount before heading home. It was a good arrangement.

Of all the Rustlers, Jorge liked Bil-ee the best, but he found the others more or less agreeable in their own ways. Maybe not so much Señor Tom Pickett, perhaps, who was angry all the time, drunk or sober. And definitely not the newcomer, Señor Dave. Jorge had never seen the new man smile. He had little eyes, too, like a *roedora*, or a rattlesnake, and he didn't blink often. Sometimes Señior Dave would sit with his back against the wall and just stare, not drinking or smoking or even speaking, just glaring a hole into space.

One day, Jorge was walking through the fort, hoping Bil-ee might have an errand for him, when Señor Dave called him over. Jorge hesitated, grinding his heel into the dust for a moment. But Señor Dave beckoned again. "S'matter with you? Come here. I won't bite ya." Jorge took a step closer, but remained out of reach.

Señor Dave sighed. He was wrapped in a filthy red-and-gold *serape*, even though the air had no chill. Jorge found everything about him scary and strange. Señor Dave's hands disappeared beneath the *serape* and emerged again with small bag of coins. He held them up. "This here's fifty dollars, *comprende*? I got a little map here too. You take this little bag to where the map says, bring me back anything you find, ten of them coins is yours. You savvy?"

Jorge took a step back. "*¿Qué es esto?*"

"It ain't a trick," said Señor Dave, softening his voice and even his eyes. "And I ain't asking you to do nothing bad. It's just a long ride and I can't do it." Señor Dave tossed the little leather bag into the dust at Jorge's feet. "Map's in the bag," he said. Dave retreated into the *serape*, keeping his dark rat eyes on the boy as he retrieved the swag.

"*Mierda*," Jorge whispered, then crossed himself in hopes none of the elders heard him. Señor Dave was not telling fibs when he said it was a long ride. Almost eighty miles! Out past Otero into the middle of what seemed to be nowhere, at least according to the ugly little map. It would take him a full day to get there and back, but for ten dollars, he would make the trip twice.

Even at thirteen, Jorge was no fool. He'd loaded a sturdy horse with plenty of water and jerked beef for the ride. He'd borrowed his cousin's wide-brimmed sombrero to protect him from the sun, and even tied himself to the saddle horn so he could dose during the ride. It was almost sundown when he reached the rock shaped like a *pito*, jutting out of the desert.

At the base of the *pito*, Jorge found a note wrapped around a stack of money. The note was written in *gringo* and he could not read it. It wasn't for him anyway and he feared Señor Dave would know if he tried. The man might be a *brujo* or even a *demonio*. Jorge crossed himself, and kissed the cross at his throat, and then spat into the dust for good measure.

As instructed, after taking ten of the coins for himself, he left the bag and the rest of its contents in the crevice. Neither did he read the note inside, written by Señor Dave. If he could read *gringo*, he would not know who "Samuel King" was anyway. Nor was he about to wait around to meet the addressee.

After watering the horse and himself from his canteen, he turned the mount around and headed back. There was a long, cold, and dark trip ahead of him. But for ten dollars, the horse could ride him.

* * *

Historians agree that there is little proof that, after Webb's hearing on March 18, 1880, Mysterious Dave Mather ever returned to Las Vegas. The papers had him departing town weeks prior. By the end of the year, most of the news slingers were in agreement that Mather was wandering about in Texas. His death was also regularly reported, much to the consternation of his creditors. He'd come by his nickname honestly.

There is nothing to tie Mysterious Dave Mather to J. J. Webb's escape from *la parerra* on November 10, 1880. But neither is there anything concrete to discount his participation.

CHAPTER 15

THE MOST DESPERATE MEN ON THE PLAINS

On March 10, 1880, history in Las Vegas repeated itself. That Thursday night, several of the commission-house boys from Otero, Sellar & Co., gathered in the offices to while away the evening talking about old times. The reason for celebration was the arrival of friend James "Jimmy" Morehead. Morehead had worked with Otero, Sr., and Sellar at C. R. Morehead & Co., in Leavenworth, KS, and had travelled west in the interest of several large wholesale houses. As the evening broke up, Jacob Gross, Thomas H. Parker, and Otero, Jr., headed towards their bachelor quarters, in the same direction of the St. Nicholas Hotel wherein Mr. Morehead had taken up residence.

The previous morning, Mr. Morehead had exchanged angry words with the hotel waiter, yet another man named James Allen. It seemed that this Allen decided Morehead had descended for breakfast in too tardy a fashion and refused to bring the man his order of eggs. "Come down when we serve and not after," said Allen. "Give in not to sloth." The waiter's manner had irritated Mr. Morehead beyond the telling.

"The same thing is liable to happen this morning," he complained to young Otero, "for I am getting to bed late tonight, and I don't intend to regulate my habits to suit any waiter. Much where I am paying a good price for poor service!" He'd been like this on and off throughout the evening.

Leaving Mr. Morehead at the St. Nicholas, the gang broke up amidst more laughter and handshakes, and retired for the night.

9:30 the next morning, Mr. Morehead came down to the restaurant, bid good morning to Mrs. Hommacher, and again requested his eggs.

"We's done with breakfast," said Allen.

"No, we are not," protested Mrs. Hommacher, but Allen stepped forward. A line had been drawn. "This is a business, mister. Not your mama's kitchen."

Mr. Morehead's constitution was not a steady one. A team of horses paraded through his cranium, leaving foot-prints and manure all over his demeanor. Without thinking, he let his hand fly and slapped Allen across the mouth. "Eggs, goddamn it!" He touched his hat to Mrs. Hommacher in apology and took a seat near the door.

Mr. Morehead had only just opened his newspaper when he heard Mrs. Hommacher's scream. James Allen fired his pistol. The bullet shredded the paper and punched a hole in Mr. Morehead's chest. It would take Morehead some hours to die.

James Allen, waiter, was known to the dwindling Dodge City Gang as a fellow bunko artist and occasional cheat who preferred a short con to something needing unfolding over time. Without cover from the Judge or the Gang, Allen was remanded quickly to *la parerra*.

As if it were now some kind of biological function, no

sooner was Allen behind bars than a mob formed outside the jail, demanding satisfaction, demanding blood. Only this time, the prominent citizens were among them. The businessmen, the bankers, the Oteros, Sellars, the Vigilante Squad in all but bandwagon. Most howled for justice, but the moneyed interests remained in the back, scowling in silent judgment of all.

On August 10, 1880, having been found guilty of murder in a Santa Fe court, James Allen was returned to the San Miguel County jail to await his hanging. Also awaiting the rope was J. J. Webb, whose death date had come and gone and who knew the reason why. Webb shook his head as Allen was brought as a new bunkmate for the already crowded center cell.

"That is how all this shit got started," he told Bonnie Hommacher that night. She had no intention of stopping her daily visits. Refilling his coffee cup, she nodded at him to continue. Webb sighed. "Some waiter shooting some drummer out of spite or meanness. Only difference is, there ain't no one on that stoop to stop a mob from stringing him up. Or me. Both Daves are long gone." He took a long swallow. "Same goddamned name, too. What do you think of that?"

She didn't know what to think about that and told him so. For many months, J. J. had tried to convince Bonnie to stay away from him. He couldn't fathom her loyalty or her continued kindness, which brought him daily shame he couldn't bear to live without. He had no one to blame for his sorry state but himself and what favors was she doing herself doting on him in this way? What future did she see for the two of them? He couldn't fathom her love for him being equal to his for her. "I saw the cards in everyone's hand and I still thought I could win."

"Win what, then?" she asked.

"Damned if I know."

Some mornings, Bonnie would arrive to find J. J. bleeding from face and back. The jailers there, particularly Desiderio Romero, were not gentle turnkeys. They were convinced he knew Dave Rudabaugh's exact location. They were not shy about using their quirts and rawhide clubs to extract information. But J. J. had no information to provide, so beating him was fruitless. However, they found it entertaining, so their game continued.

For Bonnie Hommacher, there were no rough words, not from the Mexican nor white jailers. When she entered, they all touched hats and escorted her to the center cell. Rarely did they even check her basket, letting her pass to feed her beloved John Joshua.

At night, the prisoners were chained to the wall. By day, their hands were shackled, even when they were allowed exercise in the narrow yard outside. On the evening of November 9, 1880, J. J. was still moving about the cell freely, or as freely as he could amongst the five other occupants of the crowded space. When he greeted her, Bonnie hurriedly shoved her basket through the serving space in the bars. She began speaking faster than normal, and much louder than he was used to.

"Josh, I just wanted to tell you that I'm leaving here. Maybe tomorrow, by Sunday at the latest."

"Okay," he said, scrutinizing her squirrelly demeanor. She was never like this. In every situation, she was always in charge, always confident. Now her dark eyes were darting back and forth between him, the cell, and the disinterested guards who were snacking on the biscuits she'd provided. "I'm glad to hear that," said J. J.

The words poured out of her in a torrent. "My late

husband's people have work for me in Arkansas," she said. "Winslow." She repeated the town again, with emphasis. "My in-laws, the Quinlans, they have a position for me, and I intend to take it. In Winslow, Arkansas. I shan't return here again."

"Bonnie," said Webb, reaching for her hands, the motion awkward between bars and his shackles, "tell me what's wrong."

"There's nothing wrong, Josh," she said. Her eyes were wet but the tears stayed put. She looked fierce and determined. "You just need to know that you still have friends. You are not alone in there and you won't be in there forever." She pushed at the basket again, shoving it into his arms. "You eat well and get this back to me, you hear? In Winslow, Arkansas."

The basket was heavy. Heavier than bread and steak and biscuits should be. Because she'd brought enough for the guards, he noted, they wouldn't be of a mind to relieve him of his dinner—which they rarely did, he'd have to admit, out of respect for Mrs. Hommacher. "You're a good man, Joshua Webb," she said, squeezing his hand one last time. "It's not your fault you live in a world full of rats and snakes."

She left him then. He watched her vanish through that door and into the night beyond.

Sitting down on the bunk, basket in his lap, J. J. began to formulate a plan. It wouldn't be much of one. There was only one gun in the basket.

* * *

At 6am, there was a change of guard at *la parerra*. The new shift would bang on the bars to rouse the prisoners, taunt them with the smell of fresh coffee and tobacco. Today, the six men in the center cell were chained together, for no purpose other than to do so. It amused the guards to watch the men shuffle around in tandem.

On the morning of November 10, 1880, John Joshua Webb was chained by the ankle to George Davis, a horse thief who also dabbled in mules. The other men, James Allen, George Davidson, William Mullen, and John Murray, were also feigning sleep when the new guards arrived, making the usual racket, slinging the usual insults in both English and Spanish. Webb lay on the floor, his face to a corner. Davis sat on the bunk as far away as his chain would allow, so almost right on top of Webb. When the new shift arrived, Webb didn't stir. It caught the guards' attention.

A younger guard named Emilio kicked the door. "*Oye! Despierta, cabrón!*" But Webb didn't move.

The guards entered, forcing the others to their feet so they could release the ankle shackles, but the Emilio's attention was on Webb. "He's sick," said Davis. "Been sick all night. Probably dead by now, you bastards!" Davis' voice rose in pitch and speed. "Nobody came to check on him!"

The guard put his heel on Webb's shoulder to turn him over. "*Oye!*"

Webb rolled onto his back and shoved the barrel of the pistol into the guard's crotch. "*No te muevas,*" he said, and the guard did not move. "Nobody else move!" he ordered, and the rest of the guards froze. The prisoners were in motion now, liberating keys from belts, dropping their shackles. Once free, the men rushed through the rear exit, spilling into the alley.

Miraculously, they there found six fresh horses, hitched and at the ready. Webb instantly recognized Dandy, the spotted pony Mather had sold just before he'd departed. Next to it was a roan that Rudabaugh once favored. There was no time to ponder further their origins. Webb mounted Dandy and Davis the roan. By 6:20 am, all six men had vanished from Las Vegas.

* * *

Interviewing no one, Kistler would rush an article into *The Daily Optic* that afternoon:

> *The friends who assisted in the escape are the dreaded gang of killers who infested Las Vegas last winter, and made things lively for newspaper reporters. Dave Rudebaugh (sic), "Mysterious Dave," "Little Allen" Bennett and others, whose names are legion, and who are known to be the most desperate men on the plains …*

Nobody knew what the hell he was talking about. It was common knowledge that Mather had been gone for months. "Little Allen" Bennett? Was there such a person in town? And if Rudabaugh had stepped foot in Vegas East or West, he would have been set upon in a manner that would have shamed as cowards the good people of Northfield, Minnesota, who'd faced down the Younger Brothers. At least two men spat at Kistler's feet that day as he passed.

Sheriff Romero was spitting fire. Otero, Sr., offered to pay the expenses of the posses and Otero the Younger volunteered to go. The banker was, of course, ignored by the cooler heads, his father included. Before the ink had dried on Kistler's extra, a posse of twelve men were assembled and rode out of town in the supposed direction of the fugitives.

Around four in the morning of November 11, history repeated itself. The dozen men crested a hill leading towards Anton Chico, following the smoke of a campfire. Hearing the horses approach, James Allen, the waiter from St. Nick's who'd killed businessman Morehead, got to his feet to hail the riders. "*Hola!*" he called out.

The responding gunfire spilled his guts into the fire. All twelve men rode upon the camp. George Davidson dropped right alongside Allen. William Mullen and John Murray found cover behind a boulder and returned fire. Only Murray managed to draw blood, winging posseman Juan Romero across the thigh, before the fugitives ran out of ammo.

Stepping around the boulder, Murray threw down his empty gun and raised his hands. "All right! I surrender—!" The posse interrupted and shot him to rags.

"Goddamn," said William Mullen, his final word.

When the smoke cleared and the bodies stacked upon a wagon, it was noted that neither George Davis nor John Joshua Webb were among the dead.

* * *

It was bitter cold, the morning of December 8. The slapboard shack on Dan Dedrick's ranch in Bosque Grande had gaps in the wall two fingers wide, doing little to prevent the icy chill from finding its way inside, to freeze the fire burning in the iron stove.

"It's been almost a month," Davis complained, stomping around the cabin, blowing on his hands. "When's your beloved gonna come for us?"

"Watch that talk," said Webb, huddled near the stove, wishing he'd found a warmer coat to steal along the line. "I won't tell you again. As for Rudabaugh, I have no way of knowing."

With the gun and the biscuits, Bonnie Hommacher had

also included a note among the contraband. Scrawled hasty on a scrap of parchment, Dave had instructed Webb, should he get the opportunity, to meet him "somewhere" between Vegas and White Oaks. Seeing as how Dave couldn't get any closer to Vegas *than* White Oaks, Webb wasn't sure what the man was hoping to accomplish. There was a lot of land in New Mexico. There were suggestions on the page—Rudabaugh had made a hideout among the abandoned buildings of Fort Bascom, raiding the cattle in both the Waddingham and Watts stocks, so that was one possibility. The closest, however, was Bosque Grande, and the Dedrick spread.

The Dedricks were brothers, Dan and Sam, co-owners of Dedrick and West's livery. Sam Dedrick made his money up front; Dan made his out back. (Partner Harvey West straddled the fence, fond as he was of counterfeit money and uneven scales.) There was a third brother, Moses Dedrick, who kept away from the livery business entirely. All three were known sycophants of Billy Bonney and would bring him ice water in Hell if he'd asked. That Rudabaugh had met up with Dan Dedrick on occasion was no secret to Webb, and though he was not himself acquainted with the brothers, he had no doubt that Rudabaugh had extracted promise of protection by one manner or other.

Since making their escape, Webb and Davis kept on the move, realizing early that they'd made the right decision splitting off from the other fugitives. News of the nasty business of the campfire massacre outside of Anton Chico confirmed the notion. The pair knew that Rudabaugh was operating out of Old Fort Sumner and thereabouts, so moving North was also the right play. The nagging questions: could they beat a posse there? Would they be leading said posse right to Dave and his boys? The questions weighed on J. J. and kept him from making a firm decision. Paralysis was torturing his spirit, like the cold torturing his carcass. He was only thirty years old and he felt as if he'd already lived forever. He was tired for tomorrow.

Webb's indecision was also torturing George Davis. His natural restlessness already challenged, he insisted they make frequent trips to Puerto de Luna, and Alejandro Grzelachowski's store where The Kid and his fellows were known. By Davis's reasoning, they were more likely to run into Bonney, who could then lead them to Rudabaugh, seeing as how the latter had been less-than-specific about a meet-up. "He went to all the trouble to arrange your escape," Davis groused again, "but doesn't tell you where to link up?"

"Dave's never been one for planning," said Webb with a shrug. In truth, he couldn't fully explain why he'd been squatting in a shed for a month instead of high-tailing to Arkansas and Bonnie Hommacher. He told himself that he was keeping the law from Bonnie's door, certain they'd follow him. In truth, all his crimes had built into a secret shame, and his greatest fear was of spreading that shame to Bonnie. Prison was no easier for women than it was for men. So he sat in further misery, waiting for Rudabaugh.

Outside, the wind howled like an injured giant, and threw sand and stones against the shack's walls. In the tiny paddock beyond, their horses nickered and puffed steam. "I gotta get out of this goddamned cabin," said Davis, still grousing. "When'd we go last to Puerta de Luna?"

"Four nights ago," said Webb, feeling almost as constrained as he'd been in his cell. "And we're drawing attention. People are whispering as we come and go."

"Let 'em whisper," said Davis, pacing and stomping. "I want a plug of chaw. I want a newspaper. Even at the price that goddamned Grez—Grzow—how the fuck you pronounce that goddamned name?"

"Just as it's spelled."

Davis shot him a look uglier than normal. "Who cares what a bunch of greasers whisper?"

"You will if they call the law. Could be a posse out there now."

"More greasers," Davis said, and spat onto the floor. "When this fucking cold lets up, I'm leaving you, Webb."

"I'll mourn your absence, George."

"Fuck you," he said, "I'm checking the horses." Using a scrap cloth for a scarf, he braced for the wind as he threw open the door.

Outside, six white men on horseback levered their rifles and pointed them at his head. Davis' jaw dropped and he threw up his hands. "Son of a bitch … " he muttered.

"Don't you goddamned move," said the obvious authority. This man sat tall in his saddle, wide brimmed hat on his head giving him a sense of boldness, his body made bigger by the wooly buffalo coat about his person. "By the power vested in me by the Governor of New Mexico, his honor Lew Wallace, I hearby arrest you men and intend to remand you back to Las Vegas, where you will be returned—"

"Oh, shut the fuck up," came the weary voice from the cabin. Webb emerged, hands raised, holster empty. "Just take us in already. I'm just as well satisfied in jail as dodging and hiding around the goddamned country."

The big man drew himself taller in the saddle, angry at the interruption. "I am Marshal Pat Garrett," he said. "Dave Rudabaugh and Jack Allen, I presume?"

At that, Webb and Davis exchanged a glance. "Nossir," said George. "My name is Tolliver Jennings, and this here is—"

"Sam King," Webb said, growling his words. He began to lower his hands, but the posse leaned forward as a unit, so he kept them aloft.

"Bull shit," said Marshal Pat Garrett. "You're Dave Rudabaugh and Jack Allen, alias Jack Llewellyn. And I'm taking you back to Las Vegas."

"Listen, Marshal," said Davis, chancing a grin that he'd hoped was disarming enough to keep him bullet-free, "you have the wrong men. I swear it."

"Swear it to Saint Peter," said Garrett. He made a motion that no one interpreted. He gestured again, with more emphasis. Finally, two men dismounted and slapped iron cuffs on the prisoners.

Webb couldn't help but shake his head and laugh, even as the men hauled him onto the wagon. Garrett slapped the slat side. "What's so goddamned funny, Rudabaugh?"

"Everything," said Webb. "It's all just hysterical."

CHAPTER 16

THE TELL-TALE TOOTH

It was a good time for Patrick Floyd Jarvis Garrett, having only just won his election for sheriff of Lincoln County, New Mexico, on 2nd of November, beating incumbent Sheriff George Kimball by decent vote. His campaign had been mostly paid for by the Texas Cattlemen Association. Chisum and the other rich ranchers had backed Garrett and promised him he'd win. Deliver they did.

Despite Garrettt's official term not to begin until January 1, 1881, Kimball acquiesced and appointed him the position of deputy sheriff for the remainder of the year. But that wasn't enough. Billy Bonney had gotten stuck in Garrett's craw.

Few who knew Garrett understood the obsession. At Fort Sumner, the young man was known to the older, they'd seemed friendly enough; content certainly to play cards and drink together at Pete Maxwell's or Beaver Smith's saloon where Garrett had sometimes worked. This seemingly new ambition of Garrett's struck the folk at Fort Sumner as odd and unseemly. The Kid was okay, at least as far as the Mexicans in the community went. He couldn't have done half the badness the papers were starting to pin to him. Truth was, The Kid annoyed the white ranchers specifically, and the cries for blood were throaty. Garrett, most surmised, was under pressure by the Texas coalition. Or, perhaps, he just wanted a feather in his cap. He'd begin by bringing in the most-wanted Dave Rudabaugh.

Obtaining a deputy U.S. Marshal's commission allowed him to pursue Rudabaugh and The Kid across county lines. Before he could make his first move, Garrett was approached by Azariah F. Wild, a Secret Service Agent investigating the relatively new Federal crime of counterfeiting. His particular interest was the paper being spread around by Billy Wilson, whom it was suspected was the leader of this shadowy ring. Garrett had been acquainted with Wilson on and off throughout the territory and found the man blandly agreeable, hardly a mastermind.

"Personally," said Wild, "I believe it's Bonney at the lead."

Wild was a thin, wiry man, excited at the idea of serving his country like the lawmen he'd read about in dime novels. Counterfeiting may not be an exciting crime, but he'd be surrounded by outlaws, rustlers, thieves. On the train from Washington, he'd read all about Bonney via Koogler's widely reprinted editorial. For his part, Wild couldn't wait to meet the young killer.

Garrett took in the agent, sized him up, and just shook his head.

On Monday, November 29, Bonney, Rudabaugh, Wilson, and a few other rough companions Bonney had acquired along the way, labored through the snowdrifts on their way to Anton Chico. Wild made his regular report to Washington:

"The posse left Roswell under the command of Deputy US

Marshals Olinger and Garrett," he wrote. *"The force is made up of the best citizens including a deputy Sheriff, constable and justice of the peace,"* Wild reported. *"We have at the present time between one and two hundred armed men out scouting for this gang of counterfeiters and outlaws. We this day arrested Joseph Cook, between five and six P.M. He had two stolen horses when arrested. He is now chained and now in the same 'Chosa' with me. Cook is a native of Texas and an outlaw."*

A 'chosa' is a hut, a fact once pointed out to Wild offhandedly by one of his men. He felt it his duty to educate others whenever possible, by presenting the information as his own.

Joe Cook was indeed an outlaw, guilty of the usual crimes of horse and cattle thievery, and had been an infrequent member of The Rustlers in the past, but something had soured the relationship. He gave up everything but the Kid's hat size. Wild opted to take Cook back to Roswell while the criminal kept up his constant chatter.

Cook then made outrageous accusations against Billy Wilson, telling tales of buildings full of printing presses, running off twenty- and fifty-dollar bills by the bushel. While Cook blamed all on Wilson but the murder of Lincoln, Wild began to suspect that they were being followed. Cook shifted constantly in his saddle, scanning the hills behind them, yet never missing a word of his monologue.

"Who you looking for, Cook?" Wild demanded. "Who's out there? That Wilson's gang?" Wild was no marksman, but he drew his pistol and scanned the distance as the sunset stole the light and lengthened the shadows. Once they were within ten miles of Roswell, Wild spurred the horses into a gallop, nearly breaking his neck watching behind them for signs of what he'd now convinced himself was a siege of riders. He imagined Billy Wilson, eyes blood red and spitting fire, leading a team of outlaws, sub-human and armed to the sharpened teeth. Upon reaching Roswell, both horses and riders were in lather, but they arrived in town alone.

Admittedly, Wild was chagrined by his ride, spurred without pursuit, but his report to Washington was no less exciting.

In the meantime, Garrett met up with Deputy Bob Olinger, and their combined posse set out along the Pecos towards the Dedrick Ranch in Bosque Grande, expecting to find Rudabaugh at the very least, who was well-known there. Bonney being in the vicinity as well would solidify Garrett's bona fides.

Not only was Bonney not at Dedrick, they found the entire spread nearly empty, the stock having been moved to Old Mexico a few days before. A passerby mentioned that Rudabaugh had been spotted in the vicinity a month or so back. Garrett chewed his mustache as he turned the posse around.

Finding the slapboard shack outside of Bosque Grande, at the very edge of Dan Dedrick's ranch, was accidental. Indeed, Garrett had almost dismissed the tip as fraud when a little goat drover told them of the shed long-abandoned up on the mesa, now spilling wood smoke from the chimney. Garrett's gut reaction was a round *who cares?*, but finding the deserted ranch had left the men in his employ irritated and ill disposed towards him. They already saw the politician within him overtaking the lawman, but who the fuck could really tell the difference anymore?

The idea of catching the dreaded Rudabaugh spurred Garrett towards the shed. The coup would quell the doubters riding behind him. And damned if they didn't pull it off. "Make note of this success, Ashmun," he said to his well-dressed compatriot. "History will delight in it."

Ashmun Upson, the journalist from Ohio Garrett had hired special to chronicle his adventures, was huddled in his wool coat, freezing his balls off, and made no response. That night, Garrett prodded again. "Mark down that we nabbed Dave Rudabaugh and Little Jack Allen on December eighth. Make it about eleven at night. No one will question it."

***

Garrett took the prisoners back to Old Fort Sumner, placing them in the custody of officer C.B. Hoadley, a round-faced chap who seemed proper-suited for the job. With "Rudabaugh" and "Allen" ensconced, Garrett marched to the telegraph office to alert San Miguel County Sheriff Hilario Romero that he had their two most wanted men in custody, and to remind him of the reward on Rudabaugh's head.

It would take another day before the newly-deputized Francisco Romero would arrive with an ambulance and four men in tow—history gives their names in list as Baker, Ortiz, Sondoval, and Vigil. It was agreed that the Vegas posse would meet Garrett and the prisoners in Puerta de Luna.

With the Mexican coalition on their way, Garrett made sure his former neighbors, the fine folk of Fort Sumner, recognized his new importance. No longer was he "the buffalo hunter" or "the bar man at Maxwell's." He was Marshal Pat Garrett, the man whose career began with the capture of the most notorious bandit in New Mexico Territory.

Garrett and his chief Deputy, brother-in-law Barney Mason, rode tall on their mounts as they drove in. Deputy Francisco Romero was there to greet them. When he saw Webb and Davis, he too began to laugh, and it was a bitter sound indeed. "*¿Es esto algún tipo de broma?*"

"Joke?" said Garrett. "Why would it be a joke, Deputy?"

"This is Webb," said Romero. "Convicted for murder, *si*, but he is not Rudabugh. This is not John Allen. They did not kill Antonio Valdez."

"I said as much," said Webb, with a grin and a shrug, both weak.

Garrett didn't answer immediately. His mouth opened, but no words came out. He looked at the two prisoners, shot a quick glance towards Upson, then back to the lawmen laughing right in his face. "Bull shit," said Garrett through clenched teeth.

Romero glared at the Marshal then. He seized Webb's face with an enormous, filthy hand, and forced open the man's mouth. "You see? Gold tooth." He released Webb's face. J. J. scowled at him and stepped back, spitting into the dust. "Gold tooth," Romero repeated. "*Webb*. Not Rudabaugh. Señior Marshal? We in Las Vegas want Rudabaugh. These men killed whites. Who fucking cares?"

"The United States of America cares," said Garrett, puffing himself up again, but the words didn't come as easily as the posture. "That's who cares. You ask who cares? That there. That there."

"We will take these men back to Las Vegas," said Romero. "But you bring us Rudabaugh alive. I wish to cut off his head myself."

Webb shot Romero a glance. This was a cousin, he surmised, one of Hilario's endless bloodline. Therefore he resented the rough handling even more. This new Romero hadn't earned the right. He spat into the dust again. "Come, Señior Webb," said Romero, taking his arm. "We'll take you to the blacksmith to get fettered."

"Lead the way, Señior Deputy."

From behind, Davis shouted and kicked at the deputies

dragging him from the wagon. "You greasers take your hands off me!" He received a gun butt to the mouth for the epithet and gave them no further trouble.

The blacksmith was across from Grzelachowski's store and while the burly worker refit Webb for shackles, the prisoner had a front row seat to the next step of Pat Garrett's ignominious beginning.

With Deputy Romero assuming custody of the now-identified men, leaving only a disdainful sneer for Garrett, the newly-minted Marshal felt a rage building inside of him. He couldn't bring himself to meet Barney Mason's gaze, and Upson's furious note taking was like a rat chewing the inside of his skull. He opened his mouth to speak, but only a strangled grunt issued forth. There was no second attempt. He stormed off down the street towards Grzelachowski's. Half a minute later, Mason and Upson followed, the rest of the posse dismissed.

What Garrett had originally intended at the store was a mystery. He was inside so briefly, it was incredible his eyes had time to adjust to the gloom before he yanked his gun on a man perusing a catalog at the counter. "Mariano Leyma!" he shouted.

"*Leyba*," the man corrected, closing the catalog and turning. "Who are you?"

"Pat Garrett, sheriff of Lincoln County. And you're Mariano Leyba, wanted for murder in Anton Chico."

"That I am," said Leyba, "and I'd love to see some *gringo* try and arrest me."

"I'm that *gringo*," said Garrett.

"*Chinga tu cola*," said Leyba, and he drew his gun.

Both Garrett and Mason were quicker. Bullets clipped Leyba's left shoulder and hip but he managed to stumble out through the back door and into the crowd outside. The gunfire brought men running and they soon had the store and the *gringo* newcomers surrounded.

Romero ordered the blacksmith to keep an eye on Webb and the still-dazed Davis, then marched across the road to the crowd calling for blood. "Sure," said Webb, watching the sport. "Lynch the law men. Lynch everybody. Let's all get our necks stretched because the horses aren't racing today."

On the night of December 17, accessory-to-murder J. J. Webb and horse thief George Davis shared a tiny cell adjacent to Pat Garrett, Deputy U.S. Marshal and Sheriff of Lincoln County, New Mexico, alongside his deputy, Barney Mason, both arrested for armed assault.

Frequently throughout the night, Webb woke up giggling.

* * *

The next morning, Garrett and Mason were taken before Puerta de Luna's Justice of the Peace, the Hon. Walter William Bruce. Deputy Francisco Romero was called as witness, delaying the return of the prisoners to Las Vegas by approximately one hour. The J.P. quickly found just cause for the lawmen's actions and dismissed the charges against them. Free to resume their duties, Garrett and Mason walked back into the morning sunlight, sails bereft of wind. There was nothing to celebrate. Mariano Leyba had fled Puerta de Luna for parts unknown.

Garrett's eyes had barely adjusted to the light before he spied Agent Wild riding towards them, wearing a look of disgust. This event would certainly make his report to Washington.

Deputy Romero snickered as he touched his hat and bid the pair good day. He made final note of the prisoners and mounted up. As the ambulance pulled away from the Port of the Moon, Webb slipped his hand through the narrow bars and gave Garrett a little wave, smiling broadly to show off his telltale gold tooth.

"What's the plan, boss?" said Barney to a glowering Garrett.

"We're going back to goddamned Fort Sumner," said Garrett. "I know Rudabaugh is there somewhere. Or's gonna be. And he'll have the goddamned Kid with him."

"I thought you liked Bonney," said Mason.

Garrett turned on his heel and didn't answer.

* * *

There was great disappointment in Las Vegas when the Romero posse returned with not Rudabaugh but Webb. Davis was sick with sepsis from the broken tooth and upon arrival was hustled over to a doc's on the Old Town side. When Webb descended the wagon, angry old women pelted him with rotting garbage. Following the lead of their elders, children hurled horse apples at his head, most managing to miss him. They wanted *Rudabaugh, Rudabaugh!* Lino must be avenged! "*¡Lino debe ser vengado!*"

Webb didn't blame them. How could he? Life was filled with bitter disappointments and the flavor never improved. He dodged a bit of potato and let himself be led back to his home, the center cell of *la perrera*.

CHAPTER 17

IT AIN'T NEVER BILLY'S FAULT

It was Bonney's fault that Webb got pinched at the Dedrick ranch. If he hadn't picked a pointless fight with Pat Garrett, the man might not have been so eager to catch them all—gang, accomplices, anyone he'd ever met. Were it not for Bonney lighting the fire, Webb might have escaped Garrett's scrutiny.

Back in April of '79, Henry McCarty got himself arrested by Lincoln County Sheriff George Kimball. Now, when he wasn't in a mood, Henry could make a friend of a rattlesnake, and after spending three days incarcerated with the lawman guarding, playing cards and smoking, the young outlaw decided he'd enjoyed the man's company.

"You like me so much," said Sheriff George, turning the prisoner loose, "you tell all your friends to vote for me in this election coming up."

"Happy to," said Henry. "Who's running again' you? Maybe we can put enough a scare into him, you can run unopposed."

Kimball snickered at the notion. "Big fella name of Pat Garrett, from out your way last I heard."

"Garrett?" said Henry, smile growing bigger. "We stole cattle together!"

"Yeah?" asked Kimball, leaning in, interested. "Whose?"

"Never mind, that was more a joke than anything."

Kimball nodded. "Sure."

Henry squirmed a bit. "Anyways," he said, "I don't know why he'd want to be sheriff of anything. Listen, whose side was you on? McSween or Tunstall?"

Kimball laughed. "Even if I hadn't been for English John T., why would I say otherwise to you after I just gave you your gun back?"

"Hell," said Henry. "Now I think you're *too smart* to be sheriff."

Keeping his word, Henry drummed votes up for Kimball without even the shadow of a threat. Violent promise was unnecessary in wake of purchased rounds of whiskey and bawdy jokes at Garrett's expense. While it was true that Henry was suspicious of Garrett's motives, with regards to his sudden interest in politics, he bore no ill will towards the ex-buff hunter. But it was also true that Henry loved attention. His insults of Garrett's character, demeanor, parentage, hygiene, and sexual preferences were rewarded with laughter and soon the old miners were buying Henry's drinks. It didn't take long for the news to reach Garrett's burning ears.

When Garrett won the November election, Henry's insults grew even louder, more obscene, and more frequent. Whether he meant the jabs or not was beside the point. He'd taken a stance and dug in his heels. Garrett was a skunk, it was proclaimed, and McCarty wouldn't back-walk.

Throughout New Mexico territory, wanted posters hung in every law office, calling for the capture of Dave Rudabaugh. Officially, Rudabaugh was Garrett's sole priority. It was known that Rudabaugh had on occasion been spotted riding alongside McCarty, also with Wilson and Pickett throughout the area between White Oaks and Fort Sumner, including Bosque Grande and the Dedrick spread. Quickly, Garrett recruited spies. If McCarty—or Bonney, or 'The Kid,' or whatever the hell he was calling himself— farted in the wind, Garrett wanted to know about it.

* * *

It was only by chance that Barney Mason happened to be in White Oaks at West & Dedrick's Livery Stable when three men rode in. Pat had sent him to follow up on news that Sam Dedrick had in his possession a note written by his brother's partner, Jim West, confessing that he had used $30,000 in counterfeit bills to buy cattle and horses throughout the Territory. Some of that money had wound up in the hand of suspected Rudabaugh Gang member Billy Wilson, who'd passed it in both Dodge and Vegas. Counterfeiting was a new and puzzling crime, and local law enforcement weren't equipped to investigate. A week back, Garrett met up again with Secret Service Agent Azariah F. Wild, who offered further assistance in capturing Rudabaugh's gang if they could join forces and root out the counterfeiting ring.

"Simple," said Garrett, seeing an opening fitting his pragmatism, "Henry McCarty, also known as Billy Bonney, is your ringleader." Wild was on the hook.

Barney Mason met up with Dedrick his livery and received the evidence against Sam's partner West, as instructed. Afterward, the deputy opted to fill out his own supply list for his return to Fort Sumner. He was on his way out the door as three Rustlers mounted the steps to enter. Passing him, the men paid him less of a mind than a touch of their hat brim. His own supplies in a box held to his chest, big Barney Mason stared mouth-agape at Rudabaugh, Tom Pickett, and Billy Bonney, aka Henry McCarty, the loud-mouth Kid.

Only Bonney spoke to him, saying "Afternoon, Barney, nice to see you here." Maybe it was the shock, maybe it was the growing heat of the day, but Barney's heart skipped twice. Friendly as the words sounded, there was menace beneath tone. Wasn't there?

Remaining calm, Mason loaded his cargo into his wagon and then ran across White Oaks Avenue to the little jail. Inside, Deputy J.W. Bell dozed behind the desk, feet up, cells empty. It had been a slow and very quiet week, for which Bell was grateful, though less-so when Mason came barreling through the door, babbling and blubbering about 'The Kid.'

"What kid?" said Bell, rubbing the back of his skull. So startled was he by Mason's entrance he'd slipped backwards in his chair, banging his pan on the windowsill.

"That goddamned Henry McCarty. He and Rudabaugh and Pickett are up at the Dedrick Livery."

"Uh huh," said Bell, sitting patiently at the desk.

Mason gave him a look. " 'Uh huh' ? Don't you think we should do something about it?"

"I certainly do," said Deputy J.W. "One of us—meaning you—rides out to Roswell and brings back a small army. Thirty men or so, I'd expect. I'm sure you'll have plenty of volunteers just tripping over themselves to face Rudabaugh."

Mason looked to the ceiling, perhaps appealing to the Heavens for assistance. "I go to Roswell and what happens? By the time I get back, they're ghosts in the haze."

"I'm sure Sheriff Garrett will understand."

Mason peered out the window. The Rustlers' were still hitched outside, which meant the men were still in the livery. Again, he appealed to Bell for assistance.

For his part, Bell laughed and lit a cigar. "Not just no, Barney, but *hell no*."

"What kind of lawman are you?"

"A living one," said Bell. "Do I have to say that I intend to maintain this status? Listen, Barney, I appreciate your situation, but it is just us two. You think Rudabaugh will just agree to be arrested? Young Henry might go just for the sport of it. I don't know the other. Tom Pickett? Don't know him."

"He was part of that Dodge City Gang in Las Vegas with Rudabaugh."

"And a fine, upstanding bunch they was. Christ, Barney, Pickett might be meaner than any of them. Or more panicky. Or he might beg for mercy. However it would go, God gave me seven holes in my head. I ain't looking to add to 'em."

"We got 'em cornered, Bell."

The pair continued to argue. Bell suggested they run around the corner to the home of Bill Hudgens, another deputy. Mason didn't want to wait, and while the argument drew on, Garrett's deputy watched helplessly as the three outlaws emerged, mounted their horses, and rode away.

Half a minute later, gunshots rang out.

* * *

Completely unaware of the hornet's nest buzzing in the little jail, the three men completed their business at the livery. Henry took the others in a huddle. "What do you think?"

"About what?" asked Pickett.

"Mason," said Henry. "I smell a pot-bellied rat."

"So go kill him," said Dave, shouldering his burden and heading for the door. Henry studied the man's back.

Hearing the talk from behind the counter, Sam Dedrick went white. "Please don't do that, Henry. Wouldn't be good for my business."

Henry stared back at Dedrick and the shop owner fell silent. Finally, to Tom Pickett, Henry conveyed his decision. "Nah," he said. "Too nice a morning."

Pickett shrugged, not caring either way. "Should we head up to Coyote Springs?"

Rudabaugh said over his shoulder, "I need to make sure we ain't got eyes on us. Need to get supplies to J. J."

"J. J.," said Henry, singing out. "That most beautiful of names."

"Quit that shit," said Rudabaugh with a growl. For too long he'd been pre-occupied with re-uniting with Webb. Being distracted always altered his mood for the worse, and his mood had been miserable for months.

"Listen," said Henry, quickly changing the subject. "You all know who we should hit next? Deputy Bell."

"Why him?" asked Pickett.

"He's got a *remuda* full of horses. Winter's coming and we're gonna need fresh mounts, right?"

"I take it Bell was anti-Tunstall," said Rudabaugh. It wasn't a question.

Henry shifted in his saddle. "So?"

"Everyone knows 'bout your grudge," said Rudabaugh. "We hit Bell, you're the prime suspect."

"Why?"

"Because he's a lawman and you're known to be dumb enough to rob a lawman."

"I told you to quit calling me dumb, Dave."

"Yeah, you did." He kicked his horse into a trot.

McCarty stewed, his ears hot. No matter what he did or said, Rudabaugh refused to show him an ounce of respect. It was aggravating. No one else talked to him the way Dave did. He should just put a bullet right in his head. Drop him right there, feet away from the White Oaks entryway.

In point of fact, Henry McCarty pulled his gun to do just that. Just as Henry cocked his Colt, Dave turned and fixed him with a graveyard look. There was ice in his voice as he asked, "What are you thinking to do with that?"

Unable to answer immediately, Henry merely stared back. Movement caught his eye. Exiting the Pioneer Saloon was James Redman. Redman had been anti-McSween during the Lincoln County War, which meant he'd been anti-John Tunstall, and thus, anti-McCarty. Such was the reasoning. The young Owl Hooter suddenly had both a target and a change in conversation. Swiveling in his saddle, Henry called out, "Hey, Redman!"

Hearing his name, Jim Redman turned towards the riders. Upon recognition, Redman froze. McCarty fired.

The shot took off Redman's hat and he dove for cover. Laughing his donkey bray, Henry kicked his Appy and the horse tore off through the entry arch. Rudabaugh and Pickett swore and urged their own mounts to speed, gunfire and angry voices chasing them away.

"Goddamn *bok gweilo!*" Rudabaugh shouted. Henry's laugh rode the wind.

They made camp at Coyote Springs and the trio crowded the fire. The icy wind blew straight pins through them. Rudabaugh continued to curse McCarty for a fool. "Why?" he demanded. "We were home free. Nobody said boo to us. Then you take a shot at some rube? The hell for?"

Henry said simply, "It's my birthday."

"Goddamn you," said Rudabaugh.

"It was just a joke, Dave," said Pickett in a conciliatory growl.

"Joke? Let me tell you what's a joke," said Rudabaugh, angrily rubbing his chapped hands. "That *remuda* you thought we could take." They'd passed it along their hasty exit from town.

"Bell must'a found reinforcements," said Henry.

"Reinforcements? Ten men at least guarding that paddock."

"We could'a taken all of them."

Rudabaugh stared at Henry over the fire for a good long while. "Say we could. You think half a dozen horses are worth killing ten men for?"

Henry shrugged. "Who cares?"

Rudabaugh's stare didn't falter. "How many men you killed? In truth."

Henry returned the stare. "Three at least."

"Hope it was for more'n a couple of horses."

The pair stopped talking but neither dropped their gaze. Pickett was growing bored with both of them. "We should get some sleep," he said. "You know they's out there looking for us."

'They' was a mighty big number.

* * *

Bell and Mason enlisted the help of Deputy William Hudgens after all. Hudgens immediately put together a posse of ten men, himself and Bell included. It was decided that pursuing the trio into the dark winter night was too foolish to consider, and that they would wait until morning. Coyote Springs, about six or so miles north of White Oaks, lay at the mouth of the Coyote River, which was said to "curve like an eyebrow above the town." It was a known hideout for outlaws so it was decided that would be the starting point.

Hudgens' men found only a cooling campfire but the trail was fresh. It wasn't too long before the men encountered a pair of riders coming up over the ridge. Will Hudgens peered through morning gloom and saw that one of the pair wasn't dressed for the weather, freezing without an overcoat.

"Hold up," said Hudgens to the riders. "Identify yourselves."

The pair looked rough but put up their hands. "Mose Dedrick, sir," said the man on the left. "I believe you know my brothers."

Hudgens did. Quite well. "Sure are a lot of you Dedricks," said Hudgens. "Fucking freezing morning. Where's your coat?" Dedrick didn't answer. "I have paper on you, Mose."

"Like hell," said Dedrick. "Apologies, but that can't be true."

"I'll have you under arrest until we can sort it all out," said Hudgens, ignoring the man's further protests. Hudgens looked to the man on the right. "What about you?"

"Lamper," said the man. "W.L."

Hudgens looked to Bell, who shrugged. "I'm sure you're needed in a cell too."

Lamper now shook his head. "Listen, Deputy, none of this is right."

"Shut up," said Hudgens. "We're looking for Dave Rudabaugh and Billy Bonney, I know you ride with them. They were with a third man."

"Aw, hell," said Lamper and jerked a thumb over his

shoulder towards where they'd come from. "The whole damned gang is up at Cooper's Mill."

Hudgens sat back, astonished. "You give them up just that easy?"

"Who are they to me?" asked W.L. Lamper. "Turn us loose. We'll help you bring them down."

"You asshole," muttered Mose.

Hudgens didn't trust either of them and had Bell secure their hands to their saddle horns, then the posse of now twelve moved on towards Cooper's, a sawmill abandoned, sitting inside a canyon astride a dried river bed. They weren't within whistling distance before three shots rang out. Jim Hudgens, brother to Deputy William, cried out as his horse dropped dead beneath him. The other horses spooked and reared, screaming in terror. Will Hudgens ordered the others back. To his brother, he said, "You all right, John?"

"Yep," said John. James Carlyle, the young blacksmith from White Oaks, had provided him cover. "George O'Neil's gonna be mad."

"Why's that?" asked Will.

"That were his horse."

The dust settled. Will Hudgens called out. "Rudabaugh!"

There was no answer for a long moment. Then: "Who's asking?"

"Deputy Will Hudgens!" he called, peering into the distance. The mill's structure was old but solid and the chutes were intact, all providing perfect cover. "That Bonney with you?"

The voice that answered wasn't Rudabaugh's: "Me, Billy Wilson, Tom Pickett and his sixteen ex-Rangers, twenty Mex killers, and one Chinese with boiling hot soup!" Then followed the donkey bark that was McCarty's laugh.

"Son of a bitch," Hudgens muttered. Despite the chill, he was hot, he was tired, and he was getting too old for this line of work. Knowing he was out of range, and without a target, he fired anyway, emptying his gun.

The gang responded, firing back. For many long minutes, the two sides shot blindly across the canyon but racked no casualties. Hudgens ordered the posse to split. Circling around, Bell and his group climbed the canyon side, hoping to rain hell on Rudabaugh and Bonney. The angle was bad and the outlaws were well covered. Behind the mill, several horses bucked and panicked. Taking aim with their rifles, Bell and his men cut down two of the mounts just as Bonney and Wilson broke cover.

Skidding in the dust, the pair dove behind the dead animals and crouched down. On the canyon floor, Hudgens and his men pressed forward, still firing. Rudabaugh and Tom Pickett rounded one corner on their own jittery horses, scooped up the Billys, and tore out, dodging the rain of lead as the canyon swallowed them up.

Hudgens turned the air blue with his language. Too late, he realized that both Lamper and Dedrick had taken off as well. "They won't make it far," said Carlyle behind him, and while it was likely they'd pick them back up on the way back, Hudgens still stung from the loss of quarry.

The posse searched the mill for any inkling as to where the riders may have gone next. For some days, the gang had used the mill's guard shack as cover from the frigid weather. Hudgens found the rooms littered with food tins and newspapers. He also found the overcoat Mose Dedrick had left behind for whatever reason. In a pocket, Hudgens found a letter addressed to Mose, written by his brother, Sam, the corral owner, saying nothing of importance. The Dedricks had family all over—who knew how many brothers and cousins there were. Mose being acquainted with Rudabaugh's gang was no surprise.

The dead horse was equipped with a fine saddle Hudgens recognized as having belonged to Bonney. He remembered liking the Kid, not so long ago. He'd even arrested him once on a shoplifting charge and they wound up playing cards through the bars. Now he longed to put Bonney/McCarty in the goddamned ground.

"Now these are some lovely gloves," said Carlyle. He'd found a pair of yellow calfskins, soft as an infant's bare feet. Inside the cuff of the left were burned initials: *H.M.* "Think these were the Kid's?"

Hudgens shrugged. He didn't care. They might chase the bastards until Gabriel blew his horn and never catch them. Bone tired, he ordered the men back to White Oaks.

In town, the posse was met with much excitement. They were welcomed in every cantina, crowds eager to hear the tale. As the night drew on and the drinks poured forth, the recounts grew windy, the adventure more daring. By morning, Hudgens felt his spirits improve. Like the others in his midst, he'd grown to believe their versions of the tale. Hudgens also started to see in himself the great hero the town had seen, at least that previous night, amidst the drink and bravado.

"I want him," said Jim Redman, still stinging from the fright the Kid had given him. "Fucking Bonney. The son of a bitch took a shot at me."

"You shot at him all day," said Hudgens.

"And I never even winged him."

"You can have him after I get done with him," said Jim Carlyle. "Bastard insulted my mother."

Hudgens gave him a look. "When?"

"Months back," said Carlyle. "In my own shop, no less. Said his horse reminded him of her face."

Hudgens started to speak but then thought better of it. Barney Mason had come to join them, and to him, the Deputy asked, "When's Garrett meant to be here?"

"By morning," said Mason. "He's got at least ten men with him. Including some secret agent man from Washington."

"Fine," said Hudgens. "Soon as they're here, we ride out again. And if we don't get Rudabaugh, Bonney, and them others, we don't goddamned come back."

* * *

"You did it again," said Rudabaugh. Henry was riding behind him, posse bullets chasing them from the mill. "You can't never keep your fucking mouth shut!"

"What now?" asked Henry, that whine in his voice there again. "What I fuck up now, Dave?"

"They didn't know we was there! We could'a slipped away in five seconds, but you had to mouth off. Again!"

"There weren't no getting away clean," said Henry. "So I gave their balls a squeeze, so what?"

"I'm riding out to see Whiskey Jim," Dave said. "I'm getting a fresh horse from him, and then I'm getting the hell away from you."

"Yeah," said Henry, with more than a little bitterness. "Go meet up with your J. J. Have kids together."

Dave reined the horse hard enough to make it rear. Henry went spilling down the horse's rump and landed on his own on the hardpack.

Circling around, Dave stared down at The Kid. "That's the last crack you make about Webb and me, you got that?"

"You two Prairie Marys can go ta Hell!"

Rudabaugh did not draw his pistol. He didn't take his hands from the reins. He simply stared down at Henry McCarty, on his ass on the frozen ground. "We can end this right now," said Dave Rudabaugh.

Out of sheer self-preservation, Henry finally remained silent as he got to his feet. Pickett and Wilson had pulled up behind them, but kept to themselves during the argument. "Henry," said Pickett, his voice even and his eye on Rudabaugh. "Why don't you and Billy here switch off? You ride with me for a while."

Wilson slid down and offered a hand to Henry, hauling him to his feet. "Yeah," said Henry. "We should do that. Best all around."

Rudabaugh didn't respond, nor did he help Billy Wilson climb aboard his Tennessee Walker. "You know," said Wilson, "I think I may try my hand at prospecting. There are strikes all over, right? Not just in the Territories?" Dave didn't answer. "Yeah," said Wilson. "They say you can just pluck the gold out of the water."

"Freeze your balls off in some creek somewhere," said Dave. "Nobody cares."

* * *

The Greathouse and Kuch Ranch was an epic spread thirty miles or so outside of White Oaks, near the Gallinas Peak. The stage stop and saloon was popular with weary travelers and drivers on their way to and from Las Vegas and parts East and West. Big Whiskey Jim Greathouse and his partner, Fred Kuch, reaped the profits. That many referred to the stop as "Robber's Roost" didn't seem to bother either of them.

Dave Rudabaugh figured that Greathouse was just

Owlhoot enough to give them cover, get them out of the snow. Like goddamned near everybody, Whiskey Jim liked the Kid. As expected, Greathouse greeted them warmly, ushering them out of the cold and into the warm comfort of the saloon.

After the booze came out, Big Jim took Rudabaugh aside. "I got some supplies out to Webb. He's been bouncing between Dedrick's and the Baker bunk house in Anton Chico." Dave nodded and gave his thanks. "I told him there's about five posses out looking for you boys so linking up might be difficult."

"Fucking impossible," said Dave. "We been fighting these bastards the last few days. I don't wanna go anywhere near Dedrick's. That'll get J. J. pinched for sure."

Big Jim agreed then clapped Rudabaugh's shoulder. Dave almost recoiled at the touch, the familiarity and attempt at comfort that foreign. Greathouse either didn't notice or ignored it. "Let's get you boys warmed up."

* * *

The next morning, Big Jim's German cook, Joe Steck, woke early, yawned, stretched, donned his boots and his wooly coat, pissed into the snow, grabbed his axe, and went to chop wood for the stoves. Rounding the woodhouse, he came face-to-face with ten men and their loaded rifles. The synchronous cocking of the mechanisms sounded to him like some infernal machine grinding its gears. "*Guten morgen,*" he said, his voice very thin.

CHAPTER 18

YELLOW GLOVES BRING HELL

As the sun rose over the Greathouse and Kuch Ranch, The Rustlers woke with it. They'd slept well on the benches, their sleep aided by as much whiskey as their bodies could stand. Dave was still semi-drunk as he attempted his feet. Before an inquiry could be made as to coffee or breakfast, there was an urgent pounding at the door. Since Greathouse had retired to his office, Henry McCarty took it upon himself to answer.

On the porch, hands laden with firewood, was Big Jim's German cook, Joe Steck, white faced and trembling, though not from the cold. Dumping the wood onto the floor, Steck shoved a note into Henry's hand. " 'You are surrounded,' " he read easily. " 'You haven't a chance. Come out with your hands up and without your guns.' " He looked up at Steck. " 'Deputy Sheriff William Hudgens.' How is old Will, anyway?"

Steck didn't respond. Dave shouted, "Will you shut the goddamned door?" Henry grabbed Steck by the collar and dragged him inside.

"They said that they would kill me unless I gave you that note," said Steck in his heavy accent.

"I'm sure," said Henry.

Wilson's head was pounding. "What's going on?"

"We're surrounded again," said Rudabaugh.

"Perfection," said Wilson.

" 'You haven't a chance,' " Henry repeated. "Somebody find me a pencil."

* * *

Some minutes later, while Hudgens and his men blew on their hands and stamped their feet in the snow, Jim Greathouse came tramping up through the drifts, bundled in a grizzly bear coat, his hands raised above his head. "Don't shoot and good morning!" he called.

Hudgens stepped forward, his gun ready. "We know they're in there, Jim. Turn them out to us and maybe we can get through this without gunfire."

"Well," said Greathouse, "maybe you should read this note first." He held out the same paper Hudgens had given Steck. "It's Bonney's response."

Cautious, Hudgens leaned forward and snatched the paper and opened it. Beneath what he'd written, the Kid had scribbled three words: "*Go to Hell.*"

"That little cocksucker," said Hudgens. He crumpled the note and dropped it in the snow.

"Hold on," said Greathouse, taking a step forward. "Just ... hold on one minute. There's no need to shoot up my place, all right?"

"I aim to bring them all in. That's the offer," said Will Hudgens. "Come in with us or die in the fucking snow." But it was empty bravado. Hudgens took a look at the men behind him and read the looks of terror on their faces, even on that of his own brother. They were miners and ranchers.

They were Sunday Afternoon deputies. Inside that saloon there was at least one hardened killer, another the papers say is not shy about murder, and unknown quantities making up the rest.

Then James Carlyle stepped forward. At a young age, James Bermuda Carlyle had ventured west, starting from Trumbull County, Ohio. As a teenager, he worked a spell as a buff hunter in Texas, and over the course of six days in the summer of 1874, he fought in the Second Battle of Adobe Walls. Alongside Bat Masterson and thirty other men—and one woman, Mrs. William Olds—together they held off Chief Quanah Parker and near a thousand Comanche, Kiowa, and Cheyenne. He was right alongside Billy Dixon, whose "lucky shot"—a 1,500 yard kill with a .50-90 Sharps rifle, taking the head off a brave—ended the battle. The thought that their enemy's weapons could reach that range scared the hell out of the Indians and sent them scattering.

The teenager from Ohio had more than held his own at Adobe Walls. As an adult, facing four outlaws in a shady saloon was nothing in comparison. "I'll go," he said. "Let me try to settle this mess."

There was some argument. Though Carlyle was known to both Bonney and Rudabaugh, they shared little affection. John Hudgens offered that they'd be likely sending the blacksmith to his grave.

"I'll stay here," said Greathouse. "Keep me hostage. They won't kill Carlyle with me out here."

"They love you that much, do they?" said Will Hudgens.

"Everyone loves me," said Big Jim.

"Fine," said Hudgens. He turned to Carlyle. "Tell the Kid, if you're not back out here by two o'clock, it means a fight, and his dear friend Greathouse will have the benefit of the first shot." He stopped a moment, staring at the structure housing his quarry. "They are surrounded. It is useless and hopeless for them to attempt an escape. We will wait here to doomsday if necessary."

Carlyle nodded. "I'll … tell them as much of that as I can." Then he turned and made himself seen, rifle raised high and away from him. "Hey Bonney!" he called out. Then slowly, he removed his gun belt and handed it back to Hudgens, along with the rifle. "I'm coming over!"

"Come on then," The Kid called back.

Carlyle tramped through the deep snow, taking long and deliberate strides, hands up, meaning no harm. The posse watched as he disappeared into the Greathouse and Kuch stage stop saloon.

* * *

Wilson opened the door for Carlyle, and the blacksmith brought snow and cold in with him. "Kick them boots in the corner," said Bonney. "Don't go tracking mud all over."

Carlyle didn't move but took stock of the room. It smelled like a stable, for one, but he had no stones to throw in that regard. In addition to Kid Bonney, he observed Rudabaugh lounging in a bench along the wall, slouching low in case bullets emerged through the walls. Wilson and Pickett stood behind Bonney but not quite near him, removed at least from Rudabaugh's line of fire. Pickett boasted a fresh bullet burn across his right cheek and held a bloody kerchief to it against the pain. In his left hand was a heavy Walker Colt and the barrel bobbed now and then as his wrist complained. Wilson's hands were empty and shaking, he shifted his weight from one foot to the next, all nervous energy. With such a welcome, James Carlyle did as instructed and kicked the snow from his boots. He spoke quickly, relaying Hudgens' message and the two o'clock deadline.

"Let's see your warrants, then," Bonney said.

Carlyle shook his head. "We've been chasing you all over the Territory. No time to get warrants."

"That's your problem," said Pickett from the corner. Lowering the hammer of his Walker, he dropped it to his lap. He never wore a holster and kept the gun jammed in the front of his pants. Dave often wondered how the ex-Ranger rode without the barrel stabbing his nethers.

"Well then," said Bonney, "how are we to be sure you're not some damned mob here to murder us?"

"Surely you recognize some of us?"

Bonney smiled wide. "Surely." He sat down at a table by himself, bottle and two glasses before him. "Come on and sit. Have a slug."

Carlyle paused a second, weighing his response. Should he accept? Decline with dignity? Stand strong in principle? Now that he was inside, Jim Carlyle realized he didn't have a plan. Casting his eye across the room again, updating the guns and positions, he snapped himself upright and stiffly took a seat across from Bonney. The Kid holstered his piece and pushed a full glass to him. Carlyle took it and knocked it back.

The Kid beamed. "There you go. Now we's friends, right? Right fellas?" There was some mumbling of agreement. "Or have we met already?"

Carlyle cocked his head. "Certainly we have." He recalled the incident at his store—where Bonney defamed Carlyle's mother for no reason other than a mean spirited joke—but did not relay it.

"We must've," said The Kid. "I'm not always good with

faces, though. Dave, you're good with faces. We met Jim here before?"

"Yeah," said Rudabaugh.

"That's Dave," said Bonney. He had an audience now. "He could win an argument with an echo. See, Dave's been all over and met damned near ev'body famous. Doc Holliday, Bat Masterson. Who else, Dave?"

Rudabaugh didn't answer. Wilson, nervously, offered, "Wild Bill Hickok?"

Rudabaugh nodded. "Black Hills in '76," he said. "I was going as he was comin' in. I spent a night at his camp. Quiet guy. He was traveling with this queer duck by the name of Utter, dressed like a peacock, dragged a tin bathtub around with him."

"Guess we could all use a bath 'bout now, huh?" said Bonney, still cheerful, showing off his bucked teeth in his grin. "Remember when you met Jesse James, Dave?"

Rudabaugh shook his head. "Never met James."

Bonney half-turned in his seat. "Oh, now, that ain't true. I know for a fact you met Jesse James because I'm the one'd introduced you."

"When'd you dream this?" asked Rudabaugh, sounding vaguely interested in the answer.

"Must'a been last Summer, in Vegas. At Anderson's. You came in with a sack of grain on your shoulder and Big Jim said, 'I want you to meet Henry McCarty.' And we shook hands and I said, 'And this is my friend, Mr. Howard.' Though we wasn't *really* friends at the time, you see. But I thought we could'a been."

Dave frowned—it wasn't as scary as his normal scowl. "Tall guy, yellow hair? Blinked like the sun was always in his eyes, even indoors?"

"That's the man."

Rudabaugh let that settle. "Hm," he said.

Bonney laughed and slapped the table, causing Carlyle to jump a bit. "Ain't that something? Just rolls off his back. Dave, I just added to your celebrity and you can't even appreciate it!" Rudabaugh didn't answer. "Yeah, me and Jesse I think could've been friends. I treat my friends well, Jim. Don't I, fellas?" No real response from the gallery. Rudabaugh spit on the floor. "I feel the love, Dave."

Carlyle spread his hands and The Kid stared right at them. "What's this all about, Billy?"

Bonney's eyes snapped back up. "Oh, see there, too? 'Billy.' My friends on this side of the Territory call me Billy. In Lincoln County, I'm Henry McCarty. So we must be friends."

Again, Carlyle thought of their encounter in his own store. "Certainly we're friends."

"Mm hm, I knew we was soon as I saw them gloves."

God shot an icicle through James Carlyle's chest. He'd forgotten all about the yellow calfskin gloves on his hands at that very moment. They were tight on him. The Kid had small hands.

"Last time I saw those gloves—those are my favorite gloves, by the way. They fit me like shoes. Anyway, last time I saw them, they was being returned to me by my good friend, Mose Dedrick. And to thank me for the loan, Mose was to lend me his warm winter coat, since I'm a poor ranch hand and can't afford my own."

Carlyle kept his face stone. No longer playing to the room, Bonney locked eyes with the deputized blacksmith. The air between them was starting to boil.

"Thing is, before I could gather up these clothes—which I would need to protect myself against this cold winter—some rude, disrespectful men came along and tried to murder me and my friends. They killed one of my favorite horses and all

I was doing was getting in out of the chill." Bonney smiled then, but all the warmth had iced away. "Of course, you know all about all that, don't you, Jim Carlyle?"

It was all Carlyle could do to keep from swallowing hard as a final prayer. The Kid leaned back, waved a hand. "Now, now, you're gonna say, 'I didn't know.' Or, 'No, these are mine, you got it all wrong.' Except we both know you roll down the left cuff, you'll find my initials. And since they was given to me in White Oaks originally, them initials would be 'H.M.' Of course, you been kind enough keeping them warm for me."

No one in the room moved. Only Rudabaugh had a gun out, but that was well enough. Carlyle opted for a change in tactics. He got angry and shoveled some coal into his voice. "Mr. Bonney," he said.

"Ah," said The Kid. "It's 'Billy' to my friends."

Carlyle set his jaw and spoke through his teeth, removing the gloves, slapping them on the table. "Billy, it's my great pleasure to return these fine gloves to you."

Bonney didn't move. "Appreciated, Jim."

There was a pause. Carlyle felt heat creeping up his collar. "What do we do now, Billy? Do you kill me?"

Bonney shrugged. "I guess we'll see what happens come two o'clock." He nudged the bottle forward another inch or so. "Have another."

Jim Carlyle, the blacksmith from White Oaks, sat for another two full hours with the desperados. He talked and played cards with the Kid, and he imbibed far more than he should have. Though the tension had abated somewhat, he had no entitlement to dulled senses. Outside, the posse was freezing its collective balls off, waiting for those inside to make a move. "Can we send out a note or something?" he said to Bonney. "Let them know how things progress?"

"And spoil the surprise for everybody? Don't even think such a thing."

Again and again, Carlyle scanned the room, searching for any weakness to exploit that might get him out of that building alive. Bonney smiled again, and the devil winked within his eyes. "Careful there, Jim. Me and Wilson wear our guns for protection. Pickett's a trained lawman, so his gun's a tool of his office. But Dave?" The Kid jerked his head in Rudabaugh's direction. "Dave wears a gun 'cause he likes it." He looked back again. "Three guns. Thrice the fun."

Time passed at a molasses creep. The closer it got to 2:00 pm, the worse Carlyle's fear worked against him. There had been no indication from any of the men, Wilson aside, that he was going to be released peacefully. Several times, Rudabaugh mentioned that it would be easier to kill him and slip out the back. "They ain't gonna do spit to Jim Greathouse," he said.

Despite the chill there in the saloon that the fire could not reach, Carlyle was sweating. He knew there'd be no reasoning with Bonney or Rudabaugh. Pickett he didn't know. Wilson, then, was his only hope. "Listen, Bill," he said to Wilson, "you're up on a counterfeiting beef. That's it. You're not looking at the rope."

Wilson had been pacing for the better part of the visit. He didn't stop once addressed. "Still looking at Leavenworth. And it was goddamned West's fake fucking money got me into this!"

"That's correct," said Carlyle. "Garrett doesn't even have jurisdiction over you. Hudgens neither. You'll be remanded to Agent Azariah Wild. You'll go to Washington on a private train car." Carlyle had no idea if anything he said was true. Looked past Wilson to Rudabaugh and saw the man's grim expression and then thought of Adobe Wells, the Indian warriors that kept coming in, wave after wave. He thought of the bodies piling up around the fort. Eyes watering from the gunpowder clouds about him and still firing and levering and firing. Again he smelled the sulfur and blood and shit. He heard the all of the screams competing with the throbbing in his ears, the pounding of his adrenaline-fueled heartbeat.

At that moment, Rudabaugh's hellfire gaze was scarier than the entirety of those six horrible days at Adobe Wells. He wasn't that reckless child any longer, and in that saloon, Jim Carlyle felt very, very mortal.

"Don't listen to him, Billy," said Pickett to Wilson. "Law spin all kinds of lies."

"I ain't lying!" said Carlyle in panicked protest.

"I didn't say you were," said Pickett slowly. "I'm saying, you might not know you're lying. Trying to save your skin here, boy."

Wilson wasn't listening anyway. Bonney leaned back and checked the gilt-trimmed clock above the bar. It had come all the way from Philadelphia and was one of Fred Kuch's most prized possessions. "Two o'clock," said The Kid, pulling his Colt. "Now, it's fun."

Amidst historians, there is much debate as to what happened at the Greathouse and Kuch spread that afternoon. All anyone inside the building knew was that just after two, a shot rang out from the treeline, splitting the afternoon quiet.

The Rustlers exchanged glances of surprise and horror. Rudabaugh jumped to his feet. "They fucking killed him?"

"Guess that's it for Big Jim," said Bonney.

Carlyle looked to him in desperation. "They said they would! That's what Hudgens promised. But—"

"The hell with you!" said Rudabaugh. Then everybody moved.

Ducking down, Carlyle flipped the table and heaved himself backwards. Pickett dropped to the floor while Wilson, Bonney, and Rudabaugh drew down. In a panic, Carlyle hurled himself through the saloon's front window, crashing through the glass. Gunfire erupted from either side.

John Hudgens would swear later that the hail of bullets held Carlyle's body aloft for five full seconds. Will Hudgens would warn him to never again speak of Carlyle's death, nor that the bullets pulled from his chest outnumbered those in his back.

* * *

The tragedy of it all: the devastating shot that sparked the violence had been fired by accident, by Jim Greathouse himself. The jovial reprobate bode his time with the posse-men, most of them known to him at the stage stop. They smoked cigars and passed flasks. Posse member John Moseby was a muler and drover in his spare, and he'd recently acquired a brand new Colt. He'd taken it out for Greathouse to admire. Playing like Bill Cody, Whiskey Jim spun the piece on his finger and dropped it like a fool. The butt struck a snow-hidden rock and discharged into the air, the bullet zipping harmlessly into the distance.

It was a sudden noise that gave birth to a deafening silence. And summoned Hell.

The posse rained fire upon the stop. They saw Joe Steck hie through the trees and their bullets chased him into the shade. Yet while the front of the house was besieged by chaos, the Rustlers simply vanished out back through the kitchen and stores. Snatching up fresh horses from the corral, the four men sped off unseen into the early winter twilight.

When the horror before them hit, some of the posse scattered, opting to head home and away from such misery. This hadn't been the adventure they'd imagined. For an hour after, Will Hudgens stared off into the distance, in the direction of Jim Carlyle's body, but not at it. Not at the crumpled heap of blood and meat that had been a young blacksmith and hero of the Indian Wars, steaming and cooling in the snow.

Greathouse was apologetic as all get out, but they brought him in anyway, charging him as an accessory and an abettor to the gang. Hudgens would have brought in Joe Steck, too, if they'd found him.

Later that night, Deputy Sheriff Will Hudgens rode alone to the Greathouse and Kuch and burned the stop to the ground.

CHAPTER 19

MANUELA MADE CHILI

At thirty-two years of age, Charlie Bowdre was the oldest hand in the bunkhouse at the T.Z. Yerby Ranch, and he'd killed more men than the rest of them combined. But that was during the so-called Lincoln County War, which had ended in 1878, accomplishing nothing.

The collective of ranchers calling themselves "The Regulators" had put in mind to avenge the death of fellow cattleman John Tunstall by hunting down the murderers employed by the moneyed interests, Lawrence Murphy and James Dolan. They further swore to uphold the business rights of Alexander McSween—who'd left the pair of villains to work for Tunstall, committing a cardinal sin among Capitalists. For all The Rustlers' efforts, the results had been thin. In the end, McSween was executed anyway and The Regulators scattered, many of them with murder warrants hanging over their heads.

Bowdre's longtime partner had been Josiah Scurlock, an educated man who went by the nickname of "Doc." Together they had run a number of legitimate businesses— ranches, a mail service, not to mention an infamous cheese factory on the Gila River that hadn't paid off as well as it should have. Both Rudabaugh and McCarty had worked for Charlie and Josiah at that very factory for a short spell each, tied in fact at two days apiece.

In between, Doc and Charlie lynched rustlers and fought off Indians. They and fellow Lincoln County ranchers, the Coe Brothers and Ab Saunders, broke the bandit Jesus Largo out of the jail there and brought him to justice via rope and tree just outside of town, without a peep of complaint from Sheriff Saturnino Baca.

During the Dolan-McSween debacle, Bowdre and Scurlock were among some forty workers recruited by shopkeep Dick Brewer to form said Regulators. The informal outfit sent to ground at least six men they deemed responsible for Tunstall's death in one way or another. Having received special dispensation to do so by county authorities, they'd been in truth little more than a murder squad. Vengeance by any other name.

In early '79, Scurlock and Bowdre became brothers-in-law when Josiah married María Antonia Miguela Herrera, and Charlie her sister, Manuela. In November, Doc and Maria moved to Texas, so Doc could try at respectability again. With Scurlock gone, Bowdre woke up every morning with less fire in his belly.

Manuela doted on him; she'd made a fine home for them within Old Fort Sumner and he was growing fat from her food and a good job on the Yerby ranch. Even so, time was stealing his hair little by little, adding aches to his joints without permission. Still, he reckoned he'd killed everyone he was ever mad at, and had no intention of adding to the list. One killing he was wanted for, the old mule-rider, Buckshot Roberts, had been in point of fact self-defense, yet bothered him still. There'd been many nights in the bunkhouse, sleeping alone and far from Manuela, where he considered riding out to surrender in penance.

Typically, after such dark times, the morning would arrive in tow by Henry McCarty and whatever scabs were following him at the time. Henry would be all grins and buck teeth, excited about some criminal venture on the horizon. Every time, Charlie would say *no*, and *no*, and *fuck no*, and would go along anyway. Of the original Regulators, only Henry and "Bigfoot Tom" O'Folliard were still lurking around. Charlie couldn't account for his affection for the pair. Reason left him when they uglied his threshold.

For her part, Manuela tolerated Henry. She knew him as "Bil-lee," as did her many cousins who swooned over the half-handsome young man, whose complexion had not yet been weathered by wind and cold, whose spine was not yet bent by ground-sleeping and trudgery. He was kind, he was silly, and he was respectful, and his *queridas* loved him for it. But Manuela did not like the effect he had on her husband. When Billy was in town, Charlie was dark, not sweet, and troubled, not gay. She thought little of Tom O'Folliard. He was too tall. She had to lean back to see his face and there she found little of interest.

Yerby's Ranch was located at the head of the Arroyo Las Cañaditas. Thomas G. Yerby had come to New Mexico in 1872, working first as a merchant with Charles Ilfeld, and his business in Las Vegas made his ranch the perfect hide-out spot for the Rustlers. Yerby's wife, Nasaria, was particularly taken with young Henry, and doted on him when he was about, particularly when her husband was not. For Henry, Nasaria was just another young *madre* to him.

When Henry rode up to Yerby's with three fellas in tow, Charlie felt an icy chill in the pit of his stomach, nipping at his onions. The group was ridden out, too tired for revelry.

Charlie found them bunks to collapse on. During the winter, Yerby operated with a skeleton crew, leaving it to foreman Bowdre to keep things running. Rudabaugh had worked there on and off the past year, coming and going as he was wont to do. Unlike O'Folliard or other infrequent employees, Rudabaugh had no bunk he called permanent. The two Mex hands they'd kept on were out on a mesa, but weren't likely to mind the company regardless.

Seeing Rudabaugh, Charlie took the man aside. Once out of earshot, Charlie offered the man a bottle. "Garrett and Mason combed through Dedrick's a few weeks back," he said. "They pinched that friend'a yours, Webb."

The news hit Dave in the gut and he sat back against the wall harder than he'd meant, cracking his head on a log. "Goddamned *bok gweilo* cocksucker … " he muttered, and then took a long pull from the bottle. "Okay, I got about four thousand dollars in a hole up at Coyote Springs," he said, mostly to himself. "Another thousand in Fort Bascom …"

Bowdre held out a hand, told him to relax. "They already took him back to Vegas."

Dave felt the dark of the room overwhelm him. He trained his eyes on the lantern beside the door, its weak yellow light barely creeping up to his boots. "I go back, a thousand Mexicans will cut my head off. Then my balls. In that order if I'm lucky."

Moon, an old bluetick hound, plopped down at Dave's feet. Animals still liked him, at least. Absently, Dave reached down and gave the hound's ears a scratch. He hadn't heard from Dave Mather in months. The last note he received via young Fernandez, Mysterious reported that he was heading first to Dodge City, and then points unknown. The newspapers Rudabaugh could scrounge were of no help, frequently mis-identifying Mather by placing him simultaneously in towns hundreds of miles apart. But when your nickname is "Mysterious," you expect that kind of thing.

Dave saw the problems before him. He would have to arrange entirely new go-betweens whose movements in Las Vegas would bring about no suspicion, to bribe jailers and smuggle tools. The logistics of that staggered him. He took a deep breath and let it out in a sigh. "I go anywhere near there," he said again, "I'll get J. J. killed."

At that, Charlie adopted a sad smile and reached for the bottle while Rudabaugh continued. "When we first met, I was a skunk on the Owl Hoot and he was one of Arthur's knights. He made you wanna be better, because he was good without effort. You know?" Charlie nodded and passed the bottle back. Dave took a pull and went on. "When we was in Vegas, I wore the badge. You believe that? And when I wasn't … robbing stagecoaches outside of town, I wasn't a half-bad deputy. I don't think. Because for some goddamned reason, I wanted Webb to be proud of me. What's the sense in that?"

Charlie let out a long sigh. "When Scurlock was around, I tried to be as big as he was," he said. He ran a hand through his thinning hair. At thirty-two … "Doc was a hundred-foot tall when he wanted to be." He gestured down his own lean frame. "People don't think small men can be hard cases."

Rudabaugh nodded himself. They were both slighter men, towered over by many. Henry, for example, was taller than both, and it was hard to reconcile that they were older. Bowdre and Rudabaugh both still felt like kids too often, when everyone older was taller. Tall was authority and righteousness and power. Short equaled youth, inexperience, greenery. Guns, of course, made all men equal. Kinda equal.

Thinking of Scurlock, then thinking of Henry, a queer look came over Charlie. "We all got friends we can't explain," he said. "You know, when the whole Regulator business got started, me and Scurlock was just ranchers. We owed on land to Dolan, so that put us automatically on the McSween side, and not much else. Why pay if you don't have to?" He jerked a thumb over his shoulder, indicating the room where the others lie snoring. "Henry was just another hand on Tunstall's spread. We'd see him riding with one of the Coes, we'd wave, he'd wave. That was it. He was a kid on the ranch. Tunstall had girls on his team too, and half the time I'd see Henry in the distance and think he was one of them: Sally Sue or Sadie McGee. Tunstall knew talent when he saw it, gotta give that up to him." He took a pull. "And it wa'n't never 'Billy the Kid and his Regulators.'"

"That's the goddamned papers for you," said Dave. "They don't even aim for 'mostly true.'"

Charlie nodded and passed the bottle back. They drank in silence. They rolled cigarettes and smoked in silence. "What do you think you'll do?" Charlie asked, finally.

Dave shook his head. "I can rob Chisum's cattle and drive them south until I turn to dust. I can make a play on the jail. Or I can just hope J. J.'s luck turns and get my sorry carcass to old Mexico and fucking stay there."

"Those are choices," said Charlie, nodding. "Especially that last."

"Except I'm fairly certain that the Romeros and the White Caps could find me all too easy."

Charlie nodded again, the whiskey having an effect. "That would be a worry." He thought for a moment. "Ever think about giving up the life?"

"White Caps would hunt me anyway," said Dave. "Besides, I'm no good keeping someone else's schedule. Just to make them money. Rather line my own pockets and set my own hours."

Charlie laughed. It was grim, but it was a laugh. He thought a bit, then said, "About a year ago, couple of fellas—Stilwell was one name I caught. The other was Spence, Spencer, something."

"What of them?" asked Dave.

"They's up from Texas, headed t'Arizona. Apparently the rustling's real good out by Tombstone. Mining town. Got a lot going on there, too. On both sides'a the street."

Dave shrugged. "Nobody looking for me in Arizona, I reckon."

"It's a thought, anyway. You might wanna get something going outside of the Territory."

"Thanks, Charlie," he said, draining the last drop without a thought. "Maybe I'll stick around through the end of the year. Henry can cut head from herd, I'll give him that. Pickett's all right."

"Bigfoot Tom is good in a pinch," said Charlie.

Dave shrugged. Tom O'Folliard was another of Henry's apostles and Dave couldn't stomach it. Big personalities, like Henry's, had been the bane of his existence. Little men with big personalities become lawmen and judges, if they don't make corpse first.

"You know, Henry … " said Charlie, and then trailed off for a bit before continuing, "Hell, I didn't even know he could read 'til his name started showing up in the papers. Damned journalers *made* him."

"Made a lot of us," Dave answered. "We's all just their … what's the word?"

Charlie looked up. "Fabrications." He grinned.

And for the first time in he didn't know how long, Dave felt the urge to smile back. "That's the one."

With a sigh, Bowdre sat back in his chair. "You should at least come to the winter festival in Sumner tomorrow,"

Charlie said. " 'S'a big dance, lotsa food. Manuela made chili."

In response, Dave only grunted. The idea of the noise and crowd made him uneasy. He didn't know how to act around people, and people noticed. Still, he hadn't been with a woman in he couldn't think how long, hadn't eaten more than beans and jerky in half that amount of time. History would support that, on rare occasion, when the alcohol and the atmosphere was right, the music was bright and the company light, Dave Rudabaugh would dance. He thought of one spring night with Lightning Jenny, outside in the ally behind the Close & Patterson's—the negro maid unwelcome inside—where he twirled her in the moonlight to the music pouring through the doors. Until the band wore down. Maybe after all the hard travel between him and Las Vegas, he'd earned himself a little fun. "Manuella's chili something special?"

Charlie gave him a wider grin. "Best you'll ever have."

To that, Dave had no argument. Among the Rustlers, aside from being an excellent cook, Manuela was considered as sweet, kind, and even-tempered woman you'd ever like to meet.

* * *

"*¡Pinche pendejo, whey!*" screamed Manuela Bowdre. "*¡Que El Diabolo te come culo por siempre!*"

"Goddamn it!" shouted Lon Chambers, yanking his hand away from her face, blood dripping from the webbing between thumb and forefinger. "Bitch tried to bite off my goddamned thumb!"

"*¡Chinga tu madre, cabron!*" she spit at him. It took both "Poker Tom" Emory and Jim East to hold her down on the bunk in the corner while Lon struggled to tie her wrists to the frame.

They were all in her own room in Sumner's old hospital building, constructed to help the Navajo years back when the land was the Basque Grande reservation. Manuela spat fire and bucked worse than any hornet-stung bull. Louis "The Animal" Bousman and "Tenderfoot" Bob Williams worked to secure her feet. Lon let one of those bastards with the consumed names affix the gag. Let them risk a thumb or two. The woman was fierce as a cornered puma. He heard Bousman yip and the woman's foul language then came muffled.

Chambers stomped over to the other side of the room to where Garrett sat, one ass-cheek on a windowsill. If there had been hope for clandestine control over Mrs. Bowdre, her curses had dashed that to bits. All of Fort Sumner could hear her, even over the sounds of the celebration in swing. "God-damn that woman," said Chambers, sucking his thumb.

Garrett ignored him. He was in rapt conversation with a goatherd standing outside the little stone shack that the Bowdres had made their home. The goatherd was actually a *vaquero* named Juan Roibal, a man who'd volunteered to spy for Garrett. "You're sure they're coming here?" said Garrett, again, to Roibal.

"*Si*," said Roibal, with a tired sigh. "I met them on the road. Two of them followed me for a while down the trail, to make sure I was who I said I was."

"And who'd you say you was?" asked Chambers, earning him a stern look from Garrett.

"A goatherd," said Roibal. As far as Chambers was concerned, the man certainly smelled the part. If asked, Roibal would say Chambers smelled no better.

"And why was you so quick to volunteer to us?" Chambers didn't give a goddamn what Garrett thought of the question.

"We don't need more *gringos* causing trouble around here. The sooner you take them with you, the happier we'll all be."

Chambers spit on the floor. "You don't like whites, I take it?"

"Gringos ruin everything," he said. "And that damned Bil-lee gets men killed."

"All right," said Garrett. They'd already determined the Rustlers weren't in town. The boys were known to corral at A.H. Smith's and the stables were empty at present. Barney Mason had reported earlier that they might have been at nearby a vacant shack near the home of his father-in-law, or possibly the Gayheart ranch, or but neither played out. They were just throwing darts at a map.

They'd spent weeks searching places the outlaws had just left. A few mornings back, Bousman and Emory traded shots with O'Folliard out by Anton Chico, but the big Texan managed to shake them. That was as close as they'd gotten to the Los Portales Gang, or the Rudabaugh-Bonney Gang, or the "Ruda-Bonney Gang," as some of the men had taken to calling them. It saved time and just tripped off the tongue.

For days, Garrett been trading notes with men familiar to The Kid, like rancher Brazil. Manuel Silveira Brazil had gone in with brothers Erastus and Tom Wilcox to establish the Wilcox-Brazil Ranch. It was another known stopping point for outlaws, and the owners were weary of it. The same couldn't be said of other men like ranch hand Bob Campbell or his partner, Jose Valdez. They weren't as eager to sell out Bonney and needed more persuasion. As a gambit, lies were scrawled onto paper to be passed along to The Kid. Whether the bait would be taken remained to be seen.

"What makes you so sure they's coming here?" Chambers interjected yet again.

The inquiry elicited yet another weary reply from Roibal. "*La celebración*," he said, spreading his hands, indicating the music and laughter already in the air, mingling with the many aromas torturing the starving posse there in the shack. "Who would miss it?"

Garrett leaned forward. "Why would they risk it?"

Roibal laughed. "Because they do not fear you."

Chambers spat on the floor. "Then they's just plain stupid."

"*Quizás,*" said Roibal. "*Tal vez no.*" And with that, he left.

Chambers gave Garrett a look of his own. "What'd he say?"

" 'Maybe, maybe not.' "

"And what's that mean?"

"I don't know, Lon," he said. "Why don't you go chase him down and ask him?"

"You really trust that greaser to tell us the truth?"

Garrett looked over at Manuela, still bucking on the cot, cursing him in muffled shouts and damning him with her eyes. Not too long ago, he'd attended her wedding to Charlie.

Towering over most of the men in the room, Garrett felt very, very small.

* * *

December 19, 1880. Bringing up the rear, O'Folliard was singing badly, in mangled Spanish and at the top of his lungs, a ballad he'd learned in Old Mexico, *Romance del Conde Olinos o Niño.* He hadn't much idea what the song was about, but he'd learned it by heart, listening to mariachis practice it over and over outside his bunkhouse.

Rudabaugh found the man's pronunciation amusing enough to lift his spirits a bit. His Spanish might not be perfect, but it was a damned sight better than what came stumbling out of O'Folliard's mouth. "*Ella es hermosa. Ella es un escritorio*," Tom sang. " 'She is beautiful, she is a desk,' " Dave translated, making Henry laugh. Tom sang another verse and this time Dave laughed. " 'She is a corpse I will never touch again.' That can't be right."

The Rustlers rode in a trail line, Henry at point, Dave on flank with Billy Wilson, Charlie Bowdre, then Tom Pickett, with O'Folliard riding drag. Fort Sumner rose up before them like the Promised Land, just as the sun was setting. Already, the smells of dinner reached their nostrils.

As the evening golds and purples began to glint off the adobe buildings and paint the new-fallen snow, all seemed right with the world. Yet, Henry got a funny look on his face and slowed his horse. Dave looked back. "What's wrong with you?"

Henry took a moment to answer, staring down at the town before them, the arch welcoming them to Old Fort Sumner. "Nothing," he said quickly, patting his pockets. "I just want a chaw. You all go ahead. Tom, why'n't you sing a little louder and let 'em all know we's coming."

With a nod and renewal of voice, O'Folliard nudged his sorrel to the head of the line. Dave stared back at Henry. Out of the corner of his eye, he caught the moonlight glint off steel, a rifle barrel peeking around the corner of the old hospital building at the mouth of the Fort. Hell was their greeting.

The gunshots came quick, the sounds of a drum player in spasm. Dave's Appy-Walker screamed, her head whipping to the right, collapsing under him. As he hit the ground with her, he watched Tom O'Folliard explode over and over again, the bullets lifting him from his saddle and spilling him into the snow. The Rustlers all shouted colorful variations of profanity, returning hasty fire and reversing their mounts. Using his poor dying horse as a springboard, Dave leapt forward and onto Wilson's, then skinned his own pistol to send lead into the grey smoke billowing from the mouth of Old Fort Sumner.

With bullets zipping past them like angry hornets, the Rustlers spurred their horses into gallop and tore off in the direction they'd come. Within minutes, they'd gained enough distance to deter pursuit. Dave imagined Garrett cursing them as they made their escape. Then he wondered just what had made Henry pull up just in the nick of time.

* * *

It took an hour for Tom O'Folliard to die. The posse had dragged him, tattered and screaming, on a sled into the hospital building. "Oh, fuck, Goddamn Hell!" He cried. "You've killed me, Pat! You've killed me for sure."

"True enough," said Lon Chambers.

"And you ain't killed bad enough!" said Bousman, thumbing one of Bigfoot Tom's bullet wounds, showing the dying man how he'd earned his nickname, "The Animal."

Garrett slapped the vicious man away. "Where they going, Tom? You have a plan after all this? Do some good in your last minutes."

"You go to Hell, Pat Garrett! You sold-out mother-raper!"

There was some discussion among the men as to whether they should put him out of his misery or set him out in the snow to die more quietly. Garrett didn't partake in the vote and O'Folliard spared them all the effort with a final gurgling gasp.

"Closest place for them is either Stinking Springs," said Jim East, "or maybe the Wilcox land. They won't make it any further with two riding double."

At that, Garrett turned, feeling disbelief. "These sons of bitches vanish into thin air the minute you take your eyes off them!" Which was what he'd wanted to say. Instead, he kept silent. East was a smart man. He knew the territory better than just about any other man among them and it was best to listen to him. They'd managed to whittle down the opposing numbers by one, so that was something. Still, the weather was vicious and a coming storm would make chasing the bastards nigh impossible. Their lead was increasing.

Daybreak and none of the men had slept. Nor would they for some time to come.

* * *

Cresting the ridge, the men scattered. Pickett's horse made it another twelve miles before it collapsed under him. The poor mare had been running with two bullets in her side and she died mid-gallop. Somehow, Tom made it on foot to the nearest hole-up, the Wilcox and Brazil spread. Beating the others, he hunkered down within a hay pile, watched the road for his compatriots. They arrived some two hours later.

Amidst the arguing and finger-pointing—blame for Tom going round in circles but always landing back on Bonney—the gang rejoined in the bunkhouse. The ranch owners were not allies, but they were absent. At the corral they were met by friendly faces that could distract a posse if necessary. It gave them cover to rest and properly mourn ol' Tom O'Folliard. After the bickering subsided and their flesh warmed by the fire, they were all able to grieve and relate their favorite stories about the man. Dave had barely known the big Texan, and therefore did not partake, not even to mention the wrangler's deplorable Spanish.

Fatigue hit hard. Wilson and Pickett had each picked up a bullet burn across thigh and back, and while they licked their wounds and Henry sought sleep, Dave tugged Charlie's sleeve and took him aside. "He knew," Dave said.

"Who knew what?"

"Henry," said Dave. "Knew something was up at the Fort. He stopped hard, sent Tom ahead."

Charlie gave him a look. "I don't see it that way."

"I was right behind him. He got a funny look on his face soon as the arch rose up. Maybe he caught a glint in the sunset?"

"Or maybe he sold us out, you saying?"

"What was really in those notes he kept passing with that Mex kid? Roibal?" There'd been a great trading of scrap paper over the few days at Yerby's. Young men known to Henry—Bob Campbell and Jose Valdez, and the like—came and went, or sent young kids ahead with notes, keeping Henry apprised of Garrett's posses. Not counting the baker's dozen of men coming and going at Fort Sumner, there were three other groups of deputized ranchers out and about searching the territory for the gang. If The Kid wasn't communicating directly with Garrett, who was to say his little missives wouldn't find their way into the lawman's hands somehow or other?

He'd shared one note from Valdez, reading aloud the scrawl that insisted Garrett's posse had moved on to Roswell. *There is no danger in Sumner.*

With a frown, Dave looked up and caught Charlie's gaze.

"Loyalty is a thing I value, Charlie. The only way I know to judge a man."

Charlie opened his mouth to argue, then shut it again, vexed. "That ain't Henry," he said finally.

"What ain't?"

Charlie kept his head to the wall, addressing the shadowy corners. "He loves this life. No matter how many letters he writes to the Gov'ner, what he wants is the freedom to keep doing what he's doing. He wants immunity." Finally, he turned and looked at Dave. "He doesn't want to die in jail."

"He didn't return fire."

"How many of us did? Too busy getting our asses shot off."

"Man who loves this life will sell out his fellows to keep going." *I know all about it,* he thought, remembering the Kinsey deal he made that sent Mike Roark to prison. "For... what's the word?"

"Clemency?" offered Charlie.

Dave shrugged, the word would do. "He's gonna get us all killed, one way or the other."

"You are not the first to say so."

After a long time, Dave broke the silence again. "There's a storm coming up over the mesas," he said. "Soon as it passes, I'm heading to Old Mex. I'd rather dodge the Romeros for a while than ... all this. There's four posses out for us right now. Ain't nowhere to stand around here."

Charlie nodded. "Probably the best thing for you."

"What about you?"

Bowdre shrugged. He had no idea when he could go back to Manuela now. Even visiting any of her various and plentiful family would be a risk. He shook his head sadly. "I told both Billies they should just skedaddle to Old Mex, leave the Territory entirely."

"I don't have the patience for straight life," said Dave. "Never did. J. J. kept me honest for a while… " He trailed off.

The silence overtook them booth. Charlie nodded and retreated to the bunkhouse to sleep.

* * *

That night, he dreamt of Buckshot Roberts.

They could have left the old man alone. The Regulators were at Blazer's Mill, a sawmill shanty town along the Rio Tularosa, recovering from a dust up a couple of days past. Bonney was suffering a bullet burn across his leg and had been complaining endlessly. When Andrew L. "Buckshot" Roberts rode up on his mule, he wasn't looking for a fight. He'd just sold his ranch. All he wanted was his check from the bank, then he aimed to leave Lincoln entirely. But since he'd worked for Dolan a spell, that made him an enemy of the Tunstall-McSween faction, and therefore fair game for the righteous Regulators. They were young men filled to the brim with pious violence. Plus, the morning had been hotter than Hell.

After some minutes of watching Frank Coe's fruitless attempt at talking Roberts into giving himself up, Charlie's whiskey temper got the better of him. Grabbing up his rifle, he stomped up the road towards Coe and the grizzled mule rider.

In younger days, Roberts had operated as a Texas Ranger under the name of Bill Williams, picking up along the line a spray of buckshot across his back that prevented him from raising his right arm above the belt. It hindered his shooting not at all. Sensing Charlie's ill motives, Roberts moved swifter than a broken muler should have. Levering his Winchester, old Roberts fired from the hip and Charlie fired back. Roberts' slug caught Charlie's belt buckle and threw him backwards, impact fore and aft driving the air from his lungs.

The bullet from Charlie's rifle plowed into Roberts' gut but the old man gave little more than a groan. Bonney came charging as best he could on one leg. Roberts swung his empty rifle sideways and cracked the Kid across the forehead, dropping him moaning into the dirt. Managing to dodge the returned fire, Roberts kept shooting and backed himself into an empty house.

Bleeding bad and in wretched pain, the old Ranger managed to kick furniture in front of the doorway for a quick barricade. He reloaded and resumed a barrage of gunfire. One shot creased Josiah's cheek, another blew George Coe's trigger finger clean off, doing his Colt no favors.

The Regulators regrouped under cover. Dick Brewer, their young and handsome leader, hadn't wanted any of this, but hadn't been quick enough to stop Charlie's advance. After dragging the rancher behind a stack of lumber, Brewer cursed Bowdre for a dumb bastard and checked him for holes. Miraculously, the ridiculous brass buckle at his waist had saved Bowdre's life.

Soon as he was satisfied Charlie was safe, Brewer drew his pistol and made to peek around the lumber, get a bead on Roberts. His head was out less than a second. Roberts' rifle barked and the bullet tunneled through Dick's right eye and blew the back of his head out. Brain and skull rained down over Charlie.

Their leader dead, damned near every one of them

bleeding bad, the Regulators retreated. News would come the next day that Roberts died a few hours later, following the cruelty of his wound.

None of it should have happened. They should have just left Roberts alone.

With Dick Brewer's body cooling in a creek, Charlie told himself right then that he was done. Done with the Regulators, the Lincoln County War, all of it. He was present when the Murphy/Dolan group gunned down Alex McSween and burned his house to the ground, powerless to stop anything.

None of it made a damned bit of sense. Not then. Not now.

CHAPTER 20

I WISH ...

On December 9, 1880, ten days before he'd ridden with Henry and the gang to Fort Sumner, Charlie Bowdre met Pat Garrett on the Gallinas Trail. "When's the last time you saw Henry, Charlie?"

"I ain't here to talk about Henry, Pat. You said you had a letter for me?"

Garrett reached into his big black buffalo coat and produced the missive. For some months Charlie had been exchanging letters with prominent businessman Captain Joseph C. Lea, hoping to arrange a pardon for his part in the murder of Buckshot Roberts on Indian land. The charge came with a hanging promise for both him and Henry McCarty, aka Billy Bonney. As it turned out, their legal cover as Regulators hadn't extended to the Indian Territory.

Charlie opened the letter and skimmed the contents. " 'If you vow to forsake your disreputable associates, every effort will be made by good citizens to allow you to turn your life around and become an accepted member of society.' Ain't that pretty?"

"You need to quit Bonney," Garrett said. "If you don't,

you're gonna wind up in the same cemetery as him and the rest. I promise you, Charlie, we will hound them all until we bring them to ground, dead or alive."

Charlie crumpled the letter and fixed him a look. "Wasn't we all friends, Pat? Or did I imagine all that?"

Garrett opened his mouth to speak, to issue his authority and assert his will. Instead, something else entirely spilled out.

"It all has to stop! God, Charlie, look at the country. Can't you see how it's changed? Five years ago? Ten years ago? It was all different. Country's getting smaller by the day. We have to be in a society *to live*. There is no more room for outlaws." He spread his hands, then searched the sky. "We were all bad men, Charlie, weren't we? Bonney might not want to change, but ... can't *we* be better?"

Charlie Bowdre spat into the dirt. A second later, he looked at Garrett with shame. "I don't ride with Henry. I'm foreman at Yerby's now, Pat. I got a vested interest and shares. I've been a businessman longer'n I ever been an outlaw."

"But you're still a known associate."

"Well, goddamn, men show up at the ranch, I have a moral duty to feed them, house them. 'Specially during winter."

"Explain it away all you want," said Garrett. "But your friend *will* get you killed." He drew a deep breath and let it out in a sigh, looking at Charlie sideways, gauging the man's attitude. In his youth, Charlie Bowdre had been a terror to Mexican rustlers. He'd hung or shot near a dozen men along the Border. His insistence that those days were behind him didn't measure out much confidence when facing this history. But Garrett made a play. "You swear to turn them in when you see them, a pardon might be arranged." Lacking the power to enforce such a thing, Garrett didn't feel good about the lie.

"I'll tell you what I told Captain Lea," said Charlie. "I would let every man do his own fighting so far as I am concerned, and I will do my own."

* * *

December 24, 1880. *El Ojo Hediondo*, translated from Spanish as "the Stinking Eye," was known locally as "Stinking Springs," and it came by its name honestly. Where there weren't sulfur springs leaking Satan's flatulence into the air, the great piles of owl shit beneath every scraggled tree picked up the slack.

The stone house there had been built as a military forage station by a sheepman named Alejandro Perea, who'd long since moved on. Measuring maybe twelve-by-thirty feet, if one were feeling generous, the single-room building provided cramped quarters indeed for the five men and Henry's beloved bay mare. It had a roof, but no doors. To keep out the ill wind they'd hung blankets over the doorways, front and back. Their other horses were hitched alongside, tied to jutting roof beams and out of sight from any distant travelers. Bunking down with his bay, Henry kept her near as much for warmth as quick escape.

A vicious snowstorm had given them a couple of days' cover. There was no way Garrett would be able to move his men through the weather. At the Brazil-Wilcox spread, Manuel Brazil had poked his head in to persuade the outlaws to give up, but Henry took him aside to do his own persuading. Brazil promised to head back into Sumner and ascertain the posse's intentions. He hadn't been gone an hour before Henry got a bad feeling and spread it to the rest.

"Manuel's got no stake in protecting us," said Dave, making the decision for the group. *El Ojo Hediondo* was nearby and off the path the posse would take. Moving there made sense.

They didn't realize that Brazil had stuck around nearby to watch them leave. Only then did he return to Sumner and to Garrett.

Once in the stone house they didn't risk a fire, so they hunkered down against each other and the horse for warmth. Except for Rudabaugh who of course claimed a corner for himself, his wooly goat-hair coat enough to keep him warm, and he burrowed in. For a few hours, they slept.

Charlie Bowdre awoke to the sound of hungry horses nickering. The other men, more or less heaped in a pile, didn't stir. Charlie got to his feet, keeping his once-colorful serape draped around him against the chill. He'd lost his hat during the escape and his thinning hair had a patina of frost. "Charlie," said Henry, still comfortable against his mare, "put my hat on. Keep your head warm."

Nodding, Charlie took up the Kid's large sombrero, bought for twenty-five dollars and banded with a handsome green sash given to him by some *querida* or other, and slapped it onto his head. Sweeping the doorway blanket aside, he took two steps into the open and then Garrett's posse shot him to rags.

A dozen shots rang out from the dry arroyo across the way and the gang scurried from their pile. Hugging the floor, Dave scuttled to the doorway, peered out beneath the blanket to see Charlie staggering on his feet, blood pouring out of too many wounds to count. "Jesus goddamned Christ," said Dave.

"Charlie!" Henry shouted. "You okay?"

"He ain't fucking okay," said Dave to the floor.

Charlie Bowdre rocked back and forth on his boot heels. His right hand swept uselessly across his gun belt, too blood-slick to even catch the gun.

"You goddamned killed him, Pat!" Bonney called out, his voice cracking with grief. From the corner, Billy Wilson swore, tears running from his eyes and damn anyone who'd mock him.

Charlie, blood leaking from his mouth, was saying something no one could quite catch. Dave strained to listen. He hissed to the others, "Shut up!"

" … I wish … " said Charlie Bowdre, husband of Manuela, who was now a widow. "I wish … " he said again.

"Take a couple out with you, Charlie!" shouted Bonney.

To which, Charlie replied, " … I wish … " He took another step forward and collapsed dead in the snow, his blood turned into steam.

* * *

"Oh, God," said Pat Garrett, watching Charlie Bowdre die one step at a time. Lon Chambers cursed him, told him to get down, all of which he ignored. "Oh, Charlie," he said again, under his breath. Once again, the wrong man was dead. It was his fault.

He'd told the men: "We'll never get The Kid alive." He told them: "He'll be wearing a big sombrero with a green sash." He told them: "If you see him poke his head out, cut him down. The others will surely surrender."

Already, Pat heard Manuela's mourning wail. He could picture the hatred for him burning in her eyes. After he brings her husband's body home.

A voice in his head insisted: *Charlie made his choice. He*

threw in with those bastards. Garrett found that voice and stared it down. *I did this. I killed Charlie Bowdre.*

"That's payback for Carlyle," said Chambers.

"We should burn that goddamned place down!" said Tenderfoot Williams.

"That's a rock house, you asshole," said Jim East.

Williams spit in the dirt. "That roof is slat and pitch! We can smoke them out then murder them and we can go the hell home!"

There was some support for the suggestion. The men were freezing. They were exhausted. Bowdre's blood didn't satisfy them. They wanted Bonney. They wanted Rudabaugh. "Justice" didn't make it anywhere near the top.

Debate was interrupted by a pair of shots from inside the house. The bullets passed into the trees and the posse returned fire. Garrett took his time. With his Winchester, he managed to shoot two of the ropes from the roof, freeing the horses. His third shot dropped a gelding in front of the door, blocking the entryway and pulling the blanket down with it.

Through the door, Garrett could see a horse stamping and rearing away from the dead animal in its eye line. Someone in the shadows wrestled it back. Whoever had that horse thought they might make a clean break, maybe charge the posse. That plan was now as shot to Hell as the dead gelding.

Garrett held up a hand and the men ceased fire. No further reports issued from within the house and the air went still.

"Let's rush the bastards," said Williams. "Go at 'em in a line—"

"No," said Garrett. Glancing again at dead Charlie, Garret determined then to take the men alive, Bonney's wishes be damned. The wagon that would soon return

Charlie Bowdre to Fort Sumner would not be stacked with corpses. "I got a better idea."

"That idea better include graves at the end of it," said Williams. Garrett stared down at him. Williams averted his eyes.

"I'm gonna end this without more blood," said Pat Garrett.

* * *

Inside, Henry struggled to keep the panicked mare under control. He couldn't mount her—she'd bolt for the doorway and knock his head off on the lintel. Seeing the dead horse put the mare in a panic and killed his plan to charge the posse, lead them away from the house or die in a hail of gunfire. Either way would have made for a hell of a news story.

Pickett and Wilson were hunkered down in a corner and Dave still hugged the floor. "Goddamn," said Henry, grinning wide and his eyes even wider. "We're in a spot, fellas." He had his Colt and he had his Winchester. Dave had his three pistols. Wilson and Pickett a pistol each. "How many men you count out there, Dave?"

"I saw three. Garrett and Lon Chambers, and some other dude."

"There's gotta be a dozen men out there," said Wilson, who'd been counting shots while secure in his corner.

Rudabaugh agreed. Then said to Henry, "How'd they find us?"

"Hell should I know?"

"You're the one passing notes. 'Garrett's hunkered down in Sumner with two men,' 'Garrett's run off to Roswell.' How many spies you think he has?"

Henry turned from the jumpy horse and gave Dave a hard stare. There were wet streaks on his trail-caked face, leftover tears for Charlie Bowdre. Anger flashed in his eyes. "What are you saying to me, exactly?"

"I'm asking how they found us, Henry!"

"Don't matter!" said Pickett. "They's here!"

"Hell," said Henry, "You're worth more than I am, Dave. I could have turned you in back in White Oaks!"

"Not and live."

"I'm not even gonna respond to that," said Henry. He checked his Colt. "I got six cartridges."

"I have ten," said Pickett. Wilson didn't answer.

Henry looked over to Rudabaugh. "Dave? You well heeled?"

"Not enough for a dozen men."

From outside, a voice called out. "Hey, Bonney!" Garrett sang. "How you fixed in there?"

The Kid slid up to put his back to the wall and called back through the door. "Pretty well, Pat. Afraid we don't have wood for breakfast, though."

"You should come out and join us, then," called Garrett. "We're heading back to Brazil's. Get some food in you."

The Kid laughed. "Can't do it, Pat. Business, you know, it's too constraining. No time to run around. Got places to be!"

"Weren't you to come in on us at Fort Sumner?" Garrett shouted back, trying a gambit. "Give us a square fight, set us afoot, and drive us down the Pecos?"

"Goddamn," said Henry. He looked to the others. "That's what I told Brazil we was gonna do."

Rudabaugh glared at him. "Did you mean that as a joke?"

Henry shrugged and broke into a bigger grin. "I guess we found that spy of yours, Pat!"

No response, thus Henry was further emboldened. "You fellas go on ahead and eat. Don't let us hold you up. Bring me back a shot and a beer! For old time's sake!" Risking a peek at each taunt, Henry pulled his head back in, shaking it. "I didn't get a good enough look. You might be right though, Dave, there has to be a dozen. Maybe more. Definitely more'n we faced at Whiskey Jim's."

"Oh, sweet Jesus," said Wilson, his voice high with fear. Beside him, Pickett mumbled something no one caught.

"I still say we rush them," said Henry. "At least a run to the wall where we can get a bead on 'em."

"Surrender," said Dave.

The room went silent. Henry stared at him. "Fuck," he said, "no." Dave didn't respond. "That's gotta be the worst idea I ever heard. They'll hang us here and now."

Dave shook his head, "They won't." He thought of J. J. "*Don't die for these fools, David.*" He thought of the posse they'd formed to bring in Joe Carson's killers. J. J.'d sworn protection until they were remanded back to the jail. It tore at Dave's insides the whole way back, but he too upheld that promise. He didn't know Garrett well, but he seemed cut from the same kind of cloth as John Joshua Webb. If they surrendered under condition of protection, Garrett would hold to the promise, Dave was sure of it. It would be a much bigger boon for the ambitious lawman to bring in the desperados alive. Surrender was the only smart play. Bonney would surely send the rest of them to their deaths should they not.

"Once we get to Santa Fe," Dave continued, "it's no matter to carve our way out of that jail. Place is built of mud and hope." He cast his eyes about the room, taking in the silent votes. The jury was hung. To Wilson and Pickett, he said, "Anything Federal on you?"

Wilson shrugged. "Dedrick's goddamned counterfeit money's my undoing."

"They don't hang for bad paper," said Henry. Pickett didn't say anything, just shook his head.

Wilson sat up like he'd leaned against a hot stove. "We turn state's evidence!"

"What's that?" said Henry.

" 'S'where you pin your crimes on former associates," he said. "Ain't that what you did in Kansas, Dave?"

Rudabaugh gave him a look but didn't answer.

"Hell," said Henry. "I have lots of enemies I'd like to see in jail 'stead of me."

Pickett remained silent, and Wilson returned to his brooding funk. Rudabaugh looked to Henry, "So it's you and me they want most. We're worth money alive."

"And I have a half-promise from Governor Wallace," said Henry.

"It's all worth the white flag."

"I dunno," said Henry, and addressed the pair in the corner. "What do you think, fellas? Pat the kind of man who'll give horse thieves a safe escort?" Ever helpful, the pair remained silent. Buzzing with nervous energy, Henry bounced from a squat, crazy grin and crazy eyes. He pointed his pistol at the entranceway. "Dave, I still think if we just all rain lead—"

"Henry," said Rudabaugh, his eyes narrow and steady, "you try that and I guarantee you won't make it out the door."

At that, Henry giggled. "Naw, I can take..." then he quickly went silent, catching Dave's deeper meaning.

The aroma of cooking food began to waft through that

gaping doorway. The posse was eating well. "Lord, don't that smell like Heaven?" said Wilson. Grumbling stomachs agreed. None of them had eaten since the previous night and only beans and bread at that. The allure of breakfast cinched the deal.

Working in silence, they dug a hole in the far corner and buried all the cash they had on them. No reason their hard-earned loot should fill the pockets of the possemen. There was a moment of remorse as they adding the contents of Charlie's saddlebag: a small money clip, a tin of dice, and an old watch that held a photo of Manuela. The covered it all up the best they could, even leading the mare over to stamp the dirt down.

After that, they held an election. There were no straws to draw, though horsetail hairs were considered. One of them would have to go out and face the posse under the white flag. Henry immediately withdrew his candidacy. "Yeah," Dave said. "They'll like to cut you down with or without Pat's say." Pickett and Wilson formed a union and both voted Dave. In the end, so too did Rudabaugh, eager to get it all over.

The promise of hot stew was again on the cold air. Dave's own stomach protested. He took a breath. "Ain't no jail ever held me," he said to himself. He yanked a handkerchief from his pocket, none-too clean but white enough, and moved to the door.

* * *

The gang's deliberations had given the posse enough time to travel to and from Wilcox & Brazil's for breakfast in two shifts. Garrett went last, enduring haranguing from Manuel

Brazil as he ate. "Why you moaning about Bowdre? He told me hisself he would have loved a shot at you."

Garrett ignored him. He instructed Manuel's cook to ready food for a chuck wagon. The "smoke-them-out" suggestion had given him the idea. Averse to further violence, he determined to use breakfast.

It was closer to dinner by the time all was arranged, but the wagon rolled into its position to entice. Then it was just a matter of waiting. The afternoon hadn't melted the snow, but it had warmed the air a bit. With full bellies, the men were eager for action.

They didn't have to wait long. "Hey, Sheriff!" came a call from the house.

"Who's that?" Garrett answered? "Wilson?"

"Rudabaugh!" A hand appeared in the doorway, waving the white flag. Three guns were tossed one by one into the snow. Garrett counted the thuds. "I'm coming out!" Dave said. "Don't shoot me 'til we talk!"

Nodding, Garrett looked around the arroyo at the men, motioned to keep their guns at bay. "Come on over, sir. It's safe."

No one in his entire life had ever called him 'sir.' Rudabaugh emerged one body part at a time until he was full exposed and a clean shot. With each step, he expected a bullet, but kept the white flag above his head as he crossed the thirty or so yards to the arroyo.

"You all had enough?" said Lon Chambers, still seated at Garrett's hip like an ugly dog.

Rudabaugh ignored him. "We're ready to surrender, Sheriff, if you can guarantee our safety."

Garrett cocked his head, keeping his smile friendly. He opened his mouth to speak, but the Lon dog barked again. "You accusing a posse actin' under the authority of the

United States of America of being murderous, hanging bastards?"

Slowly, Dave turned his head to acknowledge the man speaking, but he didn't respond. He simply stared. Without turning, but to Garrett, he said, "We'd all rather reach Santa Fe alive, if it's all the same to you. There's good money on us living."

"We ain't bought-out whores!" said Chambers.

"Lon," said Garrett, quietly, "enough." And the dog lowered its head. Garrett kept his attention on Rudabaugh. He'd been passingly acquainted with the man in Fort Sumner, and they had been friendly enough, or as friendly as Rudabaugh could ever be said to be. He wasn't known to be a liar, nor a backstabber. His devotion to Webb, ensconced in Las Vegas, was admired and puzzled over throughout the Territory. Garrett weighed all this against the notion that this was a trap and the Kid was waiting in ambush. Finally, he nodded. "You have my word, Mr. Rudabaugh. You and the others surrender to my custody and you'll receive our full protection."

"How you planning on taking us?"

"Through Las Vegas," said Garrett. "Then on to Santa Fe."

Rudabaugh rolled his eyes as Fortune played with him again. "You might as well shoot me now," he said. "Mexicans want my head on a plate."

"Full protection," Garrett repeated.

With a nod, Rudabaugh returned to the stone house. After a short interval, all four men emerged, hands empty, followed by Bonney's fine horse. Suddenly, as if some magical spell descended upon the posse, the same men who'd been eager for Bonney's blood were now high-stepping through snow to introduce themselves and shake his hand. They complimented the four for the fine chase.

"Sure," said Bonney. "'S'all in fun."

"Good Christ," said Pickett, "he's got himself another audience." Minutes later, they were shackled, fed, and led back to the Wilcox & Brazil for the night.

Charlie Bowdre's body, loaded almost gently onto a small wagon, brought up the rear.

* * *

The journey with the prisoners was a series of stops for food and rest that would have rivaled that of Odysseus, and with each one its own bit of melodrama. The first was the quartet balking at riding in the same wagon as poor Charlie's blue-cooled corpse.

"So walk," said Garrett.

Into the wagon they climbed, hugging their knees to avoid touching the body and catching death.

At the Wilcox & Brazil, Rudabaugh and Bonney were shackled together, but the bolt around Dave's left hand wouldn't hold. The Kid took that for a terrible portent. "Oh, mama," he said, "that surely means that I will die and Dave will live." Rudabaugh couldn't tell if Henry's moan was serious or not.

On the way back, possemen taunted the outlaws, promising death and worse. The prisoners ignored them best they could as they rode towards Old Fort Sumner. Long before the posse breached the fort's threshold they could hear Manuela Bowdre and her family wailing for Charlie. Upon seeing her poor husband's body, Manuela came at them all with a fireplace poker, landing a crease across Jim East's forehead and dropping him flat. She cursed them all,

Bil-lee included and for much longer than the rest of them. For his part, Bonney remained shame-faced.

"I want to see Paulita," said Bonney to Frank Stewart. "Tell her goodbye." The deputy promised he'd arrange it.

Paulita Maxwell, youngest sister to Pete Maxwell, one of the richest residents of Sumner, was the object of much teasing throughout the Fort, referring to her as *"Bil-lee's querida."* The taunts never failed to bring the young woman's face to red. Quiet by nature, she had a temper when pressed. Yes, she knew Bil-lee and found him as handsome as the others surely did, but she didn't know why he'd requested her presence and told her father so.

Pete Maxwell shrugged. "Maybe he'll tell you something worth money."

"We don't need money," said Paulita. Muttering profanities under her breath, then crossing herself in apology to Santa Maria, she went alone to the old hospital building. "This place is such bad luck," Bil-lee said to her. She didn't know why. "This house was built to help the Navajo, but after one died in here, the Indians refused to come in."

She stared at him. He was still tethered by heavy chain to the smaller Rudabaugh, who she had seen around the Fort and had no desire to meet. She cast a look at this man, and Dave shrugged back at her. Quickly, her head swiveled back to Bil-lee. "So?"

"Just bad luck, is all. Listen, I need to tell you something in private," said Bil-lee.

"You want me to stick my fingers in my ears?" asked Dave, disgusted.

Bil-lee pulled Paulita close and whispered to her. Dave couldn't hear and didn't strain to listen. His mind was otherwise occupied on who he still knew that could lend them aid once they got to Santa Fe.

Paulita looked flummoxed as she pulled away. She spread her hands in a gesture of helplessness. "I cannot, Billee," she said, and rushed from the room.

Rudabaugh cocked an eyebrow at Bonney, or Henry, or whoever, who just spread his own hands as wide as the chains would allow. "I didn't ask her anything dirty."

Dave shook his head. "Don't care."

None too eager to return to oppression, Henry rocked back and forth on his heels, whistling tunelessly for a minute. "I think I'll give my mare to Frank Stewart. Seeing as how I'm going to be otherwise encumbered for the foreseeable." He looked back at Dave for response. He didn't get one.

* * *

"We reached Gayheart's ranch, with our prisoners, about midnight, rested until eight in the morning, and reached Puerto de Luna about two o'clock P.M., on Christmas day. My friend Grzelachowski gave us all a splendid dinner." So wrote Pat Garrett in his memoirs, via the loyal Ashmun Upson. *"With a fresh team, we got away from Puerto de Luna about four o'clock, broke our wagon, borrowed one of Capt. Clarency, and reached Hay's ranch for breakfast."*

At each point along their journey, Garrett paid special attention to the care and treatment of the men under his arrest, even inquiring each as to the quality of their meals. While the other three found him amiable, Rudabaugh found it suspicious. As the others joshed with Garrett, Rudabaugh was content to study in silence. There was definitely a bit of Webb in Garrett, though *which* bit it was too early to say. Pat the Great was riding tall in his saddle, and for once a lawman's sanctimonium was working in Rudabaugh's favor.

The group got whittled down from a dozen to only a handful: Garrett, Frank Stewart, Barney Mason, East, and "Poker Tom" Emory.

"Five-hunnert dollars on your head, Bonney," said Emory. The Kid shrugged.

So did Rudabaugh. "In '77, I was worth twenty-five hundred. They's getting a discount with you, Henry."

The Kid responded to neither.

At Hay's ranch, the decision was made to transfer the prisoners from horses to a single wagon, both for efficiency and optics. For a time, Rudabaugh almost shared in the odd good nature of his fellow prisoners, and even the possemen joined in with their own jokes and bawdy songs. He could almost forget that their final stop along the way to the Santa Fe jail was the Las Vegas *perrera*.

But as they crested the Gallinas Hill, Dave could already see the angry, buzzing throng forming at the mouth of the town. To his surprise, as the wagon crossed into Vegas, he saw only open space out in Llano Plaza. In his absence, they'd torn the windmill down. A blessing, he thought, as he passed one scowling angry face after another, faces of all colors, all sharing the same judgment: "the villain should die." Occasionally, a piece of trash or rotten vegetable or horse apple would splat the side of the wagon, but for the most part the radiating hatred was silent and yet all the more potent.

"This the homecoming you expected, Dave?" asked Henry.

"Pretty much," said Dave, stomach sour and wondering if he'd survive the night.

CHAPTER 21

RETURN TO LAS VEGAS

As young men, still learning the ways of rustling and thievery, Dave Rudabaugh and Dave Mather found themselves one night creeping through a corral of cattle on a Kansas ranch. Their plan was to cut out three head each and sell them to a fence they knew of outside Dodge. Mather went left. Rudabaugh went right. It was after midnight and a crescent moon was high, giving them just enough light to work. They moved silently, though certain no drovers were about.

As Rudabaugh stayed low, he worked his way down a tight row of beeves standing shoulder to ass, tails flicking hard against mosquitos and blowflies. Coming to a break in the herd, Dave checked his left side. There he saw the Comanche.

The man was lean, invisible in the dark, save for the bright whites of his eyes staring back at Rudabaugh. Dave froze and he was certain that's what kept him alive. He made no move towards his gun—he only wore one in those early days—nor did he move at all. The Indian's eyes never left him, silently weighing the benefit of murdering the white thief then continuing with his night.

After a long time—Dave could never say how long, though he was certain at least one of his birthdays passed in the interval—the Indian finally turned its back on him, swung up onto a steer, and moved it away from the rest of the beeves. In moments, cow and Comanche were gone, swallowed by the night. Only then did Dave allow himself to breathe.

That was the most scared he'd ever been in his entire life. Until the cell door slammed shut on him in *la perrera*.

How would it happen? he wondered. How would the Romeros get their revenge? Would they poison his food? Or would they simply take him in the night and hang him somewhere convenient?

Any hope Rudabaugh had had about a reunion with J. J., however brief, was quickly dashed. Webb was being held in solitary, awaiting news of a retrial or a potential pardon. Having already escaped once, then a half-hearted subsequent attempt, Sheriff Desiderio Romero thought it best Webb be placed somewhere secure for his own safety. Rudabaugh, Henry, Wilson, and Pickett were held in chains in the common cells. "Like coming home again, eh *Señior Dave*?" the Sheriff said, all smiles around a thin cigar. "Oh, and *Feliz Navidad.*"

Dave nodded back but didn't reply further.

"Don't you worry, Dave," said Henry. "We'll keep you safe tonight." They fell asleep almost immediately. Dave kept his eyes open, waiting for the inevitable mob.

After an hour or so, they got their first visitor. Lute Wilcox arrived with note pad in one hand and a thin cane in the other, tapping before him as he slowly made his way into the dark building. "I'm here to take statements for the press, gentlemen," he said. "Feel free to spill your guts proper."

Rudabaugh called Wilcox over. "Lemme belay your duties a moment," he said. "What's the atmosphere?"

"Towards you?" said Lute. "Anger and resentment fomenting."

"Listen, you all have been blowing all this out of..." he sighed.

"Proportion?" Lute offered.

Dave nodded. "Seems like anyone killed anywhere in the Territories got dumped on Henry's head." Lute stared at him. "Our ... " his mouth opened and closed. "Damn it, our ... "

"Depredations?"

"Sure. Them. They's greatly exaggerated."

"Certainly."

Finally, Henry's patience gave out. "Listen," he said, sitting up on the bunk. "I thought you was here to get the truth square from Billy Bonney."

Wilcox smiled and nodded. For weeks, *The Gazette* had been running a serialized story, "The Forty Thieves," starring Billy Bonney, aka Billy the Kid, the most ruthless outlaw boss the West had ever seen. This title secretly irked both Silva and Hilario Romero, who despite their relative retirements to private life resented the misappropriation. The serial was the paper's most popular feature, and an interview with the subject would be quite the boon for Koogler's rag. Lute and Bonney talked for more than an hour. The next morning the pair would continue their conversation, only this time for *The Optic*.

Wilson and Pickett continued their hangdog routine and pouted to sleep. Henry was soon with them. Dave Rudabaugh watched the moon pass by the cell's single

window and waited to hear the click behind his ear, or feel
the cold blade across his throat.

* * *

*Our readers are familiar with the depredations committed
in the lower country by a gang of desperados under leadership of Billy the Kid, and the repeated and unsuccessful
attempts to capture them. They have roamed over the
country at will, placing no value upon human life, and
appropriating the property of ranchmen and travelers
without stint. Posses of men have been in hot pursuit of
them for weeks, but they succeeded in eluding their
pursuers every time. However, the right boys started out,
well mounted and heavily armed, and were successful in
bagging their game.*

*Yesterday [Sunday, December 26] afternoon, the town
was thrown into a fever of excitement by the announcement
that the Kid and other members of his gang of outlaws had
been captured, and were nearing the city. The rumor was
soon verified by the appearance in town of a squad of men
led by Pat Garrett, deputy sheriff of Lincoln county, and
Frank Stewart of the Panhandle country, having in custody
the Kid, Dave Dudabaugh [sic], Billy Wilson and Tom
Pickett. They were taken at once to the jail, and locked up,
and arrangements made to guard the jail against any
attempt to take the prisoners out and hang them. Feeling
was particularly strong against Radabaugh [sic] who was
an accessory to the murder of the Mexican jailor in an
attempt to release Webb some months ago.*

*Dave Rudabaugh looks and dresses about the same as
when in Las Vegas, apparently not having made any raids
on clothing stores. His face is weatherbeaten from long*

exposure. This is the only noticeable difference. Rudabaugh inquired somewhat anxiously in regard to the feeling in the community, and was told that it was very strong against him. He remarked that the papers had all published exaggerated reports of the depredations of the Kid's party in the lower country. It was not half as bad as reported.

The party of men who risked their lives in the attempt to rid the country of this bloodthirsty gang of robbers and murderers are deserving of unbounded praise and should be rewarded handsomely for their services. They will undoubtedly obtain the reward of $500 offered by the governor for the capture of the Kid, and it remains for interested citizens to raise a purse of money and present it to the sixteen men, as they paid out money and endured hardships in the endeavor to hunt down and bring to justice one of the most desperate gangs of outlaws that ever terrorized the Southwest."

— *Las Vegas Optic*, December 27, 1880.

Reporting by Lute Wilcox.

Additional reporting by Russell A. Kistler.

* * *

Garrett was already irritated when he arrived at *la perrera*. He'd slept awkwardly, woke up with a kink in his neck that wouldn't rub away. His hotel coffee was dreadful. He'd remembered the food at the St. Nicholas being so much better not so long ago. The whole affair just put him in a mood.

He was eager to get on to Santa Fe. The Atchison & Topeka train was waiting for them. Keeping on Emory, East, Stewart, and Deputy U.S. Marshal James W. Bell, Garrett wanted to collect his prisoners and be on his way. Sheriff

Desiderio Romero was resolute, shaking his head, always smiling but his voice stern. "You can take the others with my blessing," he said, "but Rudabaugh stays with us."

As it happened, Pickett was the one to be left behind, unwanted as he was for any federal charge, only rustling and vagrancy. There was no need for him to accompany the party any further. Rudabaugh, however ... Aside from the warrants, Garrett had given his word to deliver the man to Santa Fe. The main wrinkle in the tapestry was that he would not be a Federal Marshal for another week. He had no authority to enforce such a warrant. He suspected Romero knew that as well.

Still, he was Sheriff Pat Garrett and would puff up and soldier on. "Rudabaugh, Wilson, and Bonney are being bound under federal warrants. Which I assure you supersede any charges you have—"

Romero held up his hand. "Don't care. Rudbaugh stays."

Shorter than his cousin Hilario, Sheriff Desiderio was not a small man, but compared to Garrett, he was no bigger than most. But Rudabaugh and Webb both had a decent measure of respect for the Sheriff. He was proud and a man of his word. As a former outlaw, he came by his honor honestly. It all made him a big man. Much like Garrett was, in Rudabaugh's grudging estimation. The big men were now squaring off over his fate. Not for the first time, he thanked the fates that the windmill no longer stood in Llano Plaza.

"You et anything, Dave?" said Garrett.

So intent he was on Romero's posture, it took Rudabaugh a moment to register being addressed. He shook his head. "Wouldn't risk it."

"We'll get you something on the train," said Garrett. He held the door open, and both Billys emerged. Shackled only by hand, Dave held back, watching Romero. "Come on," beckoned Garrett. And again to Romero, he said, "These men are bound by federal warrants under the jurisdiction—"

Romero shook his head, waved his hand, turned his back, dismissing them all. Rudabaugh leapt to his feet and followed the others into the street.

Romero watched Garrett load his charges into a hack. Behind him, his deputies—some cousins, some nephews—emerged from the shadows to join him in watching the dread Rudabaugh ride into the early morning sun. That previous evening, they had all drunk to their victory. Their hated enemy was home. Now he was slipping through their fingers once again.

Sheriff Desiderio Romero was the singular authority in Las Vegas. Since the dissolution of the Dodge City Gang and his cousin's retirement, Desiderio presided over both sides of the river. Even when Vincente Silva was about, Desiderio Romero was the law.

Grabbing his hat and his Henry rifle, Sheriff Romero followed Garrett and the hack across the bridge. With each step, he gained another follower. As they crossed into East Las Vegas, they'd swelled into quite the crowd, white faces mixing with the rest.

From his place in the hack, Rudabaugh watched as damned near the entire town arrived to see him off. Or otherwise. "Say, Garrett," he said, and jerked his thumb at the crowd.

Seated next to the driver, Garrett looked back. "It'll be fine once we're on the train," he said.

"So you say," said Dave Rudabaugh.

Lute Wilcox was already on the platform when the prisoner wagon arrived, ready to resume his interview with Kid Bonney. Seeing Koogler's hardline stance against the young outlaw, Kistler opted for a different tact, painting

Bonney as misunderstood, perhaps even a pawn of the moneyed interests in Lincoln County. Lute's edict was to make The Kid more sympathetic in *The Daily Optic*. "Don't bother with Rudabaugh," said Kistler. "He'll be back soon enough."

Garrett got his charges aboard, secured them in a passenger car, then took his place on the platform as the train readied to depart. He kept an eye on the swelling crowd approaching the station. Sweat beaded at his brow and neck.

"I don't blame you for how you've written about me," The Kid continued, leaning out of the window, casual as can be and unconcerned about the violence brewing. Rudabaugh sunk down in his seat, keeping his head below the windows. "Dave," said The Kid, "Lute wants to know how you're feeling today." Rudabaugh grunted but didn't respond. "Put him down for 'cheerful and gay,' " Bonney said to Lute. He looked over at Wilson who had his head in his hands. "And put down Wilson for 'glum.' "

Risking a glance, Rudabaugh saw many familiar faces in the mob: Dutch Henry, ever present in case of a lynching opportunity; as many Romeros as he could count, Hilario included, filthy apron around his middle; even old Don Vincente Silva lingered beside a post, smoking a cheroot. Behind him, Miguel Otero the younger. Those faces not painted with hatred were awash with simple curiosity. He flashed back to the night they lynched Joe Carson's murderers. He thought of Dorsey, his face purple as he strangled, his britches dropping to his ankles in the final indignity. He saw his own face twisted, eyes bursting as the noose tightened.

He thought of Milt Yarberry, who didn't fear the noose. "What you do is watch the lever. Soon as they pull it, jump backwards. Then they have to let you go." Not a great legal mind, Milt.

Moving swiftly through the car, Garrett and Frank Stewart pulled down all the window shades. There were private citizens in the seats, looking just as alarmed as those in chains. "We are liable to have a hell of a fight in a very few minutes," Garrett announced. "Any of you people who don't want to be in it had better get a-lit before I lock the car."

Two men with valises hurried away. A well-dressed lady and her two tidied children followed. Several others—a couple of miners, a man in tweed—drew their weapons. One made some disparaging remarks towards the Mexicans now lining the platform.

"You ready for a fight, Frank?"

"'Course, Pat."

"Let's make it a good one, then."

"I already picked out the first man I'm going to drop," said Emory.

Jim East gave him a disgusted look. "I don't want it to come to that."

"Take these chains off, Pat, and give me a gun," said Henry, his interview concluded and the blind reporter departed.

Garrett nodded. To Rudabaugh, he said, "You feel the same?"

"I'll kill anyone meaning to do me harm," he said. "But I ain't eager."

Emory spat on the floor. "Thought you had sand, Rudabaugh."

"Sounds like he's got sense," said East.

Garrett went out onto the caboose and leaned casually on the railing, letting his coat fall open to display his gun. On the platform, Sheriff Desiderio was unimpressed. Beside him, Joaquin, his cousin and deputy, said, "Let's go and take him out of there." There wasn't an unarmed man or woman at the station.

"You don't want do go this way, Sheriff," said Garrett, using his mildest tones. "You're putting your people in danger."

Something passed between the two men. Desiderio nodded slightly, taking in Garrett's words. But then the men to his sides cursed and surged forward to rock the train, forcing Garrett to retreat back inside.

"Just saw the engineer skedaddle," said Stewart.

"Goddamn it," said Garrett. Outside, Sheriff Romero and Miguel Otero were trying to appeal to the crowd, but blood-lust made them deaf to reason.

Lying on the floor, Rudabaugh stuck his head out. "Pat, you got a smokeman on the other car!"

"Who's that?"

"Mobley or Morley, or something."

"How the hell do you know?" Emory demanded.

"Right," said Rudabaugh, "what would I know about train men?"

"They're gonna derail us!" said Stewart.

As the car rocked, Garrett threw open the door between train cars. He called out for Morley and didn't have to wait for a reply, the former engine-stoker was already making his way back. "You know how to get this train moving?" Garrett asked him.

J. Fred Morley looked much older than his thirty-eight years, thanks to his time shoveling coal into engines. His lungs were weak and his shoulders were bowed. He nodded, "Yes sir, I can." He then dropped off the side of the train, opposite the platform, and crawled on his belly snake-wise beneath the cars until he reached the engine. Leaping into the cabin, he hurled his body against the throttle and the train jumped forward, spilling everyone aboard into the aisles. There was much profanity as the train sped out of Las Vegas.

To the howling mob, Billy the Kid leaned out of the window and waved both shackled hands. "Adios!" he called. "See y'all real soon!" Billy Bonney, aka Henry McCarty, aka Kid Antrim, would never return to Las Vegas.

He sat back in his seat behind Rudabaugh, kicked the back of the seat in sympathy. "Don't you fret, Dave. You're safe for now," he said in gentle tones, without mockery. Dave appreciated that. Humming to himself, Henry watched the world speed by him at the breathtaking speed of 50 miles per hour. "This is my first train ride," he said. Dave grunted in acknowledgement. "You say you took thirty trains?"

Rudabaugh shrugged. "Probably less, but don't let on to Animal Emory."

"You got a story to share? We got the time."

Dave Rudabaugh thought a moment. "I should tell you about the Kinsey job … "

CHAPTER 22

TERRITORY VS. DAVID
RUDABAUGH

December 28, 1880, Rudabaugh, Wilson, and Bonney arrived in Santa Fe and were arraigned the next morning. A clothier in town donated new suits to the prisoners in exchange for a modicum of publicity, which he got in spades after telling every one who would listen about his generosity. "Get them poor boys out of those filthy duds and into something top-of-the-line." Nobody retained his name.

Garrett checked in on them as they dressed. "You planning on feeding us?" asked Bonney. Garrett cocked an eye at the jailor, a man named Silba, who still had grease in his beard.

"My men were also hungry," said Silba. Another jailor, a white man named George Parker, tried to stifle a laugh.

Garrett cursed them as deplorable examples of lawmen and ordered more portions to be delivered from the restaurant across the street and to hurry. All three men were due to appear in court.

Throughout his stay, Bonney was never without an audience, and he played to every crowd. He moaned in melodrama about the deplorable conditions of the jail—"Lice just jumping off the ticking, it's hot, the grub's just beans and water . . . " To prevent escape attempts, the three men were chained to the floor with three-foot lengths, forcing them to sleep bent over, heads on knees.

Lawyer Edgar Caypless was just one month younger than Rudabaugh but had impressed so many around him that it took the influence of Wilson, Waddingham, Elkins, Otero, Morley, Springer, and Catron to talk him into joining the Maxwell Land Grant headquarters at Cimarron, and hang out a shingle. Not too long after he arrived, Caypless realized that Cimarron would never be the thriving metropolis promised, and thus moved to Santa Fe to set up as a freelance lawyer. In his choosing to take on Rudabaugh's case, the savvy Caypless quickly understood that Rudabaugh didn't stand a chance. It was that which made the case appealing. Certainly more interesting than interstate commerce law.

The outlaw faced the Federal Court on two charges: robbing the U.S. mail from a train in Las Vegas and a stagecoach in Puertocito. If convicted, he would serve forty years, twenty for each. Caypless advised Dave to plead guilty in the hopes of avoiding the Las Vegas charge of murder.

"I didn't pull the trigger," Dave insisted.

"Yes, but that does not matter, David," said Caypless. "Las Vegas passed an accomplice law. You were present at the time of the killing, and you left *with* the murderer."

Dave opened his mouth to speak, but didn't have the words. Not a one. Finally, he said, "Well, ain't that a shit hand."

* * *

The prosecutor demanded, "Who was with you on the stage robbery of August 30, 1879?"

"Marshal Joe Carson, deceased. I forget the name of the other man."

"Marshal Joe Carson of Las Vegas? He's dead."

"That's what 'deceased' means."

"How convenient."

"For him or me?"

"Objection."

"Sustained."

"What about your other accomplices?"

"I had no other accomplices."

"John Joshua Webb, Jordan L. Webb, Jonathan Pierce, Selim 'Frank' Cady."

"None of those men were with me on either job."

"You never robbed with these men?"

"Objection."

"Sustained."

"Allow me to rephrase. Neither Webb accompanied you?"

"Objection. Asked and answered."

"Hang on," said Dave. "Did you say 'Pierce'? Slapjack Pierce?"

"I did."

"All right. Wanted to make sure you didn't mean 'Bullshit' Nicholson."

[Gallery bursts into laughter. Judge L. Bradford Prince gavels for order.]

"He didn't ride with us neither, by the way."

* * *

> *Dave Rudabaugh (sic) boldy testified that he led the attack on the stage and was quite certain that Jordan L. Webb, one of the accused on trial, was not present. He refused to divulge the names of the robbers, whom he claims to not know. Rudabugh (sic) says that if severe punishment is ever meted out to him … he will make it hot for some of his old chums who are now at large, and laughing up their sleeves at him, in his solitary confinement in the Santa Fe jail."*
>
> — *The Daily Optic*, Feb 14, 1881.

* * *

As Caypless expected, Judge L. Bradford Prince denied Rudabaugh's attempt to avoid the death penalty. He remanded the outlaw into the custody of Desiderio Romero to return to Las Vegas and stand trial for murder.

Shocked, but not surprised, Dave allowed the bailiff to take him by the arm. As jailer George Parker attempted to take over, Dave swung his chains into the man's face. "Eat that," he said. But with broken teeth, Parker would find food of any consistency a challenge for some days.

"I still have money," Rudabaugh said to Caypless. Which was true. The "Save J. J. Fund" had morphed into the "Save Dave Fund." In addition to the materialization of cash squirreled away in a dozen holes that Caypless refused to inquire about, a few small donations had come in for Dave via past friendlies in Dodge City. Jordan L. Webb, who had played no part in Rudabaugh's drama, contributed more than $50, in apparent gratitude for clearing his name in the robbery charge. Caypless accepted the money but insisted the case was hopeless.

Caypless turned down representing Billy Bonney any

further. He spent some days trying to unravel the ownership of the mare Bonney had given to Frank Stewart, in the hopes of securing it back to pay for his defense. Stewart had sold it to Susan McSween, now Susan Barber, having married young attorney George Barber. Mrs. Barber was in the process of taking over some 1,200 acres of land on the West side of the Mescalero Apache Indian Reservation. In the near future, she would divorce Barber and begin her ascent to the title of "Cattle Queen of Montana." Since she held Bonney responsible for the death of her husband, Susan refused to return the horse. Caypless, too, quickly reached his fill of the attention-whore, William H. Bonney.

Bonney had fully expected Governor Lew Wallace to uphold the veiled promise of clemency, despite having surrendered under duress. In his final letter to the man, Bonney wrote, "I expect that you've forgotten what you've promised me."

By the time the letter arrived, Lew Wallace was no longer Governor of New Mexico, having resigned his position in order to focus on his newfound career as a successful author, *Ben-Hur: A Tale of the Christ* having become a best-seller. Stopping briefly in Las Vegas, Wallace spoke with Lute Wilcox, who broached the matter of Bonney. Lighting a mighty cigar, Wallace coughed a laugh. "I can't see how a fellow like him should expect any clemency from me." And that was the settled matter.

On February 15, the jailers discovered that Bonney, Wilson, and Rudabaugh had almost dug themselves free of their cell, carving a large hole in the wall with broken tin cup handles, hiding the dirt and mortar in their mattresses. The trio were broken up and stuck in solitary cells, with watchmen increased. None of the three would ever see the others again.

On February 16, Sheriff Desiderio Romero arrived at the Santa Fe jail to take Dave Rudabaugh back to Las Vegas. The ride was long and silent.

* * *

Las Vegas Acorn [unaffiliated with Koogler or Kistler], February 16:

Today Sheriff Romero returned from Santa Fe in charge of desperado Dave Rudabaugh, whose name is legend under every western roof. It is well remembered that the bad Rudabaugh was captured last December in company with the young killer Billy the Kid, brought to Las Vegas and taken to Santa Fe, Dave is back to stand trial for complicity in the murder of Antonio Lino Valdez of this city last April, in which Little Allen figured as chief actor. Rudabaugh was brought up in irons and showed a restless, uneasy condition of mind when he was taken from the cars. He retained a stolid, hang-demeanor and showed no disposition to recognize any of his old acquaintances. He is poor of flesh, and does not weigh by twenty pounds as much as he did a year ago, while prancing up and down the streets of Las Vegas. What a change a year has brought forth! Then the free man—now the chained culprit, doomed to the decree of justice or possibly Judge Lynch's mandate, for we hear the grumblings of men who have revenge in their hearts...

* * *

Leaving the sunlit world behind, Dave's eyes were still adjusting to the darkness of *la perrera* when Deputy Joaquin Romero shoved him into the cell and slammed the heavy door closed. He stood exhausted and defeated and stared at the manacles around his wrists, the ones he'd worn since Christmas Day. Hopeless and friendless, he expected that these chains would accompany him to the gallows.

"My god, David," said a voice in the dark corner, "you look half a scarecrow, young man."

Tears leapt to Dave's eyes, and he didn't care who saw. "Good afternoon, Josh," he said, his hands seeking and finding Webb's in the dark. "So goddamned good to see you."

* * *

On February 6, the New Mexico Supreme Court declined J. J. Webb's request for a new trial and acting Governor William G. Ritch signed Webb's second death warrant. On March 5, as one of his last official acts in office, Governor Lew Wallace commuted the death warrant of John Joshua Webb to life in prison.

> *In consideration of the fact that the decision of the Supreme Court reviewing the case on appeal was a divided one ... and in consideration of the very large petition forwarded to the executive office by intelligent and respectable citizens of East and West Las Vegas praying commutation of the sentence to imprisonment for life, and in consideration of a letter received from the Chief Justice who tried the cause, the undersigned is disposed to grant such commutation.*

It was the Accomplice Act that damned Webb as it had done Rudabaugh. Whether or not J. J. pulled the trigger on Kelliher, it didn't matter. He was present when the man was killed, in company with the murderer. At least he wasn't facing the noose. Just the remainder of his years baking in a filthy, lice-infested clay box.

* * *

A week before trial, Edgar Caypless, esq., came down sick with influenza. He'd been debating whether or not to remain counsel to Rudabaugh, as the "Save Dave Fund" had dried up entirely. The illness made the decision for him.

The court appointed M. G. Gordon Posey as Rudabaugh's replacement counsel. He was a round-faced, red-faced man, who puffed when he blinked, and shuffled his notes throughout the trial. He'd had less than a day to prepare but was a capable lawyer when it came down to it. Rudabaugh had no complaints in the end.

Hilario Romero was the first witness called by the prosecution. "How did you know it was Rudabaugh with Allen?"

"White men don't all look alike to me," answered Hilario. "Rudabaugh is much taller than Allen. Rudabaugh was known to me as a so-called policeman in New Town."

"'New Town' being East Las Vegas?"

"Correct."

"As you call it, 'the *gringo* side?' "

"*Objection.*"

J.C. Cauldewell, hack driver, testified in Dave's trial: "I was rather suspicious of the way Allen was acting. When they got out of the cab and told me to wait for them, I didn't want to. I moved the cab a little further west but soon they were out running for my hack. They got in the back seat and Allen took out his gun and began to play with it. I turned around and he said 'You s.o.b., if you make a movie, I'll blow your brains out.' Rudabaugh said to Allen: 'Don't make a fool of yourself. I will drive.' He saw that I was nervous and he felt that Allen would not dare shoot if Rudabaugh were driving. He took the lines and drove to the hardware store. When they came out of the store, Rudabaugh sat in the seat behind the driver and Allen sat in the seat behind Rudabaugh … "

J. Maria Tafoya: "I carried Deputy Valdez from where he fell to the kitchen, where he died."

"Do you remember what the coroner said regarding the wound?"

"He said that the pistol was fired on the breast, belly and body of Antonio Lino Valdez—with malice and forethought. And that the bullet had penetrated six inches. William Mullen and the brothers Stokes assisted me in carrying him."

William Mullen: "I was living in Las Vegas at the time of the shooting."

"And what was your address at the time?"

"Cell number three, San Miguel Jail. Served nine months off a year term for train robbery. I was in the cell next to Webb for about four months of that time. I knew Rudabaugh as Webb's friend. He visited three-four times a week. Brought him newspapers and tobacco. Sometimes for us, too."

"How would you describe the relationship between Deputy Valdez and Dave Rudabaugh?"

"Objection. Speculation."

"Over-ruled."

"Valdez and Rudabaugh were known to each other and seemed cordial. Sometimes, Rudabaugh would bring Valdez coffee when he visited. They played cards with Webb several times. My chains wouldn't let me join."

"What do you remember of the day of the shooting?"

"Well, the details are fuzzy now … Allen was to the left of Rudabaugh when the shot was fired. Rudabaugh greeted

Webb with a handshake, through the bars, which Webb took left hand over right. Rudabaugh greeted me as well, bid me morning and tossed me a fresh baked rye roll. The Stokes Brothers were still asleep and I asked for theirs, but Dave hadn't brought them any, as he didn't care for them. Then Rudabaugh asked Webb: 'How do you feel? Do you need anything?' At this point, Allen turned to the jailer and said, 'You s.o.b.—give me the keys.' And I apologize to any ladies present for the rough language. Anyways, they were in the jail about a minute when the shot was fired. Then both ran out and in came Sheriff Romero, smoking a cheroot. I'm sorry, but I can't think of anything else."

Carl Stokes testified: "When Tafoya needed help to carry Valdez from where he fell to the kitchen table where he could be laid out. Bob and I, we came out the cell and assisted in carrying him. We made no attempt to escape."

"Did escape not occur to you?"

"The shooting was a surprise. We didn't know if we'd be mistaken for being in on a plot. If we stayed put, less likely we'd get shot or strung up. Safer back in the cell."

"Do you believe that's why Webb remained as well?"

"*Objection.*"

"*I'll allow it.*"

"Maybe. He didn't confide much in us afterwards. They moved J. J. to solitary confinement that morning and we didn't see much of him after that. We was released later that week."

"Who released you?"

"Sheriff Romero. Said he spoke to a judge about getting us a pardon for our help."

"Which judge?"

"I don't recall."

Finally, it came time for Dave Rudabaugh to take the

stand. The gallery was packed three deep with spectators. Lute Wilcox lingered by the window and took notes in his strange scribbled hand, unreadable to anyone but him.

"I was a police officer prior to the time of the killing and I was a personal friend of John Webb," said Dave. "Valdez never refused me admittance when I went to see Webb. The jailor and I was good friends."

Whether Dave still felt shame about the failed breakout was unknowable. His testimony rings largely true save for small differences. "I went earlier to the Summer House Saloon in West Las Vegas. On the way I met Allen, who asked to go along with me. I did not refuse him and we went in together. I went there to see a man who owed me money. His name was Tom Pickett. I was told that he was home, sick in bed. I went to the place where he lived and talked to him for about twenty minutes. He decided to get up and go to town. We stopped at the Summer House and Allen had some drinks. He had been drinking some before we met on the street. Pickett decided to stay in town while Allen and I went to the jail to see Webb.

"While I was asking Webb how he felt, I heard a shot. I saw the jailor fall. I said to Little Allen: 'What did you do that for?' 'The jailor drew a pistol on me and I jumped out of range,' he said. There was a knocking on the front door, I opened it and ran out. The hack had left the front door. I ran down the street and I overtook it at the plaza. I asked the driver why he didn't wait.

"By the time I got back into the hack, Allen was there. He got in back. He was a bit drunk. He took out his pistol and tried to load it. He couldn't. He asked me to. We drove down the street to Goodlett's saloon, where Allen had left a double-barreled shotgun. We then drove to the hardware store. Allen told me later that he was acquainted with the

Stokes brothers and had tried to get in to see them but was not admitted. He knew of my visits to Webb and came looking for me. That is how we got together that day. He was slightly acquainted with Webb ... "

Dave ended his story with the hack leaving town, omitting the shoot-out on the mesa road. When questioned about it, he responded: "I was being pursued by men intending to kill me. It made sense to return fire. Since I was the better shot, I was able to get away without inflicting any other injury."

Judge Prince agreed to take Rudabaugh's slowness to violence into consideration as he considered sentence.

*** * ***

On March 8, 1881, *The Optic* reported on the trial:

The entire time of the District Court was taken up yesterday in the case of the Territory vs. Dave Rudabaugh, indicted for murder. The crime for which the prisoner was tried was committed in Las Vegas and was the killing of the jailor of the place. Major A. Breeden and Col. Wm. Breeden for the prosecution. The hearing of the evidence took up the time of the court until about six o'clock p.m., when the court counsel was heard and the case was given to the jury about half after eight o'clock. After about an absence of one hour and a half the Jury brought in a verdict of murder in the first degree. Rudabaugh appeared perfectly calm throughout the trial, giving no evidence of excitement or agitation of any kind. His manner was serious and impressed with the fact that he fully realized his situation, but had no occasion to resort to an assumption of that stolid indifference behind which prisoners frequently strive to hide their feelings in such cases. M. G. Gordon Posey, who was appointed by the court to defend Dave Rudabaugh yesterday, did so very ably, notwithstanding that he had no time whatever to prepare for the trial.

When put upon the stand Rudabaugh told a very probable story of the murder, and the parts which he and Allen took in it. […] The story was very consistent with the facts as they appeared in evidence, except that it threw the blame on Allen. All the statements made by witnesses except as to the actual killing and who fired the fatal shot, were dovetailed in very cleverly and if the account had come from a man of better character than Rudabaugh's, and under different circumstances, it would possibly have carried conviction with it. As it was, however, it had no good effect and Rudabaugh stands a good chance of swinging. The appeal to the Superior Court will carry the matter over until next winter so that the prisoner will have time to look after his opportunities to escape…

* * *

Judge Prince delivered his expected verdict, taking his time so that his voice could be adequately recorded. "David Rudabaugh, you are indicted by the Grand Jury of San Miguel county at the term of August, 1880, for the highest crime known to man—that of willful murder of a fellow being, In this case, the crime as alleged is made, if possible, even more grave by the person killed being a public officer engaged in the performance of his duties. A change of venue was taken on your application to the county in order that an absolutely impartial jury might be impaneled to try your case. And such a jury was obtained, all its members being acceptable to your counsel. Although the counsel originally assigned for the defense were prevented by sickness from attending, yet others of marked zeal and intelligence conducted the defense, and labored with ability and earnestness to secure for you every right and privilege which the law provides.

"The jury, in the performance of their duty as judges of the facts, have found you guilty of murder in the first degree, the punishment for which is the penalty of death. Nothing which I can say or do could add to the solemnity of this verdict or of the criminal circumstances which now surround you as its subject. Certainly I am far from desiring to add a single word, which would increase the profound sense of sorrow, which now must fill your heart. For some years your life seems to have been one of lawlessness, By your own admission in open court you were a prominent actor in two outrages against society and the laws, in the stage robberies between Las Vegas and this city which attracted so much attention a year or two since, and after the commission of this murder you were found in the company of notorious breakers of the law in the southeast part of this Territory.

"Let us all hope that this awful example of the result of such a course of life is one whose natural abilities might have led him to success and honor; this evidence that the law is strong to punish as well as protect, and that in the long run it is sure to overtake even those who are most successful in avoiding it; power and penalties. This will be the means of restraining others from a similar course of violence and crime, which might lead to the same fate, And let me here admonish you to use well and profitably the time which the laws of the Territory still remain to you in this life, so that you will be prepared as fully as possible for the other life in another world so soon to come.

"It now only remains for me to perform the sad and impressive rite of pronouncing the dread sentence which the law imposed in your case, which is, that you be conveyed hence to the county of San Miguel and delivered to the custody of the sheriff of that county and there kept safely until Friday, the 20th day of May, 1881, and on that same day you be taken by the sheriff of that county to some suitable place within said county of San Miguel, and there between the hours of ten a.m. and twelve p.m be hung by the neck until you are dead. May God have mercy on your soul!"

* * *

Santa Fe New Mexican, April 22, 1881:

> *The above sentence however will not be carried out into effect, at least on the day mentioned, as the counsel for the prisoner have taken an appeal to the higher court; all motion for a new trial having been overruled, and, as is well known, such an appeal stays sentence. David Rudabaugh, therefore, has until next winter to await execution as his appeal cannot be heard until that time.*

* * *

Rudabaugh made several attempts to remain in Santa Fe pending appeal. While Webb was safe in Meadow City, Dave would certainly not be and he made his concerns known publically. Kistler was the first to take offense:

> *Chief Justice Prince has decided to return Rudabaugh to the Las Vegas jail as ordered. Previous to his decision in the matter, a considerable pressure was brought to bear upon*

him to prevent the order. It was argued that the people there were greatly incensed against him (i.e., Rudabaugh), and that he would surely he lynched if returned to this County. Judge Prince took a more sober and hopeful view of the matter and relying upon the love of good order and the law-abiding character of the people of Las Vegas, decided that this was the proper place for Rudabaugh, and that there was no reasonable or well-grounded fear that he would be dealt with illegally. Judge Prince, we are of the opinion, has taken the right view of the question. We express the general sentiment of Las Vegas in saying that Rudabaugh will not be lynched when brought here. The people of this city are strongly inclined to frown down and prevent mob law. We have reached a condition of society wherein the laws of the land can be enforced with due regularity, and we apprehend, successfully. Besides that we have a sheriff and deputies who will neither permit prisoners to escape nor allow a mob to take them out and butcher them. We have confidence in our officers that prisoners will be protected both ways. They will not escape from justice nor be mobbed. We should hate to form one of the party to take Rudabaugh or anyone else out of the Las Vegas jail unless the prime requisite for a requiem was a desirable object. The jail is well guarded by capable men who will defend the law. There is no feeling on the community against Rudabaugh, which would have sufficient strength to overcome ordinary means of protection. Let the laws be strictly en-forced with evenhanded justice and with certainty and crime will decrease and mob law disappear. Judge Prince is right in his estimate of the good character of the people of Las Vegas"

   – The Optic, March 4, 1881.

* * *

"Don't that sound like a letter of intent?" said Webb, finishing reading. Dave grunted. He'd been remanded to *la perrera* on February 27, the *Optic* hit piece came out a week later. Lute had attempted to get a quote or two on the day but Dave decided he had nothing else to say.

"Go away, Lute," he said, lying down on his bunk and turning his face to the wall. "And tell Kistler to take his 'mostly true stories' and go to Hell."

CHAPTER 23

THE WRONG SINS

They never should have tried it.

Dave was still sick, recovering from fever. He'd lost another twenty pounds from the lousy food. He and Webb both looked like shadows drowning in filthy striped pajamas.

Every morning, Dave woke up wondering if this was day the White Caps would come for him with a noose. Every night, he went to his bunk wondering if they'd slit his throat while he slept, so quiet as to not even rouse Webb, his now-constant guardian. "How many lynchings we stop?" said Webb. "No one's hanging you while I'm around."

"Except the Territory," said Dave.

"Except the Territory," Webb agreed.

News came down that on April 28, Henry McCarty, aka Billy the Kid, escaped from his cell in Lincoln County, killed Deputies Jim Bell and Bob Olinger, and then lit out proclaiming himself to be the bad man they all said he was. Dave didn't mind hearing about Olinger. The pious Bible-thumping asshole who'd harangued them in Santa Fe got what was coming to him with both barrels.

Lute Wilcox stopped by on the 16th of July with news. "Garrett got Bonney a couple of days back." Dave looked up from his bunk but didn't respond. "Bonney had been staying at Pete Maxwell's, waiting for Paulita, rumor has it." Lute tossed a paper through the bars, the pertinent bit circled in lead pencil. "Garrett cornered him there. Shot him twice."

Dave glanced at the article, then dropped it to the floor. "Paulita weren't his sweetheart," said Dave. "And Pete likely sold Henry out. Put that in your paper, Lute."

"You're still being named as an accomplice," Lute said.

"Of who?"

"The Kid. Should I put you down as part of his gang, or him part of yours?"

"Wa'n't no gang," said Dave. "Was more of a clump." He rolled over, then rolled back. "What day that say Henry died?"

"The fourteenth," said Lute. "Two days ago."

Rudabaugh grunted. "Henry got his wish on my birthday." He went back to sleep, oddly aggrieved to hear that Henry McCarty was no more. The sadness caught him unaware and held on longer than it should have. Truth played out. Henry would never be taken alive, and Garrett was no match for him in a fair fight. He would have had to ambush The Kid in the dark. Indeed, that is what occurred.

Webb and Lute jawed for a while, then the newsman left, clattering his cane ahead of him. A while later, Rudabaugh roused, found Webb smoking the last of a butt bummed from who-the-hell-knew?

"Dave," said J. J. "you didn't shoot Lino and I didn't shoot Kelliher."

"Yet here we are, Josh."

"We're being sent to Hell for the wrong sins."

Dave nodded. "I don't want to die in this outhouse."

"So let's make a real plan."

* * *

They should have waited. Between July and September, much was discussed. They'd confided in other *gringo* prisoners, hardcase Thomas Duffy first. Duffy had killed a clerk named Thom Bishop in Liberty, completely unprovoked. Duffy himself couldn't explain his actions. "Just went mad for no reason," was his explanation, still slathered with Bishop's gore.

As always, Dave's vote was for digging. The walls of *la perrera* were soft adobe over slat, forever crumbling on their own. To compensate, the prisoners were never without their chains, and many spent their nights lashed to the floor at the ankles as well, with only a few feet of leeway to get to the piss pots. Digging, though, was risky and could rarely be accomplished quickly, even with good tools. With cup handles, things would take longer.

* * *

Once Rudabaugh was secured in the jail, the anger Hilario Romero had felt towards the man seemed to dissipate. No longer could he see the murderous outlaw within the skeletal prisoner. The fire within the killer gone, that chill affected Romero's own passion. They'd gotten their man and they'd gotten him using the law. Whether or not Rudabaugh was hanged for his crimes or not no longer interested the Hilario. His grocery store on Plaza Street was busy every day. Like Las Vegas, the beautiful Meadow City now relatively free of organized villainy, Romero's family was growing stronger too.

By summer, Romero retired from the law entirely with Silva's blessing. An election was held and Desiderio was formerly appointed Sheriff of San Miguel County. Desiderio had changed as well, having turned his back on his White Cap past. Silva minded not at all. The White Caps would always thrive.

* * *

J. J. Webb knew every inch of *la pererra*. He'd paced it all out, as far as his chains would allow. He loathed it from corner to corner, hated it from room to room.

While in solitary, he found dreaming of Bonnie Hommacher too painful. He didn't dare imagine of a life with her. There was no angle in it besides self-torture, and he'd leave that particular flagellation to the religious.

Forcing himself to think of other things, J. J. found solace in his memories as a buffalo hunter. He'd initially apprenticed himself out to hunters in Oskaloosa, drifted further to Willow Creek, tried his hand at gold mining, then bar tending, then returning to the more lucrative world of animal slaughter. While in Willow Creek, his idle time had threatened to corrupt his character, forcing him towards cards and booze and fisticuffs. Sometimes worse. On the plains, he was a better man, though the buffalo had other opinions.

Joining up with a Federal surveying party as a teamster, J. J. took up the Sharp's rifle again, traveled with the party from Baxter Springs, KS, moved south along the Neosho to the Creek Indian Agency, south again to the Red River, Choctaw territory, north through the Chicasaw, the Seminole, the Creek, the Cherokee. Webb made friends in each area. He was likable.

His travels had brought him into the acquaintance of

both Wyatt Earp, with whom he would work, briefly and unpleasantly, finding Earp disagreeable, as a deputy in Abilene. He thought of the great scouts like Andy Johnson and "Duck Bill" James B. Hickok.

He forced himself to think of wide-open spaces, times where he was alone on the horizon. He dreamed of the wind, the snorting buff below him on the plains beneath his sighting cliffs. He conjured up every instance in his life where he wasn't surrounded by four walls, or when another man's stinking body wasn't pressed up against him, snoring and fouling the air.

* * *

There is no evidence to connect Mysterious Dave Mather with the prison break attempt of September 20. Mather was reportedly traveling through Texas at that time. Also sighted in Louisiana, and the Oklahoma Territory. Possibly also at the center of the Earth. Be that as it may, sometime in early September, a loaded pistol was dropped over the far wall of the exercise yard of *la perrera*, wrapped in blue cloth and retrieved by John Joshua Webb. J. J. hid it well in a wall niche beneath his bunk, and kept a fine eye on it until the time was right.

The time, however, never seemed right. Too many guards most days, coming and going as Desiderio increased their responsibilities on both sides of town. This Sheriff Romero employed more deputies than Hilario ever felt necessary. Drunks and bandylegs were tossed into the common cells and were stacked deep.

Dave had taken sick over night, waking with chills and sweats and vomiting. J. J. demanded Desiderio call for a doctor. The old coot with whiskey-shakes declared it was nothing more than pneumonia and left aspirin powders behind. "Bring me cold water and a rag, at least," J. J. begged.

"You should do your best to keep your friend alive," said another deputy, Joaquin Romero. "You would not want to deprive the noose its victim."

"Rags," said J. J. "Cold water."

Through the night, J. J. tended to Dave's fever, swearing he could hear the cloth sizzle against his friend's face.

"You should put that over his nose and let him out of his misery," said Duffy.

"Enough of that talk," said Webb.

Dave mumbled in his delirium, but J. J. never could make out a word of it. For whatever reason, Deputy Joaquin Romero frequently assisted, bringing the sick man bread and soup. It got the other malnourished prisoners jealous. Joaquin dealt with complaints with considerably less compassion. Each time, J. J. returned the bowl and spoon with thanks. Except for the last, when only the bowl was returned.

Still, they should have waited maybe one more day. One more day, and Dave might have been strong enough to pull himself up and over the wall. One more day, and Webb wouldn't have had to consider leaving Dave behind.

* * *

September 20, 1881: Las Vegas Gazette:

Yesterday morning at three am in the guardroom of the county jail, occurred one of the most terrible hand-to-hand encounters we have ever been called upon to chronicle. Four desperate and daring criminals confined in the middle cell of the county jail, having secured a pistol from the outside and freed themselves by picking the lock of their cell, made a rush upon the three Mexican guards, who were asleep at the time in the guardroom and whose names are Florencio Mares, Guadalupe Hidalgo, and Herculano Chavez.

David Rudabaugh, the leader of the gang, fired two shots at old man Mares, one just grazing his temple. Mares sprang to his feet and catching hold of the weapon with both hands, succeeded finally in wrestling it from his grasp. Another of the prisoners, Thomas Duffy, immediately closed with Mares, and in the struggle that ensued, Mares threw Duffy to the floor and called up Chavez to shoot him, which he did in good style, the ball striking a little to the left of the center of the forehead and lodging in the brain. A fierce and determined hand-to-hand contest for the mastery then began, and finally ended by the prisoners forced back into the cell and secured.

The prisoners confined in the cell were Dave Rudabaugh, Thomas Duffy, J. J. Webb—held for murder—and H.S. Wilson and A. Murphy, held for robbery. Rudabaugh is under sentence of death for the murder of Deputy Sheriff A.L. Valdez on April 3, 1880, in an attempt by him and Jack Allen to rescue Webb from jail. Rudabaugh escaped at the time and was captured with Billy the Kid. He has been confined in this jail except when taken to Santa Fe for trial. Thomas Duffy was arrested a month ago for the unprovoked and brutal murder of Thomas Bishop, a clerk in Gillerman's store at Liberty.

Rudabaugh seemed willing to talk and was very apprehensive of his personal safety. When we suggested to him that it would have been an easy matter for him to have made his escape after opening the door of the cell without *attacking the guards, he declared that he had no intention of harming them and that owing to his weakness from long confinement he was unable to climb the wall. His manner during the interview indicated great nervousness and apprehension that he might be lynched. The man who shot Duffy is scarcely 21 and he seemed to take the whole matter cooly and very much as a matter of course.*

* * *

It took four full buckets of water to wash Duffy's brains out the door.

"Old Man Mares" must have been Lute's little joke, for "Old Man Mares" was south of forty and built like two Dutchys. He'd had no trouble lifting Duffy over his head and slamming him down to the ground. Young Chavez, with his peach fuzz lip, locked eyes with Webb as he blew a hole through the prone Duffy's head. The look was of pure malice, even as Webb called for Chavez to belay his shot. Blood went everywhere.

The plan had been to force the guards back at gunpoint. Weak from illness, Dave nonetheless took point to storm the little bunkhouse. He'd said it was to lead the charge and make sure no one suffered under Duffy's rage, but the truth was as he'd told Lute: if they had reached the yard and tried to climb over the south wall of the jail, he never would have made it. As it was, the old Colt was as heavy as his chains, and the weakness in his limbs is what caused his aim to stray. He'd meant to put both shots over Mares' head, but the second creased the man's temple, sending him into bull-vision. Thinking the wound would slow the older man down was Duffy's fatal error when he attacked.

Upon Duffy's demise, the others fell back. Webb grabbed

hold of Dave around his narrow chest and dragged him backwards on his heels, retreating from the oncoming guards. That the Colt dropped from Dave's hand was the only thing that stayed Chavez from adding him to the bloody mess. Chavez forced them back into the cell and Hidalgo slammed shut the door.

Kistler sent a photographer over to immortalize the corpse. Lute ambled over sometime later. "Did it ever occur to you to not hurt anyone?"

"Of course it did," said Dave, irritated. "I had no intention of hurting anyone."

"You never seem to," said Lute. And Dave had no response to that.

* * *

There is no evidence that Mysterious Dave Mather was even in Las Vegas between September and December, 1881. There is no reason to suspect that he was responsible for passing digging tools—a pickaxe minus handle, a case knife—to the prisoners over the south wall of *la perrera*. There is also no explanation as to how John "Texas" Quinlan was incarcerated in cell number two with Webb and Rudabaugh with a barely concealed railroad spike in his possession.

After the first attempt in September, Rudabaugh and Webb were separated, shoved into solitary cells on opposite ends of the jail. This solitary lasted approximately one month, until over-crowding demanded their return to the general population of the number two, where they were ensconced with nine other men, Texas Quinlan included. The papers identified them in yet another list of names as: "Griffin, Rogers, Fogerty (aka Cutler), Jack McManus, Goodman, Kelley, Schroeder, and Kearney."

When interrogated later, the guards admitted there was much whispering and conspiring among the near-dozen desperates in the center cell, but in what prison would you find otherwise?

Quinlan was a large man with a big personality. His imprisonment seemed more amusing to him than anything else. As he conspired with the others, he spoke often of "Mrs. Quinlan," who would be waiting for them at the St. Nicholas. Mrs. Quinlan herself had been by to visit her husband the morning following his arrest, arriving in a big black hat and dark blue dress, her face veiled. The jailers refused her entry and she left without a word. Texas Quinlan nudged Webb's disintegrating shoe with the toe of his own. "A fine woman, my Mrs. Quinlan," he said with a wink. Webb nodded but added no opinion of his own.

The prisoners must have been working at the wall for some time, hiding the dirt within their thin mattresses and beneath blankets. The four guards, the icy Chavez included, admitted that they'd heard nothing, not even when waking to use the outhouse, passing the cells on the way. The prisoners were not missed until breakfast time the morning of December 3, 1881.

Using the contraband tools, Dave and the others managed to carve out a hole measuring seven inches by nineteen inches. They'd all had to squeeze out naked, wrapping their duds around their chains to keep them silent, pushing the bundles before them. Rotten food and illness had slimmed them all down. Dave went first, wriggling through the hole like a nightcrawler after a rain.

Slapping down into the mud, Dave helped pull Webb through the narrow hole, then the pair dragged Quinlan to his freedom. Rainless lightning lit the sky, throwing the prisoners into brief and sharp relief and blanching the shadows, putting both Dave and J. J. in mind of that horrible night at the windmill as they sent Dorsey and his friends to their maker. Quinlan reached back and dragged through Griffin, then returned to Webb and Dave. As silently as they could, they crept through Old Town, hugging walls and keeping to alleys. Crossing the bridge was the biggest challenge, lit as it was by gay gaslights, but they finally reached the rear kitchen entrance to the St. Nicholas.

Throwing open the door, Mrs. Quinlan was there to meet them. Tears leapt to John Joshua's eyes as he saw the radiant face of Bonnie Hommacher. "Mrs. Quinlan," said the man called Texas, "I believe you know my good friend Josh Webb."

The pair fell into each other's arms with an abandon bordering on scandalous, it had been so very long.

Quinlan moved through the kitchen and found the clean duds stashed beneath the stove, along with the two Colts, of which he helped himself to one, and tossed the other to Dave. "We don't got tools for the chains," he said. Rudabaugh nodded, and Quinlan hurried back through the door, hurrying further down the alley, towards Anderson's livery.

Taking it all in, Dave realized he'd been giving Mather more credit than was warranted. Certainly the man was waiting for him in Naranjo, but it was obvious who possessed the brains for this job. Watching Webb virtually melt into Bonnie, a strange understanding descended over Dave Rudabaugh, and with this understanding came a calm. Standing in the mudway, half in and out of fresh trousers, hands still manacled, Dave watched J. J. Webb and Bonnie Hommacher and saw the life they should have had. Were it not for the Dodge City Gang. Were it not for the Judge. Were it not for Dave Rudabaugh.

Bonnie waved him to come in further, out of any prying eyes. As he moved to do so, he caught movement in the shadows beyond the low wall marking the yard's entryway. The Blanchard Mercantile Co. was across the way, and Carl Burrows, the night watchman, was alight with a lantern, investigating the noise outside his door. Dave raised his pistol and waved the man away. Without a word, Burrows vanished back into the shadows. Back to bed or to the law, Dave didn't know. He would err on the side of caution.

"Dave, get inside!" said Webb, but Dave didn't move.

"We need to get you both inside," said Bonnie. "Quinlan's coming with a hay wagon. We'll get you under and concealed and—"

Walking backwards, Dave shook his head. His face had affixed upon it an odd smile. It split his prison-grown beard, lit up through the filth on his face.

"David?" said Webb.

"Loyalty is a big thing with me," said Rudabaugh.

"That's always been clear," said Webb.

"Loyalty means not getting your partner killed," he said. "And that's surely what I'll do if we stay together." He continued his backwards journey. To Bonnie Hommacher, Dave Rudabaugh said, "You take him the hell out of here and you get as far away as you can."

Wordlessly, she nodded, taking J. J.'s arm and pulling him back further into the kitchen.

Webb nodded and continued to nod, the words escaping him totally. "You come find me, Dave."

Dave nodded. "Soon as it's cool enough."

"Soon as it's cool enough."

Rudabaugh stumbled a little, missing the final step down into the yard. But with a final nod, he tipped his invisible hat to John Joshua Webb and Bonnie Hommacher, who closed the door behind the man she'd waited for.

Again keeping to the shadows, Dave raced down the alleyway and out of Meadow City.

Dave Rudabaugh and J. J. Webb would never see each other again.

* * *

Governor Sheldon, recognizing the importance of the re-arrest of Dave Rudabaugh and his companion desperado John Webb, who with a number of others escaped from the Las Vegas jail on Friday (Oct. 2) night, has deemed it proper to offer a reward for their apprehension and yesterday Secretary Rich was furnished a proclamation of which this is a copy: "Whereas David Rudabaugh and John J. Webb, convicted and confined in the country jail of the county of San Miguel, have escaped from custody and are now at large—Now, Therefore, I Governor Lionel A. Sheldon, Governor of the Territory of New Mexico, under, and by the authority of the power in me vested by the laws of the Territory of New Mexico, do offer and proclaim in the name of the said Territory, a reward of $500 for the said Dave Rudabaugh and $500 for John Webb to be paid out of the treasury of the said Territory upon satisfactory proof of the capture and the delivery of the aforesaid—December 5, 1881.'" This should induce the officers of the law to exert their utmost to try to capture Rudabaugh and Webb.

Dave Rudabaugh has a pair of U. S. Marshal's shackles, which he might return if politely inclined as they are of no further use to him. Doubtless Dave will not care to return them in person.

— Santa Fe New Mexican, Dec. 21, 1881.

Chapter 24

Lute Wilcox Kept Good Records

Dave Rudabaugh and Wyatt Earp eyeballed each other from across the streets of Tombstone, but they only met face-to-face once, on March 24, 1882, at Iron Springs, in the Whetstone Mountains of Arizona. They locked eyes just before Earp emptied the barrels of his shotgun into Curly Bill Brocious, cutting him in two and spraying the outlaw leader all over Rudabaugh. Dave escaped without a scratch. Earp too.

On the night of the great Las Vegas jail escape in December, after Dave and Webb said their goodbyes, Rudabaugh made it on foot six miles to Naranjo, where Dave Mather was waiting at a livery, the owner bought off handsomely. Mather got Rudabaugh unshackled, fed, and on a fresh fast horse within an hour.

"I appreciate you risking your neck for me," Rudabaugh said.

Mather smiled. "The papers are still saying I'm in Texas," he said. "Of course, I may have fed them that information. So there is less risk for me than you, I'm afraid."

Time was tight. There was no telling if the prisoners had

even been missed. The sun was still some two hours from rising and there was as yet no baying of hounds on the wind. They risked a quick discussion.

"J. J. is heading towards Texas, then to Arkansas and Bonnie's people," said Mather. He and Mrs. Hommacher had been communicating for the better part of a year, under her assumed name of Mrs. Quinlan, should their letters be intercepted by prying eyes.

"Texas" Quinlan was a cousin of hers, well up for the gag. Sometime later, Garrett caught up to him in a Santa Fe cantina and brought him back to jail. It's unclear what happened to him after that. *All history is endless lists of names.*

Rudabaugh nodded. "So it would be best for me to head the opposite direction."

"Old Mexico?"

Rudabaugh shook his head. "The Romeros, the White Caps, they'll be looking for me down there."

"So would Garrett or any posse."

"Because it's the smart play. Get out of the territory, get out of the States."

"So?"

"How's the action up in Tombstone? I read about some great fight between the Earps and the local skunks."

"I've heard it's a daily war zone," said Mather. "I've also heard the papers are being consistent with their exaggeration."

"Earp hunted me for years," said Rudabaugh. "Maybe it's time we were introduced."

Throughout the winter, Dave rode through Arizona with outlaws calling themselves The Cowboys, led by the handsome and vicious Curly Bill Brocius, rustling beeves and horses, selling them below the border. There is no evidence to indicate that Dave Rudabaugh played any part in the assassination of Morgan Earp in Tombstone by parties unknown, nor the attempted murder of Virgil Earp by Frank Stilwell. Being part of a murder squad would not have been in his character.

Morgan Earp was shot in the back through the window of the Campbell & Hatch Billiard Parlor. Following this, Wyatt Earp used his righteous mantle as lawman to declare himself the vengeful fist of God. Earp, Doc Holliday, and a veritable platoon of angry volunteers chased the Cowboys across Arizona.

Resting up from a hard ride, Brocious and the remaining Cowboys were washing up in Iron Springs when Earp and the posse came up upon them unawares, the Springs running ten feet or so beneath a ridge. Earp dismounted and was halfway towards the water when the two factions saw each other. Gunfire erupted immediately, and two halves of Curly Bill splashed down into the water, painting Rudabaugh with the gore. Dave yanked his gun and fired, his bullets piercing only Earp's great flapping coat. Scrambling up the bank, Rudabaugh and the surviving Cowboys made their escape in opposite directions.

Dave lost his taste for Arizona after that.

* * *

Lute Wilcox kept a small office on Front Street, working as a full editor on *The Optic* only, following a fire at *The Gazette* that had Koogler refiguring his business. His eyesight but gauze and shadows now, he'd taken to working with one of Mr. Edison's experimental creations, the Dictaphone, speaking his thoughts into a cone, recorded onto a wax cylinder, and then transcribed the following morning by a young copyboy named Linus Bell. By 1887, the Dictaphone would be available commercially throughout the United States. Wilcox thought it a marvelous invention.

He rose early every morning, usually with the sun, and he made his way to his office by use of his cane and his impeccable memory. On May 1, 1882, Lute opened his office and heard a click of a gun. "Good morning, Lute," said a familiar voice.

"Dave Rudabaugh," he said with a smile, closing the door behind him. "Here for a look at the early edition?"

Sitting in the darkest corner of the room, Dave lowered the hammer of his Colt and stood, returning the gun to his holster. Behind him on the shelf were three little jars of formaldehyde, and in each was a pickled index finger, sent by hucksters insisting *theirs* was the genuine trigger finger of Billy the Kid. Lute found them amusing to display. If Rudabaugh noticed them, he didn't make mention.

"Apologies," he said, referring to the gun. He stood and crossed, giving the newsman the berth he needed to find his desk. "Wasn't sure what the atmosphere in town would be."

In his own memoirs, Lute would write of this evening. *"This man before me wore Dave Rudabaugh's skin, and spoke with his voice, but this was something angry and defeated, lacking the vinegar of my old compadre."*

"If you're referring to the Romeros, I'm afraid everyone's pretty much forgotten about you."

"That a fact?"

"I don't know of any active search for you."

"Or J. J.?"

Lute didn't answer.

"Shit," said Dave, feeling an icy fist grab his heart. "Who got him? Wasn't Garrett, was it? Or Masterson? Or—"

Lute held up a finger and began to feel around in the top

drawer of his desk. "Light that lamp, please," he said. Finding a matchbox, Dave did as he was asked, and cranked the wick high. It did little to chase the gloom, but it seemed to assist Wilcox a little. He withdrew a paper and handed it to Rudabaugh. "I'm sorry," he said.

Dave took the paper and held it up to the light. " 'Dear Mr. Wilcox,' " he read. " 'I am writing to you to inform you that an acquaintance of yours … suc—*succumbed* to cholera on April 12. We knew him at our ranch as Samuel King, who lived with his wife on a stretch of land of their own adjacent to our property. You knew him as John Joshua Webb, a policeman in your town of Las Vegas, identified by front left gold incisor. We … ' " Dave's voice caught in his throat for a moment. He cleared it and continued. " 'We thought of him as a good, reliable man, friendly and a friend to all who knew him. I am sorry if this letter brings you pain, but we felt it was our duty to send you news of his passing. His wife has moved on now, in the company of family. Yours, Thomas Pepper, foreman, J. D. Scott & Co., Winslow, Ark. April 18, 1882.' "

Rudabaugh finished reading, stared at the paper for a long time, then returned it to Wilcox. Though he could barely see more than the outline of the man, Lute thought that a light had seemed to dim inside Rudabaugh. Lute had never taken him for being sentimental.

Dave shook his head. "Four months."

Lute cocked his head. "Say again?"

"All's I bought J. J. was four months. We'd stayed in our cell, he might have lived longer."

"But had what kind of life?" Lute asked. Dave looked at him and didn't answer. "He died with Bonnie at his side."

"Instead of me, I reckon."

"He made a go of it," said Lute. Rudabaugh nodded.

After another long interval, Rudabaugh spoke again. "Mather still in Texas?"

"Back in Dodge, last I heard."

"Last he wanted you to hear."

Lute nodded. There was another long pause. Then Rudabaugh broke the silence for the last time. "Reckon I'll drift," he said. "You have yourself a fine day."

Then he was gone.

Lute sat for a while. He uncovered the Dictaphone and began to speak. Some time later, Linus would arrive to transcribe the wax cylinders that immortalized Lute's scratchy voice.

CHAPTER 25

EPITAPHS

Luis Terrasas had been a poor man when the revolution broke out, threatening all citizens of his beloved country of Mexico. He roused his fellow farmers, fanned the flames of their patriotism, urged them to take up arms and fight for their country. In reward, he was named governor of Chihuahua and the president of Mexico granted him extraordinary rights: "wherever Luis Terrasas drove a stake on the open range, that land would be his."

He had six ranches, and in charge of his Parral spread was a *gringo* wrangler named Dave Rudabaugh. Rudabaugh had been drifting in and out of Old Mexico, bouncing between Chihuahua and Arizona throughout 1883, sometimes working in the so-called Hash Knife outfit for the Aztec Land and Cattle Company. Two of his past associates, Billy Wilson and Tom Pickett, worked there under foreman John Jones, but having left prison not too long ago the pair were prone to drunkenness and violence. The three men got up to some familiar antics with local beeves, as well as those belonging to the Aztec Land and Cattle Company. Their employment did not last long.

Since leaving the Cowboys, Dave Rudabaugh had resumed his twin careers of rustling and drinking, often spending his ill-gotten money as quickly as he could earn it. And though Governor Terrasas paid handsomely, it came only once per month. Whiskey was an every day expense. When the Governor came to understand that he was losing stock under his own foreman, he was tempted to put Rudabaugh to the noose. Instead, he discharged the man. He was, after all, a benevolent politician now. No longer a revolutionary.

In his frequent inebriated state, Dave's humor had vanished. In Old Mexico, once Pickett and Wilson departed, Rudabaugh was utterly without friends. Though he preferred to rustle on his own, he missed even the companionship of his fellow cellmates in *la perrera*. In his loneliness and anger, he would lash out at anyone in his way. The good people of Parral were growing weary of him.

He was in a cantina, damned if he knew its name, drinking and playing cards with some rougher characters, when Desiderio Romero and two cousins entered. "*Hola*," said Romero to Dave.

Rudabaugh looked up from his cards. He held a shit hand and had been losing steadily. Seeing Romero enter, one of the players to his left got up from the table, taking his cards with him.

"I hope you are not cheating," said Romero.

"I'm losing," said Rudabaugh, his vision not quite swimming, but far from clear.

"Then you are cheating badly."

Rudabaugh let out a sigh. It rose up from his chest and rattled out like a Biblical fatigue. The Romeros went for their guns. Faster, Dave stood and emptied the Schofield. He clipped Desiderio across the hip. His other shots dropped both cousins, blowing holes in their chests and tossing them across the room.

Rudabaugh bolted for the door, bullets chasing him outside. The hitching post was empty. His horse was nowhere to be seen. "Goddamn it," he whispered, then sighed again.

Turning on his heel, he pulled his Colt. With both hands filled, he called towards the cantina. "Come on out, Romero!" he shouted. "*Chinga tu madre, bok gweilo!*"

There was no answer. So Dave walked back in.

Seconds later, his head rolled out.

* * *

Las Vegas Optic printed the story on February 23:

> *Dave Rudabaugh, who was recently killed at Parral in the State of Chihuahua, Mexico, was what might be called an 'all around desperado.' He was equally proficient in holding up a railroad train or a stage coach or, as occasion offered, robbed a bank, 'shooting up' a frontier settlement, or running off stock. He indulged in these little peculiarities for a year or two in Arizona, and inasmuch as many of our old timers doubtless remember him, some of them to their cost, the following sketch of the antecedents of Rudabaugh, communicated to the Tomb-stone Democrat Arizona, by one who knows, will prove of interest:*
>
> *In 1880 he became a member of the famous Billy the Kid Gang which eventually got him into jail. He escaped the jail in Las Vegas and fled to Arizona where he rustled with varying success for nearly two years when he was driven out of the Apache country and struck for Old Mexico where*

he became manager of the cattle interests in Chihuahua of the governor thereof. David continued to be a desperado, however, and became engaged in his final difficulty in the ancient town of Parral. He fatally shot up two persons before the buzzing ball caught him in the fatal shot that ended his life. The natives of Parral got up a procession in honor of the event, and Dave's head was severed from his body, was carried on a pole and exhibited about the streets ...

* * *

Long after he'd retired from Las Vegas and moved to Colorado, where he worked until his death with the United Workers for the Blind, Lute Wilcox heard a rumor that Rudabaugh had escaped Parral with his hide intact. A drummer from Butte had run into a rancher in Oregon. The man was at the end of his run, a heavy drinker and a widower at that. His poor wife had been part Indian—or maybe a colored gal—regardless, she had some sort of grapevine scars that ran from her forehead to her waist, but was fine to look at otherwise. The rancher mourned her loss, but the gal had given him three strong daughters.

"This rancher," said the drummer, "wore a tan Stetson with a wide brim. He said he'd been a lawman in Las Vegas some years back. "Sam King, he said his name was."

If true, this rancher would die penniless in 1928, some years after Lute, surviving Pat Garrett by two decades. Like Doc Holiday, this rancher, this perhaps-Rudabaugh, would die in bed, boots off. But unlike Holiday, this rancher had people at his side that loved him.

Would that we could all be so lucky.

* * *

Henry McCarty was only 21-years old when Sheriff Pat Garrett shot him from the dark in Pete Maxwell's home at Fort Sumner on July 14, 1881, Dave Rudabaugh's birthday.

It took Garrett several months to bring Billy the Kid to St. Peter, and many speculated that Garrett knew all along the whereabouts of the young outlaw, but lacked the passion to kill him. Only after he was pressed by the moneyed interests, those that made him who he was, that he finally made a personal call to Fort Sumner. With this execution, Garrett made Henry immortal.

With his friend and journalist Marshal Ashmun "Ash" Upson, Garrett wrote and published *The Authentic Life of Billy, the Kid*. Though deemed authoritative at the time, Garrett and Upson filled the book with inaccuracies, embellishments, and, in keeping with Upson's career, outright lies. It was not the best seller that had been Lew Wallace's *Ben-Hur*.

On February 29, 1908, a much older Garrett rode with his business associate, Carl Adamson, returning from Las Cruces, New Mexico, in Adamson's wagon. Jesse Wayne Brazel, who'd been leasing land from Garrett but misusing the leeway in some manner, approached them on the road and they got to arguing. Dismissing the normally good-natured hand, Garrett descended the wagon, and went to the side of the road to make water. As his back was turned, either Brazel or Adamson shot him in the back of the head.

Brazel's trial for Garrett's murder concluded on May 4, 1909. As Adamson was the only witness and failed to appear, Brazel was acquitted for the murder.

* * *

Whiskey Jim Greathouse was charged as an accessory to Jim Carlyle's murder and was arrested in March, 1881, released on bond two days later. Acquitted but near penniless now, his station stop gone, his cattle seized or otherwise driven off. In December 1881, Greathouse rustled some forty head of cattle from Joel Fowler of Socorro. Fowler gave chase and cornered Big Jim in the San Mateo Mountains. Following the big man around for almost a day, Fowler took an opportunity to shoot Greathouse twice in the back. Fowler would be lynched for other crimes by the good townsfolk of Socorro in January, 1884.

* * *

Billy Wilson was convicted of counterfeiting and sentenced to ten years in Leavenworth Prison in Kansas, from which he escaped. He rejoined with Tom Pickett and the pair resumed alternating under lawful and otherwise employment throughout the Southwest and Mexico. In 1896, at the behest of former Lincoln County sheriff Pat Garrett, President Grover Cleveland granted Wilson, aka Dave Anderson, a full pardon. Wilson became sheriff of Terrell County, Texas, in 1918 and was killed by a drunk cowboy the same year.

"Scarface" Tom Pickett wound up a deputy U.S. Marshal, resigned his commission in 1922, after an illness resulted in the amputation of his right leg. He made it all the way to 1934, an old man of 76 in Winslow, Arizona, where he died of nephritis on May 14.

* * *

Lucius "Lute" Merle Wilcox was born in Pennsylvania on August 30, 1858. Wilcox married Henrietta Stiles of Washington, Indiana, on June 18, 1890. Though completely blind by 1890, he was a prolific writer, having authored the books *Irrigation Farming* and *Frontier Sketches*, as well as editorials, short stories, articles, and founded the magazine *Field and Farm* with Captain L.W. Cutler. Wilcox spent ten years as president of the United Workers for the Blind of Colorado and died in his sleep in 1930.

Wilcox enjoyed noting how the great Meadow City changed from day to day. On February 7, 1880, he ran the following headline in *The Daily Optic*:

> *ALL THE DANCE HALL GIRLS TO BE BAPTIZED*
> *SUNDAY!*
> *THE MILLENNIUM HAS COME!*

The headline caused much ruckus and was a deliberate shot across the bow strictly to annoy George Close, but for no reason anyone could fathom, save it amused Lute. Close, the co-owner of Close & Patterson's, was content to be seen in public now that the stench of Judge Hoodoo had cleared from his establishment. One February weekend, a Baptist minister had come to town, and as most pious organizations tended to, concentrated his attention on the dance-hall girls.

"I am going to shut up shop," said George Close, grousing in Lute's vicinity. "Those missionary bastards are trying to take all the girls away and get them to join the church. A dance hall can't run without girls, can it? They are back there holding services now."

As Miguel Otero, Jr., would recount in his first autobiography:

> *Entering one of the rooms, the trio found all of the girls*
> *rounded up and corralled, so to speak, in line corner, and*

entirely at the mercy of two clerical-looking gentlemen and a group of lady satellites who were assisting in conducting the services. The dance-hall flock looked as demure and innocent as so many lambs and seemed much affected by the earnest words they had just been hearing. Sadie was noticeably demure; Big Hattie looked as sorrowful as though she'd lost her "man;" Careless Ida had penitence written all over her countenance; while Lazy Liz, and Nervous Jessie, were wiping their weeping eyes. The scene was indeed a touching one, and had the reporter stayed there much longer, he, too, would have been numbered among the converted. Even French Pete, the notorious gambler, was there, and he was overheard to say, "I guess I will have to quit rolling high-ball and turn missionary, too."

George Close was upon tears as well. Beating his breast, he said to his crowd of men in the saloon, "Boys, I guess Saturday night will be my last show, as all the girls propose to be baptized Sunday. What I dislike about it is on account of the musicians and rustlers, for they will surely have to rustle now in dead earnest."

Following the baptism, amidst much weeping and joyousness and proclamations that they'd been "saved," the girls all returned to their duties on Monday, under the watchful eye of Lady Mabe. Giving Sunday to the Lord was all they would spare. Much to the relief of many, George Close included.

Harold Patterson would not be reached for comment.

* * *

Miguel Antonio Otero II served as a delegate to the Republican National Convention, where he met Ohio Senator William McKinley in 1892. After winning the election for President in 1896, McKinley appointed Otero governor of the Territory of New Mexico. After McKinley's assassination, he survived a particularly brutal election with Thomas B. Catron to earn reappointment by President Theodore Roosevelt, and retained office until 1906. In 1899, he chartered Santa Fe High School, the first secondary school in Santa Fe.

Having befriended Henry McCarty during his famous trial in Santa Fe, Otero revisited his past and published *The Real Billy the Kid; With New Light on the Lincoln County War*, edited by Marshall Latham Bond, whose father, Hiram Bond, had been an old associate of the Otero family from Denver. In addition, Otero authored a three-part autobiography: *My Life on the Frontier, 1864–1882*, *My Life on the Frontier, 1882–1897*, and *My Nine Years as Governor of the Territory of New Mexico, 1897–1906*. He died on August 7, 1944.

* * *

Milton Yarberry, who'd been born John Armstrong and offered no explanation for his unusual consumed name, and who'd recommended to Dave Rudabaugh to, should he ever stand upon the gallows, "just jump up," was himself hung for murder in Santa Fe on February 9, 1883. Ironically, he was "jerked to Jesus" via a new method where a dropped weight hoisted the condemned into the air. In this case, Yarberry was yanked upwards with such force his head stoved in on the cross beam.

* * *

Most sources agree that Mysterious Dave Mather was reported as dead on or about March 16, 1887. Means, location, and manner of death always varied. Prior to the reports he hadn't been seen by anyone reputable in over a year. He'd drifted in and out of Texas, never to return to Las Vegas, working both sides of the law as he'd always done. He'd failed to appear in a Dodge City court to stand trial for the murder of David Barnes, for which his brother, Josiah Mather, was also accused. Neither Mather could be located thereafter.

On February 9, 1988, *The Weekly World News* ran the following headline:

UFO SHOCKER; DID ALIENS KIDNAP OLD WEST LAWMAN IN 1889?

Jorge Hernandez, none other than the young boy used as a go-between in Fort Sumner by the two Daves, reported at the end of his life that he was "the last person on Earth" to ever see Mysterious Dave Mather.

Having reached the tender age of 105 by 1971, Hernadez told reporters that, when he was just 23, "sometime in 1889," he'd ridden as a member of "a posse of ranchers and lawmen—including the mysterious gunfighter and peace officer Dave Mather." A silver object in the sky, "measuring some seventy or eighty feet in diameter, hummed across the Arizona sky one evening, moving like ball lightning and brightening up the land like a midnight sun."

"The amazing chase continued for three grueling days. It included at least one encounter with an extraterrestrial who appeared to be armed," read the article. *"Hernandez then 'fired several shots from his .45. When he did, the little man flickered like the flame of a candle and disappeared.'*

"Later that day, Mr. Mather rode to the same spot alone and

never came back. He vanished at the same time the spaceship rose 200 feet into the air and took off over the horizon, never to be seen again."

ABOUT THE AUTHOR

Mike Watt is an author, journalist, and filmmaker from Pittsburgh, PA. With his wife, producer and director Amy Lynn Best, Watt has written and produced a dozen independent features and short films through their company, Happy Cloud Media, LLC, including the 16mm zombie-noir, *The Resurrection Game*, *Demon Divas and the Lanes of Damnation*, and *Razor Days*.

As an entertainment journalist, his work could be found in *Fangoria*, *Cinefantastique*, *Film Threat*, *Femme Fatales*, and the *Movie Outlaw* book series. He was the editor of *Sirens of Cinema Magazine*, *Taxi Driver: The 40th Anniversary Edition Screenplay*, working with Paul Schrader and Martin Scorsese's Sikelia Productions for Gauntlet Press. He continues to publish the bi-annual digest *Exploitation Nation*, focusing on all aspects of genre entertainment.

His non-film related work includes the collection *Phobophobia*, the novels *The Resurrection Game* and *Suicide Machine*, and the Encyclopocalypse Press publication, *Hot Splices: The Author's Cut*.

Dave Rudabaugh is an obsession of his, and not even he can explain why.

www.ingramcontent.com/pod-product-compliance
Lightning Source LLC
Chambersburg PA
CBHW011149310726
48973CB00010B/2838